A VOLCANIC

RACE

LIZ YOUNG

ISBN-13: 978-1979086578
http://lizy-writes.blogspot.co.uk
Living Rock Books

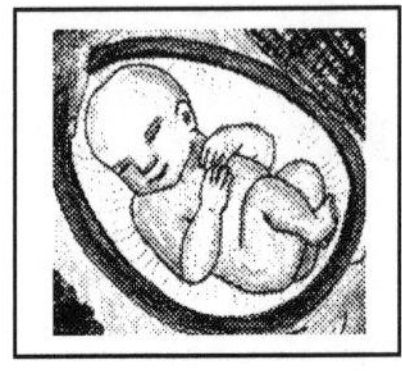

For Dan, who told me to write it,

Mandy, my alpha reader and first critic,

Helen Baggott, proofreader extraordinaire,

all Talkbackers for their invaluable advice,

and for the island of Tenerife,
my home for fifteen years,
whose fantastic rock
formations and colours
inspired this story.

CONTENTS

PROLOGUE

Picture the scene – a world dotted with volcanoes and cut by rivers of fire that glow bright gold under a dark sky. Dinosaurs graze and hunt, tiny creatures scuttle, insects zip and pester.

Then a meteor the size of a small moon screams a fiery path through the fume-filled atmosphere and bombs a mile-deep hole into the earth's surface. A billion tons of pulverized rock fountain skywards and the explosion flings an ellipse of mountains around the crater.

The impact creates a hair-line fissure that zigzags down the continent, and the land immediately spews lava in a frantic effort to weld itself back together. Burning vegetation pours smoke into the thickening atmosphere, the stars vanish, and morning never comes.

All grazing creatures starve and the predators follow them to a premature grave, insects eat their flesh until that, too, is gone, and there is no life left on the face of the earth.

For centuries the world is in darkness. The fissure scabs over in time, and the crater, two hundred miles long and girded by mountains high enough to be ice-clad even in summer, is gradually filled by rain, snow-melt and glaciers until it becomes a vast inland sea, from which three rivers spill south. The dust-cloud settles, and in this deep layer of fertile soil long-dormant seeds crack open, and the earth shines with new green.

Eventually a few fish crawl out of the sea on muscular fins and the slow process of evolution restarts, but when water seeps into the underground lava-flows, the impatient earth mixes it with minerals to create instant life. Before apes learn to walk upright, a race formed of liquid rock has spread out to inhabit the lands divided by the three main rivers.

Near a tributary of the most easterly of those rivers stands a small mountain which, when viewed from the plain, resembles a recumbent giant. Half-way up its steep side, just where the giant's mouth appears to be, is a cave.

A VOLCANIC RACE

CHAPTER ONE – THE HUNT

The three hunters were nearing home when Tomboro spotted the small cave. He must have passed it a dozen times before and not noticed it, but today the angle of the sun cast a shadow – and he could have sworn it was moving. He blinked and looked again – everything was still. He turned away, thinking he must have been mistaken, until he sensed the thump of a slow heartbeat and heard a deep fluttering snore. Startled, he dropped the deer carcass he was carrying and checked its body for a pulse. It was definitely dead. Straightening up, he focussed his attention again on the heartbeat, realising he could hear it through his skin rather than through his ears. In a low voice he alerted Flint and Juncal and began creeping towards the cave, his obvious caution bringing them swiftly to his side.

"What is it, Tom?" Flint whispered.

"Bear," Tom answered, "There's a bear in that cave."

"How could you possibly know from out here?" Juncal scoffed.

Flint unsheathed his knife saying, "If Tom thinks there's a bear in the cave we ought to check."

It was rare to find a bear hibernating this far south, and they approached the cave warily. Although even a bear could not outweigh an adult Rockman, it could still be a dangerous adversary, with powerful claws that could rip through the toughest skin.

Flint took the lead, entering the small cave with Juncal and Tom close behind him. There was no sound, but the smell of bear was unmistakeable, and as their eyes adjusted to the gloom they saw a huge pile of fur almost filling the space. Half-expecting a warning growl they stood very still, wondering why the creature hadn't woken from its hibernation, and sniffing the air for the stink of death. Then the heap emitted a faint snore, far too quietly for Tom to have heard from outside the cave. His heart pounded with excitement. He had found a rare prize – two or three hundred pounds of meat wearing the kind of fur coat that could keep a man alive during the cold winter months.

Moving with infinite caution, Flint insinuated his hand into the heap of fur to find the bear's head, and then his normally sombre face broke into a grin. "There are two of them!" he mouthed, "Are you ready?"

Juncal looked doubtfully at Tom's slight figure as he stepped closer. Flint and Juncal were old hunting partners, but this was Tom's first proper hunt and he was determined not to miss this chance to prove himself.

When he saw Flint's grey muscles tense to tighten his grip on the sleeping bears, Tom knew instinctively what he planned, and raised his knife in readiness. Flint jerked both heads back simultaneously and Juncal and Tom cut their throats – the bears slipped from sleep to death without a sound. As the hot blood ran down Tom's arm he felt a momentary sadness. Murmuring the hunters' prayer, "Go with the Mother," he scooped up a handful of dirt to scrub his arm. When his fingers touched the blood he had a fleeting vision of two spirit bears lumbering from the cave in the wake of Flint and Juncal, who were hauling their carcasses outside. He ran after them, just in time to see the bear spirits vanish north towards the forests which were their natural habitat. "Did you see that?" he asked, but the others were heaving the bears onto their backs and didn't hear him. Tom reclaimed the deer he'd been carrying earlier and started up the mountain track towards home, thinking back to the start of this astonishing week.

*

Only a few days earlier Tom had been deep in the winter Sleep – his volcanic race's equivalent of the bears' hibernation – and the best of his many vivid dreams was the one in which he was riding the lava flowing from a volcano. In reality, the intense heat would have melted him instantly, but in his dream he was unhurt, body-surfing the red-hot waves that flowed beneath the earth. Glowing tunnel walls streaked past him and bubbles of gas exploded beneath him, releasing flashes of incandescent light so bright they left images on his brain. He was yelling with the sheer joy of being alive when a Voice pierced the roar of the volcano – "Tomboro!"

Beneath him the lava was turning dark, with only a hint of red remaining in its depths – his dream

Voice was warning him that the clan's fire was low and it was his turn to tend it – if it died completely it would be his fault.

Jerked out of his dream by the urgent summons, he sat up too quickly and banged his head on the rock above him. Smothering a gasp of pain, he rolled out of his blankets of fur and stumbled along the short passage to push handfuls of coal into the fire. Only just in time, too – if he'd slept for another hour it would have been too late.

The Guaza Clan's cave was the mouth of an old lava tube, with a fissure in the floor that still emitted steam from the depths. This steam-vent gave heat all year round, and was the main reason that this small clan prospered in their isolated fastness. When the Cold started to bite and their bodies slowed down for the winter Sleep, the clan could seal the entrance and retreat inside their centrally-heated cave, secure in the knowledge that they would survive until the spring. Nevertheless they kept their fire burning constantly, and not only for cooking. The Home Fire was sacred – a living link with the lava that gave birth to this volcanic race – and it should never be allowed to go out. From his twelfth birthday, five years earlier, Tom had taken his turn at tending the fire. Usually hunger woke him, but several times this winter he had been roused by that Voice calling him to his duty.

After making sure the fuel had caught properly, Tom cut a chunk of the smoked sausage that hung from the roof, and chewed it while he checked on the rest of the clan. The two children were warm enough – Pedro tucked between his parents Flint and Masaya, and little Kea in Juncal and Etna's bed – but Tom was more concerned about Grandfather, who had been unwell since last autumn. Holding his hand on the old man's chest, he counted three slow, shallow breaths, and then checked on his own mother Hekla before crawling back into his furs. He rubbed his scalp again where he'd hit his head and hoped it proved he had grown during the Sleep, then the play of firelight on the smooth rock walls pulled his eyes closed, and it was several days before he woke again.

*

This morning it had been the smell of curry that woke him. Detecting a hint of goat meat beneath the scent of hot spices, he had stretched comprehensively to send the lava flowing all the way to his toes, wriggled free of his fur blankets and swung his legs onto the floor, almost landing on Pedro's feet.

"I thought you were never going to get up – I've been awake for ages," the younger boy grumbled.

Tom cuffed him, ochre hand meeting brown ear with a resounding thump that had no discernible effect on Pedro's sturdy frame. "You're only cross because you had to do all the chores."

"There wasn't much to do, really," Pedro grinned. "Mother just threw everything that was left into the pot."

At the fire, Pedro's mother Masaya was stirring a handful of spices into the bubbling pot with her strong brown fingers, answering Tom's query with a nod. "Yes, it's goat – I had to use the meat up quickly as it was starting to smell."

"If it's warm enough to thaw the meat then it's definitely Spring," Tom said happily, "Has anyone been outside yet?"

"Flint opened the inner wall to get this meat, but you know the outer seal must wait for your grandfather." Masaya smiled at the boys' eager faces.

"You can wake him now if you like – tell him breakfast's ready."

Grandfather Overo's bed was in a far corner of the cave behind a jutting rock that gave the Leader some privacy, although it also cut him off from the direct heat of the fire. Masaya, his elder daughter, had tried to persuade him to sleep nearer the fire for the winter, but Overo had insisted on staying in his own bed, where his body knew every hollow.

His leathery brown skin was reassuringly hot when Tom touched him, but the old man's chest was as still as the cave wall behind him. Tom pressed his fingers into the hollow behind Overo's ear, and his eyes widened. "I can't find a pulse!"

"Try again!" Pedro urged in panic. "Grandfather can't be dead."

"I'm afraid he might be," Tom answered.

Then the same Voice he had heard in his dreams told him, "Don't give up so soon." So he shook the old man's shoulder roughly while Pedro yelled, "There's goat curry for breakfast," directly into Overo's ear.

When there was still no reaction, Tom laid his head on Overo's chest. "I can't hear a heartbeat," he told Pedro. "But I'm sure he's not dead – I can feel his spirit in there."

Pedro gaped at him. "You can't! You're not a Seer – Hekla is." He raised his voice to shout, "Come and help us – we can't wake Grandfather!"

Within seconds the adults had pushed Tom and Pedro aside to crowd round the Leader. Little Kea peered past Pedro's hip. "Why won't Grandfather wake up?" she quavered, beginning to cry.

Etna picked her up, saying, "Hush, child – it's probably his time to return to the Mother."

"You give up too easily," Masaya snapped. "Father can't die yet."

Etna simply shrugged – she was used to her sister being short with her – and carried Kea back to the fire.

Pedro nudged Tom. "Come on, let's go too – we can't do anything here."

Tom shook him off. "Grandfather's not dead," he insisted, laying his hand protectively over the old man's heart. "Do something!" he urged the men, "I know he's alive."

Flint gripped Tom's shoulder. "What do you mean?"

"His spirit's still there in his body," Tom said, spreading his free hand on his own chest, "I know in my heart he's still alive – try harder!"

Flint frowned doubtfully as he pinched the old man's arm. "The boy could be right!" he exclaimed, "Overo's not stiffened yet – if we act quickly we might be able to save him." With Juncal's help he lifted Overo's body and carried him to the centre of the cave.

The old man literally weighed a ton, but they held him directly over the scalding steam vent while Masaya and the boys worked feverishly to rub some circulation back into his limbs. Gradually, as the heat seeped into his stones, Overo's sluggish lava flowed more freely and he began to stir. After many anxious minutes he opened his eyes and his family eased him into a seat.

Blinking at the circle of concerned faces he growled, "Why are you all standing round like idiots?"

and slapped Masaya's hands away from his arm. "Leave me alone, girl – I'll move when I'm ready." Tom and Pedro grinned at each other – Grandfather still burned with his usual fire – and, as if to emphasize his return to normal, Overo demanded his breakfast. After demolishing a bowl of curry he winked at Masaya. "Not bad – though it could have done with more chilli."

Masaya chuckled – food was never spicy enough for her father but, after this morning's scare, it was a relief to hear him complain.

While the rest of the clan ate their breakfasts, Flint watched Tom surreptitiously, wondering whether the boy really had sensed the old man's spirit. It could have been simply wishful thinking, but if Tom had the Sight he should be encouraged to develop it. That would be the Seer's task, he thought, and realised rather belatedly that Hekla was missing. "Where's your mother?" he asked Tom, "She should have known Overo needed her."

"I expect she's in her Sanctum," Tom mumbled through a mouthful of curry. "She was gone when I woke up – perhaps she felt a Sign."

*

Deep in the heart of the mountain, Hekla lay full length on the warm rock, keeping her whole body in contact with the earth, and her eyes closed to shut out the distraction of the torchlight sparkling off the flecks of gold in the black walls. Her first visit of the year to the Sanctum was always special, but this spring it was doubly important. She had been aware of the earth's restlessness since the previous autumn, and early this morning a strong Call had woken her from the winter Sleep. She had made her way to her Sanctum still half-asleep, but now that she was fully alert she could feel the vibrations as Mother Earth sought the weaker places in Her skin through which She could release pressure. The Mother was preparing to give birth, and as the contractions rippled through Her body, Hekla sensed them. She concentrated her Seer's power and the Sign came through clearly – a child was coming for the Guaza Clan, and it was her duty to make sure the parents were at the right place in time.

Hekla had been born in a land of long winters and pale skies, where only the hardiest of this heat-loving race could survive. Over several years she had migrated south with her young son, earning her living as a nomadic Seer. She had joined the Guaza Clan three years previously at a Clan Festival, and when their old Seer died she had filled the vacancy.

She sat up stiffly – her blue body was more resistant to cold than those of the Guaza Clan, but the lava that flowed in her veins was still sluggish after the long Sleep. She had been lying for over an hour in her Sanctum, making certain of the Signs, and now she needed food. She reached up to take her torch from its socket.

Clutching her cloak around her body, she hurried along the familiar passage to join the clan, only pausing at the final curve to adjust her furs and assume the dignified demeanour appropriate to a Seer. The moment she stepped into the firelight there was a stir of anticipation. She waved her hand in an imperious 'Not now' gesture and sat in her rightful place beside Overo.

Masaya passed her a bowl of hot curry and stood back, twisting her hands nervously as she waited for her to speak. Hekla peered at the group through the steam rising from her bowl – a ploy she often used to add an air of mystery – then she relented and told Masaya, "The Signs are still weak but they are definite. It is as I suspected last autumn – you will have another baby this spring."

Flint flung his enormous arm around Masaya and she looked up at him with shining eyes. "This year! I'll start packing now."

"Not so fast, woman," Flint laughed, "We don't even know where we're going yet."

"The Sign is from the west, beyond Cold River," Hekla told them. "It's not so clear after that, although I know it will be a long journey."

"We'll probably be heading for the far side of the desert," Overo guessed, "That's the only mountain range west of Cold River."

"That's what I'm assuming too," said Hekla, "The Signs aren't detailed enough yet."

"That's an awfully long way," Masaya said with a worried frown, but Etna said gleefully, "We can stop at Grand Oasis for Kea to meet Juncal's parents."

"They might be dead," Kea said calmly, "Grandfather Overo nearly was."

There was a moment of horrified silence which Overo broke by slapping his knees and saying cheerfully, "Nonsense, child – I was merely slow to wake up, that's all."

"Everyone thought you were dead except Tom," Kea insisted, "He said your spirit was still there – I heard him."

Hekla glared at her son. "How dare you say that! You know nothing about spirits."

Tom recoiled from her anger but stood his ground. "The others woke him up – I just felt certain he was alive, that's all."

"Which I most certainly am," Overo said, frowning at Hekla. "I'm glad the boy insisted, though, or I'd have woken up too late for breakfast." He peered into the cauldron. "Is this all the food we've got? That's not enough for several weeks away from home."

"The last of the frozen meat and vegetables went in there," Masaya said, "We've only a got few sausages left." She pointed to the ceiling, where a dozen or so big sausages hung in the smoke from the fire. "We'll need more than those for a long journey."

"Then Flint must go hunting today," Overo said.

"Juncal should go with him," Masaya added quickly, "We'll need lots of meat so we can dry some for travelling."

"It's not up to you to decide what Juncal does," Etna snapped, "He'll be busy enough at the mine – we'll need to take coal too."

"The mining can wait until tomorrow," Juncal said, "I'd much rather go with Flint today."

As Masaya smirked over her small victory and Etna seethed, Overo sighed. They'd only been awake for an hour, his daughters were squabbling already, and it seemed Hekla and Tom had also fallen out. If he didn't step in quickly the whole clan would be at loggerheads before the journey even began. Grunting with effort he heaved himself up with the aid of his staff and moved towards the entrance. "I believe it's time we opened up the cave," he said, adding pointedly, "Perhaps that will clear the air."

The lava tube that formed the passage was roughly twenty feet in diameter – twice the height of a grown Rockman – and fifteen yards long from the cave where they lived to the inner wall that Flint had dismantled earlier. The clan's ancestors had filled the cave-mouth with tightly-packed rocks to form the strong outer wall and reduce the threshold to a size one man could defend. Just before they entered the winter Sleep the clan blocked this threshold with a massive boulder – the gaps around it allowed smoke to escape, and the freezing air that leaked in preserved their winter stockpile of meat.

On reaching the wall, Overo peered through a tiny gap and said, "The sky's blue with only a scattering of clouds – it looks like a fine day for hunting." Amid the semicircle of beaming faces he struck the boulder with his staff, booming, "The Guaza Clan welcomes the spring!" then Flint and Juncal put their shoulders beside Overo's on the vast rock and heaved. After a long moment the boulder rolled ponderously aside, groaning as it shifted from its winter resting-place, and the men jumped clear to let it fall into its summer groove.

Immediately Hekla bustled forward to complete the ritual by sprinkling the threshold with fire-powder and igniting it with a taper, praying,

"Mother Earth – with Your sacred fire we thank You for bringing us all safely through the Sleep, and ask You to bless our coming journey."

The moment she had finished, Overo strode through the flaming powder into the spring sunshine of the plateau, followed by the entire clan.

After the warmth of the cave the air struck chill, but they hugged their furs tightly around their bodies and took deep, grateful breaths of the fresh air. This first sight of the outside world after months of darkness was always a special moment, and the excitement affected all of them in different ways. Juncal and Etna tossed their daughter Kea between them, laughing at the little girl's shrieks of delighted terror as she flew from one pair of arms to the other. Flint and Masaya walked to the very edge of the plateau to gaze west as if they could bring that distant volcano and their long-awaited baby nearer merely by wishing. Overo and Hekla sat on a rock by the entrance, soaking up the spring sunshine like the lizards that basked in the cracks of the nearby wall, and Pedro rediscovered a football. The inflated deer stomach had gone soft during the winter but he kicked it to Tom anyway. Tom simply lifted the limp bag on one toe and flipped it the width of the plateau into the rocks.

"What's up with you?" Pedro grumbled, "We always have a kick-about on our first day outside."

"I've got more important things to think about," Tom retorted, and walked away along the track that led further up the mountain, looking for somewhere he could think in peace.

Once he was out of sight of the plateau he sat on a rock in the sun and replayed in his mind the puzzling events of this morning. First there was the strange Voice that had woken him out of his Sleep dreams several times to put fuel on the fire, and he wondered if it could have been the Voice of Mother Earth Herself? He could ask his mother the Seer but, judging by the way she'd snarled at him this morning, it would be a waste of time. Then there was this business about Grandfather and how he, Tom, had known he was alive when everyone else thought he was dead. Maybe it was only the fact that the old man was still hot – everyone knew that dead people turned into cold, hard rock. And it had only been a day or so since he'd felt Grandfather breathing – perhaps that was it? Tom shook his head. No – that was what the others thought, but he knew better. He had sensed a living soul in that stiff body and there was no point in denying it, least of all to himself. Who could he talk to about these new sensations? He had no friends of his own age who might have helped.

Tom kicked a rock savagely – if Hekla had been a proper mother like Masaya they'd have stayed in one place and he would have friends to talk to. He could barely remember the clan in which he'd spent his first few years, or the father who had died – his mother's wanderlust had taken them to too many different places. On their travels Hekla used to talk to him about the insistent Call that had kept her moving south, dragging her young son along, hunting for meat to keep them alive or trading her skills for food and shelter. Tom had been too young to understand when she said Mother Earth was talking to her – now he wished he'd asked her what the Mother's Voice sounded like.

Looking round quickly to make sure no-one was watching, he pressed his hands on the rock, hoping it would speak to him, but of course nothing happened. Maybe Mother Earth only spoke when She had something important to say, Tom thought, and he'd heard the message that Grandfather was alive because Hekla was in her Sanctum out of reach. Then he remembered his mother saying she always heard messages better in her Sanctum, so that couldn't be right. Perhaps he was turning into a Seer as well? It was all very confusing.

"Is this some kind of test?" he asked aloud, and an echo bounced off the mountain which sounded remarkably like 'Yes'. Feeling oddly comforted, Tom ran back to the plateau where Pedro was kicking a rock about and wearing a sulky expression. A pang of guilt at having left his young friend alone prompted Tom to call, "Chuck me that football and I'll blow it up so we can have a proper game." A few minutes later he and Pedro were just boys – Voices and spirits forgotten.

Overo saw the boys playing together and sighed with relief – that was one worry less. It had been a dreadful shock to wake up stretched over the steam-vent like a side of venison, and he knew in his stones that he'd had a close brush with death. Rock bodies needed heat to survive, and the souls of the elderly often slipped back to Mother Earth during the winter Sleep. In a way he would have been happy to be reunited with Maipu, he thought, then scolded himself for the wish. The Mother obviously wanted him to lead the Guaza Clan westwards – maybe when he had performed that duty he would be allowed to join his mate. On that comforting thought he fetched a glowing coal from the fire and held it to his clay pipe while he brought his thoughts back to the present.

When the pipe was drawing properly he continued holding the coal to warm his fingers while he asked Hekla, "Have you any idea how much time we've got to prepare?"

It seemed a long time before Hekla answered, "I'm not sure – the Signs were very faint. I do know it will be a journey of two or three weeks. We will need a few days to get ready for that, but the Mother wouldn't send the Call if She knew we couldn't get there in time." Hekla looked sternly at the old Leader. "Will you be up to the journey? You were very close to returning to the Mother today."

"Don't you worry about me," he replied gruffly, "I was only a bit slow in waking up, that's all – there's life in these old stones yet!"

"You mustn't hold Flint and Masaya back," Hekla warned, "If they miss this chance for a baby they might not get another."

"You forget your place, Hekla," Overo huffed, blowing herbal smoke in angry clouds, so Hekla bit her lip and refrained from further comment. Turning instead to watch Tom, she repeated an earlier effort to read his thoughts but, as before, she hit a blank wall. Her grey eyes darkened – if Tom had already learned how to shut her out, she faced a major problem – there was only room for one Seer in the Guaza Clan.

Shreds of Helka's conversation with Overo had drifted through the clear mountain air to Flint and Masaya, who were still standing at the rim of the plateau.

"I thought we'd never have another baby," Masaya was saying, "Even when Hekla hinted at it last year I was afraid to hope." Her round brown face shone with excitement.

Flint tried to inject a note of caution. "It's a long way to go for a baby," he said, "Pedro was born much closer to home. I hope Hekla knows what she's talking about."

Masaya gnawed her fist anxiously. "If she's read the Sign wrong we could be too late – perhaps we should leave at once."

Flint put his arm round her shoulders in a reassuring hug, wishing he hadn't voiced his doubts. "We'll get there, love – I'll make sure of that."

Pedro groaned inwardly at his parents' public display of affection. He had enjoyed their undivided attention for ten years, and with a new baby to look after they'd have little time left for him. Then he cheered himself up with the thought that to get this baby the whole clan was going on a journey, and perhaps he'd make his first proper kill while they were travelling.

As if he'd heard Pedro's thoughts, Overo slapped his hands on his knees and said, "Right! You've all had long enough to stretch the Sleep out of your limbs. Is anyone going hunting today, or must I do it myself?"

"We're going now," Flint said immediately, and when he and Juncal turned to go and fetch their spears Tom announced, "I'm coming with you."

Flint looked at him doubtfully. "Are you sure? You've never hunted for a whole day before."

"I've grown a hand's-width during the Sleep," Tom said, standing as tall as he could, "You needn't worry – I'll keep up." He held his breath until Flint nodded and said, "All right, you can come – get your spear."

Five minutes later, when Flint and Juncal began their descent of the steep mountain track, Tom was already a good way down, determined that no-one should call him back.

Down on the plain, Tom echoed every move the two older men made, taking care to avoid snapping any fallen branches and feeling for loose stones with his toes – the last thing he wanted was to ruin the first hunt of the season. They blended well into the landscape – Flint's body was the grey of the rock for which he was named, while Juncal's colour reflected the sandstone of his native desert. At ten feet tall they were nearly the same height as the wind-stunted trees of the savannah, and each man weighed close to a ton, but after years of experience they moved smoothly, making little sound on the hunting grounds they knew so well.

A few miles from home Flint spotted a herd of deer and dropped to his haunches. Juncal and Tom instantly followed suit, their crouched shapes matching the rocks which dotted the area. Tom scanned the herd with the eyes of a hunter – mingled with the does and fawns were some young males, which were exactly what they were looking for. One or two animals lifted their heads and subjected these new rocks to a puzzled scrutiny and then, when nothing moved, returned to their grazing.

At Flint's whispered instruction, Tom crawled through the long grass on his belly, confident that his body gave off no scent and his ochre skin matched the dry stems of last year's growth. The two older men inched closer until they were only a few yards from the small herd, and as soon as Tom was in position Flint hissed a signal. With a surge of speed that gave the startled herd no time to flee, the three apparent boulders sprang upright and hurled their spears with all the power of their rock muscles. Two young bucks fell to Flint and Juncal's spears and the rest of the herd bounded away, leaving Flint and Juncal to sling the carcasses over their shoulders and move on. Tom trailed after them, kicking stones in disgust that his own spear had flown wide.

Having achieved their first kill of the year, the hunters were less alert than they should have been, and failed to spot the solitary lion stalking them. They were strolling through a copse when the tawny creature burst out of the dappled shadows and knocked Flint off his feet. The lion simply wanted the deer and was no threat to Flint, but Flint wasn't about to give up the meat. With his arms momentarily pinned under the combined weight of meat and lion, he yelled for help.

Rushing forward, Tom grabbed the lion's nose to prise its jaws apart and rescue the deer, while Juncal whipped out his knife and launched himself onto the lion's back, gripping the mane with one hand while he sawed at the animal's throat with his stone blade. The lion reared up, knocking Juncal's knife from his hand,

and Flint scrambled free, leaving Juncal still wrestling with the lion.

Tom drew his own knife and circled round them, trying to find an opening while Juncal and the lion rolled around in the dirt, well-matched in growling ferocity. The lion's tawny pelt and Juncal's skin were so similar in colour that Tom was afraid of stabbing the wrong body. Suddenly he saw his chance and darted in to slice through the animal's jugular.

Juncal scrambled from beneath its body grumbling, "I was just getting into my stride there!" but he gripped Tom's arm briefly in gratitude.

"Now you've finished playing, Juncal, we've got to get this meat home," Flint scolded, "The women won't be pleased if it's gone off before they can cook it."

When Juncal stooped to throw the lion over his shoulder, Tom asked, "What's the point in bringing that? It's no good to eat."

"I can eat anything, but I fancy a lion-skin cape," grinned Juncal, holding the fearsome head above his own, "How do I look?"

"I think you're mad," Tom replied, laughing as he picked up Juncal's forgotten deer, "I'll be surprised if you can persuade Hekla to cure the skin."

"Oh, she will do it for me," Juncal said with supreme confidence, "No woman can resist my charms."

With a shrug of acquiescence, Flint led the trio of hunters towards home. They were nearly in the shadow of their mountain when Tom saw the cave and heard that snore.

*

The hunting party took until dusk to reach home, and all three were exhausted from the long haul up the winding mountain track. Tom was carrying both deer while Flint and Juncal struggled under the weight of a bear each, and Juncal was also dragging along the lion which he had refused to leave for the scavengers.

Overo and the women and children had been looking forward to a meal of fresh venison and were delighted to see the two deer, but when the hunters dumped their loads outside the cave entrance it was the bears that grabbed all the attention.

"What luck to get two bears!" exclaimed Overo, stroking the thick winter pelts, "Where did you find these?"

"Tom discovered them in that small cave near the track," Flint told him, "Though it's a mystery how he knew they were there. He must be psychic – we were fifty yards away."

Hekla scowled ferociously, but before she could ask Tom any questions Juncal pushed the lion into view. Pedro and Kea gazed at it in awe, clamouring for every detail of the fight. Juncal immediately launched into a vivid description to which the children listened open-mouthed with admiration.

Etna's black eyes flashed angrily. "How could you be so stupid?" she blazed, "The last thing we need is you being injured when we have a journey to make! You could have cracked your head open."

"There wasn't a rock anywhere near me," Juncal said defensively, "And besides, I thought you'd be pleased to have its teeth for a necklace."

Etna could never be angry with him for long and relented enough to say, "A necklace would be nice, but you should have been more careful."

"Not only that," Masaya said, "You stopping to fight the lion means we haven't got time to roast the deer – we'll have to cook bear liver for supper."

"You should ask Hekla to fix those scratches," Etna added as she and Masaya began to butcher the meat. Juncal looked at himself in surprise – he hadn't noticed that his arms bore several deep gouges, which were already beginning to crust over.

"You'd better heat those up quickly before your lava sets any harder," Hekla said, so Juncal held his arms over the scalding steam-vent to soften the skin while Hekla hurriedly mixed powdered clay and oil into a paste. "I'm afraid the scars are going to show," she said as she stirred, "I haven't got any clay your colour."

Juncal didn't mind what colour she used. When the paste was moulded into his wounds, his own lava would burn off the oil and blend with the clay to heal the gashes – a few contrasting scars would prove he had defeated a lion in battle.

Tom, reluctant to face the questions his mother was obviously itching to ask, was hoping Juncal's story would distract her attention, but it was a forlorn hope. In the close confines of the cave it was impossible to evade her indefinitely.

As soon as supper was over she pounced. "What's this nonsense about you being psychic?" both her words and her tone of voice betraying her scepticism.

Tom defended himself with as much confidence as he could muster. "I knew there were bears in that cave before we reached it."

"How could you have known? You must have heard something."

In the glow from the fire Tom could see her scornful eyes boring into his. What was even worse, he could feel her trying to probe his thoughts. He recoiled from her intrusion and turned his face away, trying to pacify her by saying, "That must be it – perhaps I heard them snoring."

It was a relief to hear Overo say, "It's been a tiring day for us all – time for bed."

As Tom settled down in his fur-padded bed he could still feel Hekla probing for a way into his thoughts. He forced his tired mind to picture Juncal wrestling with the lion, and when Hekla eventually broke through his barrier, all she saw were two tawny bodies rolling around in the dust.

CHAPTER TWO – PREPARATIONS

The next morning Juncal went to the mine further up the mountain to dig coal for the journey, leaving Flint and Tom to go hunting without him.

When they reached the foot of the mountain track, Flint asked almost casually, "Which way shall we go today, Tom? You found the bears – let's see if you can find an ordinary herd."

Tom studied his face, suspecting mockery, but Flint was perfectly serious. Feeling the responsibility weighing heavily on his shoulders, Tom shut his eyes to concentrate. After a few moments he sensed, beyond the sounds of wind-blown grass and trickling water, the pulse of many heartbeats and the crunch and tear of animals grazing. He opened his eyes and pointed southwest. "There's a herd that way, over those hills."

"I can't see them," Flint said, "But let's see if you're right."

Several miles and two hills further on they found Tom's herd, and then there was no time for anything but the hunt.

They were on the way home with a brace of deer apiece before Flint asked, "How on earth did you know where they were?"

Although Tom had anticipated the question it was still difficult to answer. "I felt a kind of vibration, as if I was connected to them through the ground somehow – I can't explain any clearer than that." He glanced at the bigger man and added, "Don't say anything to my mother, will you?"

Flint smiled sympathetically. "She wasn't very encouraging yesterday, was she? Well, I'll keep quiet if you want me to, but it won't remain a secret for long. If you can do that every time we hunt we'll have enough meat in no time."

The next few days were a blur of activity. While Flint and Tom hunted, Masaya and Etna prepared food for the journey. They filled pottery jars with stew, sealing them with fat to exclude the air; they made meat puddings by filling skin bags with cooked meat and grain, and turned scraps and intestines into long, spicy sausages. Even Kea was kept busy drying strips of meat on the slabs of hot rock that surrounded the steam-vent.

Meanwhile Overo and Pedro repaired the sledges. Reluctant though he was to admit it, Overo was feeling his age and knew it was likely that Tom's instinct *had* saved his life that first morning. Searching for some task that would keep his mind off such dismal thoughts and prove that he could still be useful, he discovered the travelling sledge needed a complete overhaul. The big wooden sledge was fifteen feet long and half as wide –roomy enough to take all the clan's possessions on long trips. Although it was solidly made, it had been out in the open for the three years since the last Clan Festival. The smaller sledge also needed attention and, content to have found a task worthy of his skills, Overo inspected every inch of them.

Not surprisingly, the weather had rotted the leather bindings, but he was pleased to find the basic structure was still sound. He would have to check every joint and replace all the bindings, the runners would have to be rubbed smooth, and they would need new rollers. The job would keep him occupied while the younger men hunted, and should banish any thoughts about him being too old for what promised to be an exciting trip. He recruited Pedro, who was delighted not to be at the beck and call of the women, and sent him to fell saplings from which to construct new rollers.

Hekla, after sorting out her medicine bag in preparation for the trip, spent her time curing hides. When the new bearskin capes were finished, she draped them over a rock near the fire for the clan to admire their vast splendour. As a matter of course, Overo had one of them, and Hekla claimed the other. "I've done all the work of curing them so I've earned the right," she said, "And the Seer's just as important as the Leader."

There was a beat of shocked silence before Flint said, "We wouldn't have found the bears at all if it wasn't for Tom. In fact he's been locating the herds on every hunt since, and I'm convinced the Mother is helping him."

"Utter nonsense!" Hekla snorted. "For one thing he's much too young – my own Sight hadn't developed by his age."

"Tom is almost a man," Overo said quietly, "And Maipu was a Seer from childhood." Overo's reference to his lost mate was enough to silence any further argument as he continued, "Hekla is right in one respect – she worked the capes so she should have one of them."

While Hekla smirked and draped the thick fur round her shoulders, despite the fire's heat, Juncal said hurriedly, "I hope no-one is going to deny the lion skin is mine." He pulled it from its peg and wrapped it around his body, striking a pose in the firelight. Hekla had left the head and tail attached and Juncal's looming shadow on the cave wall brought the beast back to startling life.

"You look magnificent in that skin," Etna said, "You should be the next Leader."

"For heaven's sake, Etna!" Masaya gasped, "At least wait till Father's actually gone before you talk about replacing him." Realising she had overstepped the mark Etna hid her embarrassment in Kea's soft neck, but her words hung in the air.

"Well, I think Juncal looks like a real lion," Tom said quickly, hoping to defuse the moment.

Picking up on his cue, Juncal pounced on Etna, growling ferociously, "I feel like a real lion – mated to a lioness."

Etna glowed with pleasure, Kea squealed, and Masaya's irritation subsided. Soon after that the clan retired to their beds, Hekla taking her bearskin cape with her as if still afraid someone would steal it.

Later that night Tom was woken by the sound of two rock bodies clashing against each other and guessed what was happening – there are few secrets in a shared cave. After Juncal's imitation of a lion he had seen Etna slide her Bondstone into the embers of the fire. Many times on their travels he and Hekla had shared a clan's cave or a campfire, and Tom had occasionally seen couples mating. One night he had glimpsed a woman slip her glowing Bondstone between her belly and the man's, and ever since then he had wondered what mating was like. For the hundredth time he wished he had a father he could ask.

Earlier that day he and Flint had witnessed a buck mounting a doe, and Tom had ventured to ask, "Rockmen don't mate like the animals, do they?"

Flint's grey skin had turned a painful mottled colour and he'd made a great play of sharpening his spear as he muttered, "You should ask your mother about that."

"I can't ask her – she's a woman. Besides, she's not speaking to me since I found the bears."

"She's probably just busy," Flint had said. "Now – while that buck's occupied, let's get ourselves a couple of the younger ones," and the subject was dropped.

Lying in his bed now, Tom watched Juncal and Etna's shadows until they subsided into a murmuring heap, but he was no wiser.

Towards the end of the night he had a dream in which he was holding Etna's Bondstone. As he turned it over it broke in half, releasing a flood of lava which he tried to catch in his cupped hands. It writhed so much that it slipped from his grasp into a rain puddle and formed into the shape of a baby. He snatched it up and found it was attached to a shining, cobweb-fine filament that stretched far into the distant west.

Tom half-woke and lay in his furs, thinking his dream must have been about the expected baby. The only problem was that it had come from Etna's stone. Did that mean the baby the clan was expecting should be her baby, not Masaya's? He was wondering how to ask his mother when the same Voice he had heard in his Sleep-dreams said, "Get up, Tom – it's time to leave – now!" with such urgency that he rolled out of bed onto the floor.

Dragging on his tunic, he hurried to the centre of the cave, where he found Etna hauling in the line on which the meat puddings had been suspended to cook over the steam vent. "Surely that's enough food?" she was saying to Masaya, "We've made twelve of these and all those sausages."

"It should be enough with the stew and the dried meat," Masaya replied, "And it's been five days since Hekla heard the Call – if we wait any longer we'll get there too late."

"My Voice says we should be leaving now," Tom blurted out.

"What voice?" Hekla snapped from behind him.

Tom was struggling for an answer when Flint spoke up for him. "The one that's made certain we found a herd every time we went hunting. If Tom says he heard a Call, I say we should go today – and it *is* my baby."

"I am this clan's Seer, not Tom!" Hekla said furiously.

Overo's authoritative tones cut through the rising argument. "Everybody calm down!" The Leader squeezed Hekla's arm. "We're all on edge, Hekla – just go and talk to the Mother for us, please."

Hekla took a deep breath to argue further, but at the look on Overo's face she said, "All right – I'll go to my Sanctum and ask Her again, if it will make you feel any better." Draping her new bearskin around her shoulders, she stalked off.

Once she had entered the passage at the rear of the cave the clan's voices faded, and she allowed the silence to engulf and soothe her. She laid her hand against the living rock to feel the pulse of the earth. Her eyes widened – the Call had doubled in strength since yesterday! She hurried to the Sanctum, spread her cape on the floor and lay prostrate.

The earth's pulse was a strong beat now, and her lava picked up the rhythm as the minerals in her body became aligned to the increasing pull from the west. She lay still, warmed by the same Earth-heat that escaped as steam in their home cave, praying for the success of their quest. When she was absolutely certain of the Call's direction she sped to the cave, where one look at her face told Tom his Voice had been right – today was the day.

"We need to move fast," Hekla told Overo, "The Signs are much stronger now."

"I knew we should have left sooner," Masaya wailed, "We've waited years for this baby."

"Are you sure the child isn't for me?" Etna asked suddenly, "Masaya's a bit old to be a mother again."

Masaya rounded on her sister, spitting fire. "Of course it's mine! Hekla wouldn't make a mistake like that. And your Kea's only three – it's my turn."

"Stop squabbling, the pair of you!" Overo roared, "Anyone would think you were still children." Overo rarely raised his voice and he took advantage of their shocked silence to add, "Now – Hekla says we must leave straight away so I suggest you all get a move on."

"We can be ready to leave in an hour," Flint said, reaching up to unhook the smoked meat from the cave roof. "I hope you girls can pack the food without coming to blows?"

In frosty silence, Etna and Masaya began filling leather sacks with the meat puddings and sausages. Juncal started collecting the clan's fur blankets together, and Overo told the boys, "Come on, Tom – Pedro – we'll check the sledges."

Overo and Pedro went along the passageway towards the entrance, but Tom hung back with his thoughts churning. What if Hekla *had* made a mistake about whose baby it was? Etna's outburst reminded him of last night's dream – perhaps she *was* the intended mother. "Mother – I need to talk to you," he began.

Hekla waved him away like a troublesome wasp. "Can't you see I'm busy? I've no time now for more of your foolishness."

Tom could see there was no point in insisting now – he would have to try again once they were on their way.

CHAPTER THREE – THE JOURNEY STARTS

Within an hour the clan was ready to leave. The coal that Juncal had mined filled half of the large sledge, with jars and leather sacks of provisions taking up the other half. The new rollers Pedro had cut were laid on top of the lot. Masaya and Etna had packed their cooking pots and furs in the smaller sledge and tidied their cave for the long absence – there remained only one more task to be performed before they could leave.

Overo carefully selected an ember from the Home Fire and placed it in the clay Firepot on a bed of charcoal, after which each clan member in turn, from Flint down to Kea, added their own chosen ember. Hekla positioned each one with careful fingers to make certain the small new fire was burning properly – the clan never undertook a journey without carrying this link with the Home Fire. Once it was safely stowed among the furs in the small sledge, with a sack of charcoal beside it, Overo kicked the remnants of the Home Fire into the steam vent to return it to Mother Earth, Hekla said a prayer to protect the cave, and they all trooped outside.

As the massive boulder dropped into place to seal the entrance, Tomboro had an overwhelming sense that it was closing off a significant part of his life, not simply the cave. He watched the dust float up like the last wisps of smoke from a dying fire and swallowed hard. When he turned round, Overo was watching him.

The old man smiled sympathetically. "It will still be here when we come back, Tom."

"If we come back," Tom replied, unable to meet Grandfather's eyes for fear of what he might see there. "I have a premonition …" but Overo held a finger across the young man's lips. "The clan will return home, Tomboro. Now stop dreaming and give me a hand with this harness."

When Tom had helped him to settle the straps of the small sledge over his shoulders, Overo gripped his stout staff and paused to fix the memory of home in his mind, more disturbed than he cared to admit by Tom's words. Many generations of the Guaza Clan had inhabited this remote spot – the men hunting on the plain below while the women cleared the plateau and planted food crops – surely they were destined to return? He clapped his hand on Tom's shoulder. "Come on, lad, best foot forward – adventure calls!" he said, his cheerful tones lifting everyone's spirits as they set off across the broad mountain plateau.

Spring was everywhere – the sledge runners crushed scent from the fresh grass, the air was filled with the sound of birds, and beside them a stream splashed merrily to fall in a series of little waterfalls to the plain below. Masaya gazed longingly at the un-tilled soil of the field beyond the stream. Etna, who was less enthusiastic about farming, remarked happily, "We won't have to do any digging this year."

"We should be back in time to plant something – chillies and beans at least," Masaya said. She smiled when Pedro added, "And yams – we've got to have yams."

"You'd better make the most of this holiday, then," Etna said sourly, "You'll be helping in the field when we get back." Pedro scowled – in his opinion he worked hard enough already without Etna putting ideas into his mother's head – and he ran ahead to join Tom.

Tom had remained beside Grandfather, ready to help if the sledge proved too heavy for him. His heart was heavy with the premonition that they wouldn't all be coming back, and he was especially afraid for the old man.

Overo was thinking along the same lines. It was three years since he had woken from the winter Sleep to find Maipu cold and stiff beside him, and he still missed her. Only last night he had gone up to the clan's burial site to sit by her cairn and ask her who should succeed him as Leader if he didn't survive this journey. There were only two possible candidates. Etna's mate Juncal had adapted surprisingly well to life in the cool mountain air after a youth spent in the desert heat, and he was an excellent miner. Unfortunately Etna was the driving force in that relationship, and a man ruled by his mate would not make a good Leader. Overo thought that Flint, Bonded to his elder daughter Masaya, would be the better choice. Maipu had agreed, of course, although she had reminded Overo that Flint was a little overfond of the freedom of the hunt. They both suspected that Flint often stayed in the hunt shelter overnight from choice rather than necessity, but he was the more serious man of the two. A bonus was that both Tom and Pedro looked up to him. Casting a lingering look at the plateau which had been his home for so many years, Overo thought this journey would be an ideal opportunity to observe both men, because whether he returned with them or not, he was weary and more than ready to hand over the Leadership to the next generation.

Lost in his thoughts, he jumped when Tom touched his arm. "Grandfather! The big sledge is ready to start the descent." Flint and Juncal had reached the edge of the plateau and turned their sledge round to lower it backwards down the steep slope.

"Right, boys," Overo said, shaking off his sombre mood, "It's time for the rollers – this is where the real work begins."

The sledges would slide over grass or smooth ground, but on rougher ground they ran on rollers cut from tree trunks, and it was Tom and Pedro's job to position them. Lifting the first roller from the big sledge, they held it in position while Flint and Juncal eased the weight of the sledge onto it, and then onto a second roller and a third, by which time the boys had run round to the front with the first one again. It was back-breaking work, even for the strong Rockmen, but yard by yard, roller by roller, Flint and Juncal manoeuvred the heavy sledge down the first section of the trail, the boys moving the rollers from the back to the front again and again while the men strained on their harnesses to control the slide.

Overo held back until they had moved some distance then told his daughters, "You girls can help me while Hekla goes ahead to clean the shelter. I doubt those men of yours have left it in a fit state for us to sleep in."

Masaya and Etna exchanged looks of horror – Father was right, the shelter was probably littered with rubbish. They couldn't let Hekla clear that up – the shame would be a dreadful start to the journey.

"I'll go," Etna said quickly, "The Seer should stay with you to tend the Firepot." Taking Kea by the hand, she squeezed past the big sledge and hurried down the track before her father could raise any objections.

It was well after noon when mother and daughter reached the plain. Kea was tired and hungry, so Etna fished a roasted bone out of her backpack for her to chew while she made the shelter habitable. Thanking the stars that she had got there first, she dumped three years' worth of debris on the midden. There were bones the hunters had cracked open for the marrow, several broken spears and a mouldy fur, and the fireplace was buried under a huge pile of ash. Once she had cleared that, she replaced the rocks that had fallen from the fireplace before pulling up a small shrub to sweep the dirt floor on which they would be sleeping tonight. She collected kindling and dead branches for the fire, then dozed beside Kea in the hot sun to wait for the others.

First to arrive were Overo, Hekla and Masaya with the small sledge, having overtaken the others on a wide stretch of track. Overo slumped against the wall grumbling, "I don't remember it being such hard work last time," and closed his eyes while the three women finished preparing the camp for the night. Using a coal from the Firepot they soon had a fire warming the shelter, and only then did it dawn on them that they had nothing to cook.

"The others will be here soon expecting food," Masaya wailed, "We should have packed some in with the Firepot."

"Father will have to go hunting," Etna said, but Overo was asleep and obviously too tired to hunt. The sisters were looking at each other in dismay when Hekla said, "I'll find us something." She produced a slingshot from her belt, laughing at their incredulous expressions. "How do you think I fed myself and Tom all those years on the move? I used to be quite skilful with this sling – if I haven't lost my touch we'll have something cooking by the time the men arrive." Selecting a few round stones from the ground, she left her cape in the warmest corner of the shelter to stake her claim before walking naked into the surrounding bush.

Following the mountain stream that now ran gently through the grassland she found, as she had hoped, that it fed into a shallow pool. Many hoof-prints proved that it was a popular watering place, so she sat down to wait. The moment she had settled into stillness she became simply a blue rock, and there was nothing to alarm the family of dikdiks that came down in the late afternoon to drink. Aiming at one of the young bucks, Hekla whipped her leather sling swiftly to launch one of her stones, grunting with satisfaction when the small deer dropped instantly. The rest scattered in panic as Hekla dispatched the animal with a quick slash to the throat, offered its blood to Mother Earth in thanks for the kill, and returned to the hunt shelter with her prize.

Refreshed by his nap, Overo opened his eyes to the startling sight of the clan's Seer emerging from the bushes with blood trickling in streaks down her blue body. He frowned with displeasure. "You shouldn't be doing that – hunting is men's work."

"But a sling is a woman's weapon," Hekla replied, "I couldn't use a spear like a man."

"I suppose it's all right if it's only a sling," Overo allowed grudgingly, "And as you've actually made a kill, at least we'll eat tonight."

Flint and Juncal and the boys were on the last stretch of the slope when the appetising smell of roasting venison wafted up the track, the prospect of food spurring them on to reach the shelter just as the sun dipped below the horizon. Soon the whole clan was sitting round the fire, consuming every last scrap of Hekla's deer.

All three men's shoulders were chafed and aching from holding back the heavy sledges, and the fat from the meat was the perfect stuff with which to treat them. As she massaged Juncal's shoulders, Etna looked over at Hekla who was treating Overo and asked her, "Would you teach me how to use a slingshot?"

Hekla sat back on her heels to stare at the younger woman. "I suppose I could try, but it's not that easy."

"If you can do it, I can," Etna said, rubbing more fat into Juncal's back.

He grabbed her wrist. "No woman of mine goes hunting – that's men's work. Women's work is to cook it."

Angry fire flashing in her black eyes, Etna snapped, "That's what Father said, but you'd have gone hungry tonight if it wasn't for Hekla's sling! I don't care what you think, I'm going to learn – it might be useful."

"Etna has a point," Masaya said, coming unexpectedly to her sister's defence. "We can't keep stopping on the way for you and Flint to go hunting, and our stores won't last if we eat them every night."

"Pedro and I could learn too," said Tom, and his reward was the first smile he'd had this year from his mother.

Overo sealed the matter by saying, "Hekla can teach you all to use a sling – any new skill you learn will benefit the clan."

Pleased and flattered, after supper Hekla searched the midden for some leather scraps to make several new slings. Watching her fingers at work, Overo prayed the sling lessons would help to dispel the atmosphere of tension that had built up over the past week. They were a tiny clan facing a long and dangerous journey and they needed to pull together. Thinking of another way to bring them back together, he announced, "I think a bedtime story is called for."

"Which one do you want?" Hekla asked.

"Can we have the Guaza Giant story? Grandfather tells that one best," Pedro said innocently.

Hekla's pale eyes flashed with anger – it was the Seer's privilege to tell the legends that passed the Knowledge down the generations – but, with an apologetic shrug that couldn't quite conceal his pleasure at Pedro's request, Overo said, "It's only a story, Hekla – not the Knowledge," and began the old tale.

"On a vast and empty plain, one little house crouched inside a low wall. Both house and wall were built of the rough brown rocks that had been spewed out by a volcano."

"That's Guaza Mountain where we live," Pedro told Kea in an audible aside.

Overo grinned and patted the wall against which he was leaning. "This shelter was made the same way. Pepe, the Human who lived there, had carefully chosen each rock to interlock with its neighbour, filling the spaces with loose stones cleared from the field beside his house.

"That particular morning a hot wind was rippling the grass when Pepe and his young son headed for the mountain, hoping to catch a goat for their dinner. They were halfway up the slope when the ground began to shake and rocks started rolling downhill. A hot gust of sulphurous air knocked the man and boy off their feet, and a roar of sound battered their ears. Grabbing his son by one arm, Pepe dragged him under an overhang, where they cowered in fear while the earthquake raged.

"Deep underground, from the lake of boiling lava in which it had been sleeping, a spirit reached out tendrils of thought. It was preparing for life above ground, and was searching for some creature to use as a template. But all the animals had fled the earthquake – the only living creatures nearby were the two Humans – so the mountain spirit copied their shape."

Hekla couldn't stay silent. "I've never liked this story. To talk of Guaza Man – of any rock spirit – copying a Human's shape is blasphemy! If Humans exist at all they are just a kind of ape."

"For Heaven's sake, Hekla! It's only a story," Overo said, "Whether they're real or not isn't important now." Pulling his furs more closely round his body against the evening air, he continued. "One thing the spirit hadn't taken into account was size, and it overestimated, swimming through the lava to the surface on vast and powerful limbs. Fumes and red-hot rocks exploded into the air as Guaza Man somersaulted southwards, landing with his huge legs astride the stream of lava.

"Then his field-sized eyes focussed on Pepe and his son, cowering beneath the inadequate shelter of the overhang, tiny and terror-stricken. Pepe held his son to his heart and stared back, every cell in his body screaming with fear, both at the giant and at the lava which was heading straight for them. In a flash the giant understood. These creatures whose spirits called to his, and whose shape he had copied, could not live in the molten rock which had given him life. Without hesitation he threw himself full-length in the path of the boiling lava, stopping its progress towards the pair. The lava raged its frustration against his huge back in great hot waves, but he held firm until, slowly and reluctantly, the flow divided around him – Pepe and his son were safe.

"It was then that the giant discovered he couldn't move – the lava had mingled with the rock of his body and fused him to the ground. He struggled and fought to free himself but in vain – he was stuck fast. Realising his brief moments of life on the surface were over, he opened his cavernous mouth to roar his anguish, the sound drowning the noise of the eruption.

"Terrified out of their wits, Pepe and his son scrambled away from the deafening noise and raced downhill. Somehow they made it, dodging falling rocks and gasping in the overheated air, to find their house covered in ash but still standing. Pepe dashed inside to discover his woman and the baby curled in one corner, sobbing with fright, miraculously alive. Wiping the ash from their faces, he brought them outside to see the rock giant which had given its life to save them.

"The glow was just fading from the huge eyes when Pepe shouted 'Thank you,' and they watched in awe as Guaza Man's soul returned to the Mother."

Overo looked round at the circle of absorbed faces and concluded. "We believe that Guaza Man's mouth is the cave that protects our clan. Hot breath still seeps from his throat to warm us and his face gazes eternally at the sun."

"How do you know he's still here, Grandfather?" Kea asked sleepily.

"Because you can see him from the plain," Overo told her. "When we start our journey properly tomorrow we will be able to show you."

As Tom drifted off to sleep that night, he thought how fascinating it would be if Humans really existed. They were rumoured to be no taller than a boy and made from flesh like the animals. Grandfather was old enough to have seen everything – perhaps in his long life he had seen Humans. He must remember to ask him.

CHAPTER FOUR – WESTWARDS

Early the following morning they began their real journey, marching confidently over the gentle rise and fall of the scrubby grassland that marked the northern edge of the plain. Their muscles moved smoothly over their sturdy frames, echoing the semi-fluid rock that rolled at the edges of the volcanic flows which had given them birth. The men stood roughly ten feet tall and the women more than eight, yet the rock hues of their bodies blended so well with the landscape that only their movement betrayed their presence. With the sun's heat soaking into their stones, the winter Sleep seemed far away and their long strides covered the ground rapidly.

Flint and Juncal were again harnessed to the heavier sledge while Overo pulled the small one and, as the ground was smooth enough not to need rollers, the women and boys were free simply to walk alongside. The silk-smooth runners of the sledges slid easily over the fresh grass, leaving parallel tracks of crushed stems and deep grooves on softer ground.

Tomboro stared at the tracks, wondering if they would still be there when he returned, but even as he looked they faded. "That's not possible," he exclaimed.

Pedro gave him an odd look. "What isn't possible?" he asked.

Tom blinked and the tracks were visible once more. "Oh, nothing," he replied.

"You've been weird all week," Pedro complained, "I'm going ask Hekla how these slings work again – I've been trying since breakfast but I can't get it right."

Hekla was delighted to demonstrate her skills a second time and, without slackening their steady pace, Tom and Pedro, Etna and Masaya learned how to load and fire their slings. Masaya couldn't get the knack at all and soon gave up trying, but Etna hit the target quite often. Pedro was the quickest learner, hitting the mark time after time. Tom kept missing, although pride and determination kept him going, but he was beginning to despair until an inner voice told him to relax and rely on his instinct. After that his arm seemed to know what to do, and when they halted for the midday meal he was hitting the targets as often as Pedro.

That afternoon the land ahead as far as they could see was still flat enough for the sledges to move without rollers, so Tom and Pedro continued practising with their slings. They wandered ahead of the others through a strip of woodland, stopping frequently to shoot at a rock or a bird. After an hour they were so far in front of the small convoy that they sat down to wait, idly picking through the grass for ammunition. Tom was leaning back against a warm rock, basking in the dappled sunlight that filtered through the spring foliage, when he felt a pair of hostile eyes staring at him. "Pedro!" he whispered, "What's that animal?"

Pedro frowned. "What animal? There's nothing here."

"Could have sworn I saw one," Tom said, "It was all teeth and tusks – but you're right – these rocks are too small to hide anything bigger than a rabbit."

Pedro laughed nervously. "You've got Juncal's lion on the brain – let's go back and join the others." Tucking their haul of stones into their belt pouches they started back, but as they approached a clump of larger rocks Pedro clutched Tom's arm and hissed, "Something's moving in those shadows!"

Both boys froze, sliding stones quietly into their slings, and a moment later a large warthog emerged from between the rocks. Yellow eyes glowed as it stared at them, as if trying to identify these new shapes in its territory, but the boys remained motionless until its gaze slid away. Instantly Pedro launched a stone which caught the warthog behind the ear, dropping it where it stood. Pedro pranced around it chanting, "I've killed a monster!"

Tom was laughing at his antics when he sensed the animal returning to consciousness. Beneath its bristles the powerful muscles twitched and the yellow eyes flickered. As they focussed on Pedro's capering figure Tom shouted, "Look out!" and dived on the warthog, pinning it down by the snout with one hand and trying to avoid the sharp thrashing hooves as he cut its throat.

"I – I only stunned it, didn't I?" Pedro stammered, "You saved my life!"

"I was afraid it would gore you – those tusks look evil."

"And you knew it was waiting for us – you saw it five minutes ago," Pedro said shakily. His brown eyes widened as his mind assembled the clues. "You knew about Grandfather too. You really are a Seer, aren't you?"

Tom grimaced. "I'm starting to think so, but Mother doesn't believe me."

"Well you'll just have to prove it to her, won't you?" Pedro said blithely, "We'll think of a way."

*

Flint was looking for the boys to help with the rollers over a stretch of rough ground when Juncal spotted them standing proudly beside their trophy.

"We killed a monster!" Pedro said as soon as they were close enough.

Juncal scoffed, "Call that a monster?"

But Flint said quickly, "It's not a bad prize with a slingshot – which one of you brought it down?"

"Pedro did," Tom said.

Flint's face glowed with pride. "You obviously have a true hunter's instincts, son – I'll have to start training you properly."

"But Tom knew it was there ages before we saw it," Pedro said, "And he knew it was still alive when I didn't – he saved my life."

Flint turned his big smile on Tom and said, "That's why I tell you both a man should never hunt alone. But right now we need your help with the rollers, so throw your hog in the back and get to work."

As they pulled out the first roller Pedro peered into Tom's face and whispered, "You're very quiet – are you seeing something else?"

"No I'm not! I'm just cross – you shouldn't have said anything to the others."

"Why not? You *did* see the warthog before we were anywhere near it – that's the proof you need for your mother, isn't it?"

Tom could feel Hekla watching him and lowered his voice even further. "Leave it, Pedro. Mother would only say I made it up. I'm afraid it'll take more than that to convince her."

That night's shelter was only fifty miles from home – a distance set by earlier generations to allow for the slower pace of a mixed group travelling with sledges. It was one of several ancient stone huts which the clan used every Festival year, with just enough space for everyone to sleep, and when they had fixed a leather curtain over the doorway it warmed up quickly.

After unpacking their blankets, the women turned joints of wild pork over the fire while the boys boiled the warthog's head in the big cauldron to loosen the tusks. When they sat down to supper there was a curved tusk dangling from a thong round each boy's neck – proud trophies of their first solo kill.

*

Each day the clan moved further away from their own lands, hauling their sledges west past the grazing herds of cattle and deer that thronged the vast grassland. To their right, dense forest spilled down from the northern mountains. At times it was so close that they heard monkeys calling, or saw flashes of brilliant plumage. On one occasion they even caught a glimpse of a troop of apes retreating from the steady thud of their footsteps and the scrape of sledge runners.

In this sparsely-populated land the clan's caves and stone shelters had remained undisturbed since the last Festival, and on the second day Overo sent Tomboro and Pedro ahead with instructions to sweep out the dust and insects ready for the night. When Pedro protested, "Cleaning is women's work," Overo clipped his ear hard enough to hurt. "Your mother's been helping me haul the sledge, which some consider men's work – have you heard her complain?"

As Pedro rubbed his ear, muttering, Tom dragged him away. "Shut up, you dolt! We'll be ahead of the sledges, and without their noise we can creep up on prey undetected."

Tom was right, and they often welcomed the clan to the clean shelters with some fresh meat – as there was no time to spare for a real hunt their contributions were very welcome. Once the boys caught a large ground-sloth, but their regular bag consisted of rabbits or birds which the clan roasted and ate whole, small bones and all – the internal furnace that kept their lava flowing could digest almost anything.

Although no-one ever lost sight of the seriousness of their quest, particularly Flint and Masaya, the trip began to feel like a holiday. They were all enjoying the change of scene, the leather harnesses softened with use and no longer chafed, and each day the fifty miles between shelters seemed shorter.

On the fourth night the clan reached their shelter so early that Flint suggested carrying on to the next one. Overo swiftly vetoed that idea. "My legs aren't as young as yours," he said, shrugging off his harness and slumping onto a fallen tree-trunk, "I'm going to sit here in the sun and smoke a pipe – you can go hunting if you've got energy to spare."

"A large joint of meat would make a nice change," said Masaya.

Flint picked up his spear instantly, saying, "Those trees look inviting – fancy a forest hunt, Juncal?"

"No, he doesn't," Etna said, catching Juncal's hand, "I need him to help me."

Juncal flushed with embarrassment but said, "Sorry, Flint – not this time."

"Suit yourself," Flint said with a knowing smirk, "Tom and I can manage without you."

The moment Flint and Tom left the sunny plain for the green shade of the forest the temperature dropped, but they were warm enough as long as they kept moving. Flint led the way, moving so stealthily that Tom found it hard to distinguish his grey body from the densely packed trees. He kept a careful eye on him – he would be easy to lose sight of completely.

After a while Flint stopped and beckoned. Tom crept up to him, treading carefully over the thick loam. Very little light penetrated the canopy, but Flint's sharp eyes had spotted movement. He touched Tom's arm and pointed at the dappled back and pale hind-quarters of a doe, almost invisible in the broken shadows – she was cropping grass, unaware of their presence.

"Stay here," Flint murmured, melting into the trees as light-footed as a naiad. Tom stood holding his spear at the ready, tracking Flint as much by instinct as by sight, until he heard the sharp snap of a branch breaking. The deer, startled into instant flight, ran directly at Tom. All he had to do was step into its path for it to impale itself on his spear. He was pulling it free and saying the hunters' prayer of thanks when Flint reappeared. "That was a good kill, Tom – a clean thrust straight through the heart."

"You did all the work – she ran right at me when you broke that branch."

"I hoped she would," Flint said, slinging the carcass over his shoulder.

They were almost back at the camp when they were startled by a burst of noise as a pack of wild pigs crashed through the undergrowth right under their noses. Flint dropped the deer to chase after them but they vanished as quickly as they had appeared.

"Damn, I love roast pork," Flint said breathlessly, "We need Juncal to help track them down." They raced back to camp, only to be confronted by a scene of utter chaos. The small sledge was lying on its side with Overo struggling to right it, the big cook-pot was broken into several pieces, and Etna was shrieking at Masaya.

"What on earth happened here?" Flint asked. "Have you been attacked?"

"Yes – by a herd of pigs," Overo said, "They just appeared out of nowhere and ploughed straight through as if a devil was after them."

"We saw them too," said Flint, "We came to fetch Juncal. What's Etna yelling about?"

"It's Pedro and Kea," Juncal said as he tried to light a torch from the trampled remains of the fire. "They went to collect firewood and those damn pigs stampeded through exactly where they were. We've not seen them since. I was going to look for them when you turned up."

Flint hastily made his own torch, asking, "Why did you let two small children go off on their own?"

Juncal shuffled uncomfortably as Etna said, "Masaya was supposed to be watching them."

"Don't make it out to be all my fault," Masaya snapped, "You should have been looking after Kea yourself instead of sneaking off with Juncal!"

"Never mind whose fault it is now – we're wasting time," Overo said, "Flint – you're the best hunter – can you track them?"

"I hope so," Flint said, "But two children won't have left much of a trail, and the pigs have probably destroyed any tracks."

"Pedro said he could smell garlic," Hekla said, "Perhaps they went looking for it."

That set Etna off again. "Trust Pedro to lead Kea into trouble."

Masaya retorted, "That's not fair and you know it!" but then Tom shocked both women into silence by yelling, "Shut up and let me concentrate! I might be able to find them if you'd give me a bit of peace." He had picked up Kea's clay doll from the wreckage and, holding it to his chest, felt a connection with the little girl who owned it.

He was hoping he would be able to find two lost children as readily as he had located game on the hunt, but Hekla snorted, "Theatrics won't help," and tried to snatch the doll.

"Leave him alone, Hekla," Overo ordered, "We should at least give the lad a chance."

Hekla backed off, muttering darkly, Flint was held in check by Tom's wrapt expression, and even

Juncal waited when every instinct screamed at him to rush off bellowing his daughter's name.

*

Pedro and Kea had, as Hekla surmised, gone hunting for wild garlic. They had followed the pungent scent to a damp hollow, where a profusion of the spiky white flowers bloomed in the dim light. When they slid down to gather some, they hadn't noticed until it was too late the herd of pigs busily rooting for the succulent bulbs.

Two children landing in their midst caught the pigs unawares and the lead sow whirled to face the danger. From Pedro's size she assumed he was a Human hunter – one had recently killed a piglet and she wasn't going to allow another one to be taken. For a long moment Pedro and the sow stared at each other, neither of them sure what to do, then Kea screamed. The sound was so like a Human's yell of attack that the sow charged, followed by the entire herd. With a brutal yank on Kea's arm, Pedro hauled her out of the way and up the side of the hollow. They were surrounded by squealing, stampeding pigs armed with fearsome tusks, so Pedro dived headlong into a thorn bush, dragging Kea with him. Scratched and frightened, they lay there panting until the noise and crashing faded away.

"What were those monsters?" Kea asked shakily, "They were as big as me!"

"Some kind of warthog, I think," Pedro answered, "We should get back to camp before they attack us again."

They forced their way out of the bush through the inch-long thorns, and it was only when they were free of the tangle that they noticed how quiet it was. Birds chirped and bees droned, but now the panic was over there was no other sound – no comforting rumble of the clan's voices, no clatter of a ladle in a pot – their wandering had taken them further than they realised and they were totally alone.

Slipping her hand into Pedro's, Kea said in a wavering voice, "I want my mother."

"We'll go back now," Pedro said, turning in a slow circle. "All these trees look the same," he said after a while, "Which way did we come?"

The huge old trees breathed out silence and shredded the light into confusing patterns. Beneath the vast trees the two children were suddenly so overwhelmed that blind panic took over and they ran. They followed lines of light that dissolved into shadows, and flinched at shadows that were shattered an instant later by light. Spotting a larger pool of sunlight, Pedro headed for it towing Kea behind him, but when they got there it exploded into a thousand golden butterflies. A breeze of delicate wings swooped around them in a fluttering cloud, and they were entranced as the shimmering glided away on an up-draught. The children's gaze followed the butterflies' flight until they vanished, leaving behind only stark contrast. Tall treetops loomed overhead, seemingly about to topple and crush the two small figures.

"I'm scared," Kea whimpered.

Pedro squeezed her hand. "Father will find us."

"You mean we're really lost?" Kea wailed.

Pedro hugged her, determined to be brave – he was *years* older than Kea, after all. His voice trembled as he admitted, "Yes, we're really lost."

The corners of Kea's mouth pulled open into a square as her wail turned into a full-blown howl and echoed round the clearing.

*

Tom's eyes were closed but his mind was wide open, searching the moist green forest currents for a sound that was no sound – the heart-cries of frightened children wanting their mothers. He was too intent on finding Pedro and Kea to wonder how he could be standing by the camp-fire and walking in the forest at the same time. He wasn't simply seeing the forest as in a dream, or remembering it – he was actually there. His feet sank into the leaf-litter of centuries and his skin tingled from the touch of insects. He walked along the tracks he and Flint had taken, and found the pool of blood where he had killed the deer. He was about to try a different trail when he noticed a small footprint in the sticky red puddle. This was the clue he was searching for – Kea had gone this way. Looking up, his attention was caught by a cloud of brilliant butterflies flitting through a gap, and a moment later he saw Pedro and Kea, sitting in a clearing with their arms round each other, looking very small in the vast emptiness.

Tom opened his eyes and told Overo, "I can see where they are now – they're a spear's throw from the place where we killed the deer."

"Don't waste your time listening to him," Hekla scoffed, "He only closed his eyes for a second."

Overo silenced her with a gesture. "It won't take long to check, will it?" he said, and Flint and Juncal raced off with Masaya and Etna hot on their heels.

Left behind in the wreckage of the campsite, Hekla glowered at Tom. "You must have seen where they went when you brought that deer back – that trick with the doll doesn't fool me."

"Mother, it wasn't a trick – I really could see them."

"Adolescent nonsense!" Hekla spat, "If it was possible to see them, I would have done so."

Overo was leaning against the shelter wall, smoking quietly and forgotten by them both. He believed Tom's psychic power was already stronger than Hekla's but, sadly, it was obvious the guidance the lad needed wouldn't come from her. Perhaps, he thought, tapping his pipe out against his leg, they could find Tom a tutor on their travels. He sighed – what with deciding the Leadership issue and now this problem, it was turning into a difficult journey. He raised his voice to halt the argument between mother and son before it could spiral out of control. "We'll find out soon enough if Tom's located the lost children, won't we? Tom – rescue that fire, will you – the pigs ran right through it."

By the time Tom had rekindled a blaze from the scattered remnants of the fire, the relieved parents were emerging from the trees with Pedro and Kea. Kea slid out of Juncal's arms and ran straight to Tom crying, "You found us!" and planted a kiss on his cheek.

Tom flushed with pleasure. "I just followed the butterflies."

"You saw them too, did you – weren't they pretty?"

"What butterflies?" asked Overo.

"There was a huge cloud of them," Pedro said. "Thousands – they flew right past us. That's when we knew you would come."

"Come and give me a hug, you two," Overo said, holding out his arms, "You had us all worried sick." Hugging his grandchildren, Overo looked over their heads at Tom and nodded. It was just one nod, but Tom knew it signified more than thanks – it was an acknowledgement of his powers. What the future held didn't matter nearly as much now Grandfather believed in him.

Kea wriggled off Overo's knee and returned to cling to her mother, still shaken by her half-hour of being lost. Pedro, who had decided to treat the entire episode as a great adventure, shook off Masaya's attempt to cuddle him, so she returned to her cooking, only to discover the best cauldron was broken. "No!" she wailed, "Our supper was in that!" and the tears she hadn't shed when Pedro was missing flowed freely over this smaller loss.

Tom picked through the fire with his fingers, but the meat was burnt so black it was hard to distinguish it from embers. "We can't eat this," he said, "It'll have to be meat pudding tonight."

"We could always hunt down those pigs," Flint suggested, "They left clear enough tracks."

"We haven't got time for a pig hunt," Overo said at once, "Anyway, I fancy a steak from Tom's deer." As he winked at Tom, the irrepressible Juncal said, "We can always go after the pigs tomorrow."

"No we can't," Flint reminded him, "Our next stop is Cold River. First thing in the morning we'll have to fell trees for the bridge."

"What's wrong with using the ones we had three years ago?" Juncal asked.

Flint laughed mirthlessly. "They'll be long gone – I think Outclans take them for firewood."

CHAPTER FIVE – COLD RIVER

Wrapped up against the morning chill, Overo, Flint and Juncal scouted the nearest area of forest for suitable trees – they knew from experience that they needed hardwood logs roughly twice their own height to make safe bridge spans.

"I think we should use beech this year," Overo said, "Oak was far too heavy."

After locating two trees with straight enough trunks, they didn't waste time chopping them down – they simply put their massive strength into rocking them until the roots tore out of the ground. Following a rough trimming, each trunk weighed about a ton and a half, which was too much for the sledge, so they rolled the huge logs the few remaining miles to the river.

Meanwhile the boys had gone ahead to start a fire in the riverside shelter. Rather than risk carrying the Firepot, Tomboro took a burning coal from the overnight fire in his cupped hands, blowing on it and feeding it fuel to keep it alive, while Pedro carried an armful of dry kindling. As they approached Cold River, the sound of water tumbling over its rocky bed made them shiver, and when they stood on the riverbank the air felt deadly cold. They quickly ducked inside the shelter to build a fire before going in search of more fuel. They didn't have to go far – just behind the shelter they found some logs already cut.

Pedro looked round apprehensively. "Someone's been using our shelter – what if they're still here?"

Tom reassured him, "There's no need to worry – these were cut years ago."

"That's all right then," said Pedro, "I suppose you knew that just by touching them?"

"Something like that," Tom said. Seeing Hekla approach, he gathered an armful of logs, saying innocently, "Look what we found, Mother – these'll save us having to collect more just yet."

Overo pulled the small sledge to a halt a moment later and jerked his thumb at the river. "It looks a bit colder than last time, doesn't it?" he said, grinning at the boys.

"It looks freezing," Tom said, "I don't remember it being this full before either."

"That's because we crossed it after the Festival, in high summer," Overo reminded him, "The river's at its lowest then, but this early in spring it's swollen by snow-melt."

"What's snow-melt?" Pedro asked.

Overo rubbed the boy's head affectionately. "You should ask Tom – Hekla said they saw snow a few times in the north."

Tom shivered at the recollection. "To look at, snow is beautiful," he told Pedro, "It floats silently down like pure white flakes of ash, but it is so cold." He glanced at Hekla and lowered his voice to a whisper. "Mother should have foreseen the danger of crossing the mountains that late in the year – I thought we were going to die." That distant memory of the snow brought a sense of foreboding, but he shook it off. "Come on – let's see how we make a bridge."

They found Overo standing on the riverbank, sighting along his staff. He told the boys he was trying to assess whether any of their permanent bridge foundations had shifted in the past three years. If any had moved, someone would have to realign them before they could place the spans. "Not a pleasant job," he said, "This water is freezing cold and deadly." When Flint and Juncal arrived with the beech trees, Overo told them, "We're in luck. Only one boulder's out of line this year – the second one needs to move a yard upstream. You know the drill, Flint – let's get the ropes out and start."

With a rope attached to his sledge-harness, Flint waded into the icy water with Overo and Juncal playing out the lifeline. By the time he reached the problem boulder he was waist-deep in the river – he had to move it quickly before the cold numbed him. Bracing his feet on the riverbed, he put his back against the huge rock and heaved against the force of the current.

Seeing it begin to move, Overo called encouragingly, "One more shove should do it!" Flint made an even greater effort, and the boulder rolled into its former hollow so suddenly that he slipped and fell. Masaya screamed.

It was obvious the big man was having a struggle to rise, on hands and knees on the riverbed with the water swirling over his back as if he were just another rock. Overo and Juncal were hauling on the lifeline, trying to get Flint back onto his feet before he froze. Masaya stood with her hands over her mouth and her eyes wide with terror, while Pedro ran back and forth on the bank yelling, "Get up, Father!"

Tom was almost driven to his knees by the sheer volume of fear from everyone that flooded his senses. He felt a slight easing when Flint managed to stand but, numbed by the cold, it was clear he could do no more. Leaning on the boulder he had just moved, the big man stared at the gap that separated him from the bank and Tom felt the despair flood Flint's mind – those ten yards might as well have been a hundred, because he couldn't move another inch.

The need to help Flint overrode all Tom's other instincts – even his own fear of water. Without hesitation he slid down the bank and waded towards him, followed a second later by Pedro, the women too slow to stop them. The boys were chest-deep in the icy water when they reached Flint and slid their arms round his waist. Energised by their body heat, Flint straightened up a little and Tom forced words of encouragement through his clenched jaw. "Come on, Flint – it's only a little way."

Pedro added his own urging, "F-father – please t-try."

His young son's shivering voice overcame Flint's paralysis, and together the three staggered the few yards to the bank.

The near tragedy had been such a shock to them all that no-one spoke until Flint and the boys were inside the shelter, wrapped in blankets, with their feet in the fire. Overo draped his own cape round Flint's shoulders while Masaya threw every scrap of fuel on the blaze. As a cauldron of boiling water filled the shelter with steam the three rigid bodies gradually relaxed. Hekla handed round cups of chilli broth and the boys took theirs gratefully, but Flint was shaking so much that Masaya had to hold his cup to his lips.

When the fiery brew reached his stomach he let out a huge sigh, "That's better! I had a bad moment or two out there." Peering through the steam at the boys he added, "I wouldn't have made it at all without your help – you were both very brave."

Pedro looked up from his position by his father's leg. "I didn't know water could be as awful as that."

"Our little stream back home flows over sun-warmed rock," Flint said, stroking his son's head, "And you probably don't remember the last time we crossed Cold River."

"We ferried the boys over in the sledge that time," Masaya recalled, "They've never learned how dangerous it can be – we should have warned them."

"There are a lot of things we should have told the children," Hekla said, "It's time they learned some more of the Knowledge – I'll tell them the Cold legend later."

"Any stories will have to wait until tonight," Flint said, shrugging off Overo's warm cape and taking his feet reluctantly out of the fire, "We've got to get on with the bridge."

This time it was Juncal's turn to brave Cold River and he moved quickly to the first boulder. Having hauled himself onto the top, he waited while Flint and Overo dragged one of the beech trunks to the river's edge. Tom held his breath as they dropped it towards Juncal, but they had judged the length correctly and when it bounced on the boulder Juncal caught it. Their ancestors had carved grooves in the boulders to take the spans, and when the top of the log was in its groove the boys braced the landward end with rocks. Juncal ran along it back to the bank, then he and Flint took the second span up and dropped that into place.

"Right – that's the first stage done," said Overo, "If you're going hunting you'd better do it before the daylight goes."

"A hunt should warm us up nicely after our cold baths," Juncal said, "It'll be our last chance to get fresh meat before we cross the desert."

"Isn't there any game there?" Pedro asked.

"Oh, there's game all right," Juncal answered, "But no cover to speak of – we'd scare it away long before we could get within range."

*

After their evening meal Kea reminded Hekla, "You said you'd tell us a story."

"Yes, you promised," Pedro added, "The one about the Cold."

Hekla sat up straighter and pulled her fur more closely round her shoulders. Stories were a treat usually reserved for the long evenings of autumn, when there might be hunting tales from the men, or a trader would bring news of the outside world. Sometimes Overo told one of the old stories, but narrating the traditional legends of the Knowledge was the Seer's privilege which Hekla guarded jealously. Everyone settled more comfortably, watching the blue sparkle of her face in the firelight as her voice deepened to the ritual tone of story-telling.

"Many thousands of years ago," she began, "Before there was even Thought, there was only the Sun, circling in space trailing a wake of fire. Nothing else moved in the vast emptiness and the Sun's great hot heart burned with loneliness.

"He was so desolate that one day he howled his misery aloud and the Moon flew from his mouth. As it hung in the void nearby, pale gold and beautiful, the Sun rejoiced to see the smiling face of his child. For a while they were happy together, but the Sun's ancient enemy, the Cold, was jealous, and breathed its frigid breath on the Moon. The Sun's child was too small to withstand the wintry blast and was soon frozen into a ball of white ice."

Pedro and Kea shivered at the word picture Hekla was painting – even Tom huddled deeper into his furs. The last time he had heard this story he had been small enough to sit on his mother's lap and take comfort from her body heat. Tonight he could detect no trace of the mother – Hekla was all Seer as she continued with the story.

"The Sun was now even lonelier than before, and in his grief he spun so fast that a huge ball of fiery rock shot from his belly. As it hung in the heavens nearby, rivers of fire flickered red and gold over its surface. This child of the Sun – the Earth – was bigger and stronger than its sister the Moon, but it still needed its Father's protection, so when the Sun slept, the Cold swooped in again to hold sway.

"But however cold the winter, in spring the Sun always returned to warm the Earth with his breath. In time the extremes of temperature caused the Earth's crust to heave and fold into hills and valleys. Solid rock cracked open to release fiery lava which created mountains. Rain fell and rivers flowed down the valleys, drawing green life from the newly nourished soil. Gradually the Earth learned to absorb the Sun's strength in summer to help it survive the winter."

Hekla looked at the children's absorbed faces and added a warning. "Remember what happened today – even a man as strong as Flint is not invulnerable. Rockmen need heat as much as the Earth does, and we must never forget that the Cold is always lying in wait, hoping for the unwary to fall into its icy clutches."

She let her final words die away into silence, and Tom actually felt her change. The Seer who had opened a window on the Knowledge retreated, and into the foreground stepped the woman who loved the limelight. Hekla turned her ice-blue eyes in his direction and he felt a chill. The warning was clear – she would even sacrifice her own son to retain her position. She broke the spell she had woven by leaning forward to take her cup of tea from the embers.

"But where did we come from?" Pedro asked.

"That's another story for another night," said Overo firmly, "We must sleep now – tomorrow we cross the river."

*

At first light Flint and Juncal crossed the bridge by moving the spans in sequence, using the first span to make a third, the second to make a fourth and so on. A rope tied around Juncal's waist towed the small sledge, which bounced through the turbulent water with Overo and Tom on board to fend it off the boulders.

Tom watched the two men moving the huge tree trunks and knew with a heavy heart that he would never be that strong. He was only eight feet – no taller than a woman – and he was unlikely to grow much more. As his hands pushed against the cold rock of yet another bridge support, he felt a momentary connection with the men who had placed it in Cold River, and remembered that the Mother had given him a gift that would make up for being small – his strength was in his mind. He was jolted out of his reverie when Flint swore loudly and the sledge stopped moving.

"What's the holdup?" Overo called out, "We're getting wet down here."

"A big chunk of the bank has gone," Flint answered, "The river's at least twelve feet wider than it was three years ago." He and Juncal hauled the sledge alongside the last support and then Tom could see the problem – the tree-trunk bridge span wouldn't reach without another support.

Overo pointed at the far bank. "There's a big boulder over there that would do the trick if we could get it."

It was only yards away – less than a stone's throw – and Tom joked, "If we had a big enough sling we could shoot someone across." He hadn't meant it seriously, but as his own words sank in he added, "If you swing me over on a rope I can tie it round the boulder."

Juncal stared at him. "And then we could haul it into position. That's brilliant, Tom, and it might work – you're light enough."

"It's risky – do you think you can do it?" Flint asked.

Tom, with the water splashing cold over his feet, began to wish he'd kept his mouth shut, but he lifted his chin and said, "I'll give it a go – unless you can think of another way?"

"You're a brave lad," Overo said, "Stand still while I strap you into a harness – that'll keep you safe."

Grandfather's warm hands securing the knots steadied Tom's racing pulse, and Juncal hauled him onto the bridge. Giving him no time to lose his nerve, Juncal lowered him almost to the water on the downside of the bridge, swung him back and forth to pick up momentum before giving an almighty heave and letting the rope slide through his fingers. As Tom flew through the air he had an exhilarating sensation of weightlessness, then there was a splash and he scrambled ashore.

Yelling, "I only got my feet wet!" he hauled in the wet rope. He tied it round the large boulder for Flint and Juncal to pull while he pushed from behind, and after a minute it began to move. The current had already cut the earth away from beneath it, so it simply rolled down the slope to the river's edge. When it settled into place there was even a groove in the top, as if Mother Earth had carved it especially for them. Flint dropped the final spans into place, Overo's small sledge came ashore, and together they towed the larger sledge across the river with the women and children perched on the load.

The moment they landed Hekla confronted Overo. "Whose stupid idea was it to swing Tom over the water like that? You could have killed him!"

"Tom volunteered," Overo replied, "And there was no other way."

Tom stared at Hekla in surprise. This was the mother he remembered, fighting like a lion for her cub – perhaps if he approached her the right way she might help him after all. Before he could say anything Pedro said, "Well, I thought it was brilliant – I wouldn't mind having a go myself."

Masaya gasped, "Don't you dare!" and Flint laughed. "We've no time for playing games, Pedro. Now we're here, thanks to Tom, we need everyone to push the sledges up this slope."

The west bank rose thirty feet above river-level and the footing was treacherous – it took the combined efforts of the clan to heave the loaded sledges up the steep incline. It was only when they were safely away from the edge that Tom could take in his surroundings.

The contrast between the east and west banks of Cold River was startling. The plain they had just left was predominantly green, with trees and grass bright in the spring sunshine, but up here on the western bank there was barely any green at all – apart from a fringe of straggly bushes along the line of the river, it was just grey scrub hugging dry, beige coloured ground. The sibilant swish of the desert wind made the skin of his neck crawl in foreboding.

Pedro touched his arm to get his attention. "Tom, what's the matter?"

With an effort Tom shook off his mood and smiled at his friend. "I don't remember any of this from three years ago."

"We were too busy looking for marbles along the river-bank," Pedro reminded him, "And then I had to teach you how to play."

"That wasn't my fault," Tom protested, "Mother never stopped anywhere long enough for me to make friends." He cuffed the younger boy's chest. "But you're my friend now, and I was just thinking that on this side of Cold River our adventure really begins."

Relief smoothed the frown from Pedro's face. "Oh, is that all? I was afraid you were seeing things again."

Before Tom could frame a reply Overo called them to help dry off the sledges and re-grease the runners, then he sent them back down the slope to fill every container they possessed with water. It didn't take long – an hour after landing on the west bank, the Guaza Clan turned their backs on the plain and set off into the desert. Each of them in their own way was very conscious that they were far from home, separated from it by the formidable barrier that was Cold River – their adventure truly had begun.

CHAPTER SIX – DRAGONS

Tomboro fell into step beside Hekla, hoping to take advantage of her unexpected display of mother-love. The harsh laugh of a hyena from the retreating forest gave him his opening. "Hear that, Mother – do you remember the time we were attacked by hyenas?"

He kept his expression carefully guileless, but Hekla glanced sharply at him before she replied. "They wanted that antelope, but I'd stalked it for two hours and I wasn't ready to surrender it." She smiled. "Do you remember how we fooled them?"

"How could I forget? We stood in the fire eating the meat straight off the spit and they had to make do with the pile of intestines. How did you know they were coming?" Tom slipped the question in so casually that Hekla answered without realizing she had been outmanoeuvred.

"The spirit of a large pack has a distinct resonance, particularly if it poses a threat."

"So you saw them before they arrived?"

"I didn't see them – I sensed them."

Tom sighed. "I was hoping you could see them like I do." He rubbed the edge of her bearskin cape between his fingers. "I heard these bears breathing before we were anywhere near them, and I actually saw that warthog five minutes before Pedro and I killed it."

Hekla twitched her cape out of Tom's grasp, almost snarling, "Don't start that again, Tomboro! You're only trying to grab some attention with your claims, but you don't fool me."

Recoiling from the venom in her voice, Tom dropped back to help Overo with the small sledge, his face a rigid mask that discouraged any attempt at conversation.

Soon the vegetation that marked the river was merely a dark line far behind them. It was baking hot – perfect weather for Rockmen – and they removed their clothing to absorb the sun more easily. The heat sped up the flow of lava through their bodies and, only pausing occasionally to drink some water, they covered the ground at a steady seven or eight miles an hour. The sounds of their progress kept the sparse desert game at a distance – even the scorpions and snakes hid in the tiny areas of shade cast by patches of scrub – and the amount of food they had brought with them began to make sense to the youngsters.

At midday Overo called a halt. "We'll have a quick bite to eat now – in this heat we can manage without a hot meal."

"No fire?" wailed Kea – she had never eaten a meal without the comfort of flames beside her – but Overo insisted. "We're in the middle of nowhere with a long way to go yet." He smiled down into Kea's long face. "You can sit in my sledge and look after the Firepot if you like."

So they made a hasty snack of cold meat pudding and got moving again, knowing that Overo was right – it was imperative to reach shelter before the cold desert night descended.

An hour later they hit the dunes – wave after wave of seemingly endless sand in which their weight made every step a struggle. The hot desert wind blasted stinging sand into their faces, and the sledges stuck if they paused for even a second. Thigh-deep in sand as he pushed the sledge up yet another sand-dune, Tom had a vision of the desert swallowing him completely. For a nightmare moment he couldn't breathe, experiencing again the sense of foreboding he had felt beside Cold River. It was a relief when the sledge topped the rise and he was able to pull his legs free and slide down the slope to face the next challenge.

It was late afternoon when they finally left the dunes behind, to trudge across the now flat and featureless land towards the sunset. Tom was beginning to wonder if they had lost their way when the horizon changed shape. A vague hump appeared silhouetted by the setting sun, and was gradually revealed to be a low, isolated outcrop of gingery rock. With a vast sense of relief and a final spurt of speed, the clan reached their goal just as the sun fell off the edge of the world.

When the sledges stopped, Kea awoke from her doze among the blankets, wiped a crust of sand from her eyes and asked in dismay, "Is this all there is – just a pile of rocks?"

"No-o, it's not," Tom said as a memory dawned, "There's a shelter here."

"So there is!" Pedro cried, "I left something behind."

The boys raced round to the far side of the outcrop and there, soaking up the last of the day's heat, was a stone doorway. Pedro ducked inside to emerge a moment later grinning with delight at the contents of his cupped hands. "I knew exactly where they were!" he cried, waving a clutch of marbles under his mother's nose, "You wouldn't go back for them!"

Masaya rubbed his head, laughing, "We were back at Cold River before you remembered them. Besides, you found some more."

"Not nearly as good as these," Pedro grinned, "Let's have a game, Tom."

Tom agreed quickly, hoping the game of marbles would distract him, but he couldn't shake off the feeling that had been growing stronger with every mile – a conviction that fate was drawing him south-west. Mingled with the Call that was leading the Guaza Clan to Flint and Masaya's baby, he had a strong premonition of a more personal destiny. He was so distracted that he lost three games on the trot before they were called to supper.

Masaya and Etna had boiled two meat puddings which the clan ate hungrily, leaning against the warm ginger rocks and watching the last of the sunset stain the sky shades of apricot, green and purple. In fact there was nothing else to look at – the land between them and the horizon was totally empty, bleak and forbidding. With this reminder that tomorrow they faced another long hard trek, they went to bed as soon as they had eaten. The shelter was simply a curved wall someone had built against the rock-face, but the roof was intact and they made it cosy by standing the Firepot on a built-in shelf. Worn out by the day's exercise, they slept soundly.

Soon after dawn they were on the move again, Overo setting a brisk pace from the start. Noting Hekla's preoccupied expression, he asked quietly, "Have there been any more Signs?"

Hekla clearly had to drag her thoughts back from the distance. "No, I'm afraid not," she said ruefully. "The Signs were so clear at home, but I've had no more for days."

"Are you sure we're going in the right direction?"

Hekla's jaw tensed. "Of course I'm sure – I just don't know how far away it is, or how much time we have."

Only Overo would have dared to question her, but he overstepped the mark with his next suggestion. "Perhaps the Desert Seer felt the Sign. We could ask him when we meet – or Tom."

"I don't need another Seer's help, especially not Tomboro's!" Hekla snarled, and strode on ahead in furious silence.

Shaking his head in frustration, Overo looked back to check on the rest of the clan. Masaya and Etna were harnessed to the small sledge with Kea sitting on the load feeding fuel into the Firepot, Flint and Juncal were pulling the big sledge in tandem, but Tom and Pedro were plodding along with boredom etched clearly on their faces – until the rollers were needed again they had nothing to do. Overo raised his voice. "Tom, Pedro! You two can make yourselves useful by running ahead to check the next shelter."

Pedro gestured in dismay at the empty landscape. "Where is it?"

"Keep going west for a couple of hours until you see the tops of palm trees – just head straight for them."

"I'll find it, Grandfather," Tom said confidently.

"I have no doubt you will," Overo replied.

"If you miss it you can always follow your own tracks back to us," Hekla said, adding spitefully, "Pedro's good at tracking."

Refusing to rise to her bait, Tom said, "Come on, Pedro – we might even get some fresh meat if we're on our own." Taking one of the water-bags, they set off alone into the distance.

Watching Tom's slender figure and Pedro's stocky one disappear into the heat-haze, Overo observed, "The clan is lucky to have those two young men – Tom's brain and Pedro's strength are a good combination."

"They're hardly men yet," said Hekla, "And I wish Tomboro would stop inventing stories."

"Actually I'm inclined to believe him," Overo began, but stopped when he saw Hekla's scowl – the

Seer was preoccupied enough without believing he was siding with Tom against her.

Tom and Pedro jogged along steadily. Tom was as sure of his direction as a migrating wildebeest, but Pedro kept stopping to shade his eyes and look for the promised trees. It was two hours before he pointed to a faint smear of green staining the horizon. "There they are! We're not lost after all."

"Told you I knew the way," Tom said with more than a hint of self-satisfaction, "We must have walked in a dead straight line, and that cloud of dust behind us has to be the sledges – I reckon we're halfway there." He tilted the water-bag to his mouth while Pedro cut a length of sausage into pieces. The sun had warmed the water to just the right temperature and, after washing down a lump of sausage each, they continued their steady jog towards the distant trees.

The small oasis was a welcome sight after the featureless desert. The tall palms they had seen from the distance swayed over a steep-sided bowl of rock that was the same dull terracotta as the surrounding land. Its wind-scoured walls enclosed a shallow pool fed by a narrow waterfall, and a fine mist of spray watered a swathe of greenery over which hovered a permanent rainbow. It was beautiful and eerily quiet, but the expected shelter wasn't there – only the deep shadow of an overhang close to one side of the pool.

"I remember this place now," said Pedro, "But I thought there was a proper shelter."

"You're right – it was under that overhang," Tom said, "Heaven knows what's happened to it. Grandfather's not going to be happy – there isn't room for us all to sleep under there."

It only took a few moments to search the small oasis. Upstream there was nothing but the high crack from which the waterfall poured into the pool, which in its turn drained away under a pile of jumbled rocks. Staring at those oddly regular rocks, Tom had a brief vision of them tumbling in water and realised what had happened. "It's like at Cold River," he said, "The spring floods washed everything into the pool and those square rocks were the wall."

"How on earth could you know?" Pedro asked but then light dawned. "Oh, right – you had a vision, didn't you?"

"Well, yes, actually…" Tom began, but Pedro held up his hands.

"No, don't tell me – your spirit stuff is too spooky for me."

"All right – I won't tell you," Tom laughed, "But if we want to sleep in a proper shelter tonight we've got to get those rocks out and rebuild the wall."

"Let's get on with it then," said Pedro, "As long as we can do it before the others get here, who cares how it happened?"

They waded into the pool in some trepidation only to find that, although it was shaded by the tall palms, the water was warm. The rocks that had been the shelter's front wall were hand-cut sandstone blocks weighing a hundredweight each – the boys carried each one easily to the overhang to rebuild the wall. They had been working for an hour when they lifted one of the final blocks from the pool and spotted a brief flick of movement.

"Surely there can't be fish here?" Pedro gasped.

"Perhaps it was a snake," Tom said, "We've nearly finished building – let's wait and see if it comes back." They took their slings out of their belts and sat quietly beside the pool to wait.

Their labours had lowered the water-level in the pool and, as the few remaining blocks dried out, a strange creature emerged to bask in the sun's rays. Then another appeared, and another, and the boys gazed in awestruck silence until half a dozen dragons had come to life before their eyes.

"Can we eat them?" whispered Pedro. One creature swivelled its reptilian eyes in his direction and he shivered under its steady gaze. Tom cast his mind back to the walls of their home cave which were covered in paintings of animals, with a cooking-pot drawn beside anything edible.

"I think they had a food-sign," he whispered, "Shall we try?" Moving a careful inch at a time they loaded their slings with pebbles and focussed on their chosen targets, knowing one chance was all they would get. Tom blinked a countdown – one, two, three – and the stones flew from their slings, there was a flurry of movement, and the dragons vanished.

"We both missed!" wailed Pedro, "I was so sure I hit mine."

"Me too," Tom said, "And I could have sworn I sensed a death. Oh well – we'd better get the last blocks moved and finish that wall."

They waded into the pool again, but as Pedro braced himself to get a better grip on a block he yelled, "My toe touched a dragon!" and he fell back with a resounding splash.

Tom hauled him up, both of them laughing, then felt around in the water. A moment later he held aloft a grey-green body, crowing triumphantly, "Got mine!"

"How do you know that one's yours?" Pedro demanded.

"I just know, but yours is in here too somewhere," Tom told him, so Pedro searched until he found it – both their pebbles had struck their targets after all. Laying their prizes carefully in the shade to keep fresh, the boys returned to their building.

When the weary travellers reached the oasis, Tom and Pedro gave them no chance even to draw breath before they displayed the slain dragons. Juncal laughed, "What's all the fuss about? They're only lizards – I caught dozens of those when I was a boy."

The two young hunters slumped in disappointment, until Kea crouched beside the lizards, stroking their scaly bodies a tentative finger. "Dragons!" she breathed, "You killed real dragons!" and the boys' hurt pride was salved.

Later, when a fire was burning steadily in front of the reconstructed shelter, Juncal made up for his earlier remark by saying, "We should start our meal with roast lizards. If you like I'll show you the way Desert hunters cook them." Under Tom and Pedro's watchful eyes, he cleaned and spitted the large lizards, digging the spits upright into the sand to cook beside the fire.

There was just enough for everyone to have a taste, and the boys were delighted when Juncal said, "You did well to catch these – they move like lightning."

Overo crunched a leg-bone and licked his fingers. "Delicious. I'm surprised you had time to hunt with that wall to rebuild."

Tom looked at him suspiciously. "You knew we'd have to, did you?"

Overo grinned. "It has to be done every time we come – the spring floods always demolish the shelter."

"That's what Tom thought had happened," Pedro said. Tom scowled at him ferociously – he didn't want the evening ruined – but Hekla hadn't even heard; she was sitting apart from the others, watching the sky darken and hoping desperately for another Sign.

Masaya watched her surreptitiously while she and Etna prepared the main meal, eventually asking, "Have you had another Sign yet? Are we going to get there in time?"

With the same question on every face Hekla was forced to confess, "I have prayed every night for another Sign but I've had no answer."

"What if we go all that way and there's no baby?" Masaya wailed, "What if the Mother thinks I'm too old as well?"

"I didn't mean that," Etna said guiltily, "Of course you're not too old."

Masaya shook off her sister's hand, sobbing, "We've been travelling for a week, and Hekla's not even sure we're going the right way." Flint's expression echoed Masaya's fears – the Signs were usually clear and strong all the way to a baby's birthplace.

Shamed by her inability to allay their fears, Hekla hunched into her cape and walked out of the firelight into the shadows, her distress pouring out of her in a flood. Tom followed – she was his mother, after all – but at the touch of his hand on her arm she jerked away, snarling, "What are you playing at? Can't you see I'm praying?"

This was a blatant lie which Tom ignored. "Mother – it's silly of us to argue when I can feel the Call too – let me help you."

Hekla shrugged. "You're just imagining things." But there was a tinge of uncertainty, and perhaps even hope, in her voice.

Tom ploughed on. "If you read my mind, Mother, you'll see I'm telling the truth."

Hekla peered at his face in the twilight. "You've been deliberately hiding your thoughts since the Sleep, haven't you?" Tom nodded and braced himself to be invaded, but the first sensation he was aware of was the insistent pull from the south-west. He lowered his barriers to endure the unpleasant sensation of Hekla's probing and, as their two minds combined, the clan's baby Call came through strong and clear.

Before Tom could react, Hekla dashed back to the fire, announcing triumphantly, "The Call is stronger – we're on the right track."

Tom, determined not to be ignored this time, added, "What Mother says is right – I feel it too."

"My Sight needs no confirmation from a boy," Hekla spat, and Tom reeled from the shock of her betrayal. Without his help she wouldn't have heard the Call, but there was nothing he could say that wouldn't sound petulant. Pedro winked at him sympathetically – after today he had no doubt that Tom had the Sight – small consolation as Hekla clasped Masaya's hands gushing, "I am certain now that we will reach the volcano in time."

"I must admit I was worried," Masaya answered, "But if two Seers agree on the Signs, we can be doubly sure."

"I think it's supper time," Overo said hastily, "Tom – help me to a seat," and Grandfather's strong grip on his shoulder helped to steady Tom's churning emotions.

CHAPTER SEVEN – GRAND OASIS

Tomboro's legs were twitching so badly that they woke him up. Wrapping his blanket tightly around himself against the chill, he slipped outside to find that, although the night was lightening into dawn, no birds were stirring – the small oasis was eerily silent. He was standing by the edge of the pool, tense with foreboding, when Hekla appeared at his side.

"What are you doing up?" she demanded in a fierce whisper.

"Something woke me – I think danger's coming," Tom answered. A moment later a ripple splashed over his feet – with no breeze to disturb the water, that ripple could only have been caused by an earth tremor. Shouting, "Everybody outside now!" he dashed into the shelter to grab Kea, who was asleep nearest to the fire, and the rest of the clan scrambled out of their beds just as a fierce tremor hit the oasis. Holding Kea on his hip, Tom locked his free arm around the nearest palm tree, fighting to stay upright as the ground swayed beneath his feet and more ripples spread across the pool, appearing to Tom to cover the whole oasis. Unsure whether it was real or illusion, he gripped Kea so tightly that she cried out. Then the crash of falling stone brought him back to reality as the wall that he and Pedro had built collapsed into a heap of rubble.

The tremor had lasted less than a minute, and they were just congratulating themselves on having escaped injury when Pedro cried, "Grandfather's still in the shelter – he'll be crushed!"

Flint and Juncal dashed to the rescue, tossing the huge blocks aside as if they were pebbles. Masaya stood wringing her hands in anguish and Kea began to cry, but Tom was unconcerned. "It would take more than a few stones to kill Grandfather," he told them, "And I'd know if he was dead." Masaya stared at him as if he was crazy, but only moments later Overo emerged unscathed, covered in dust and grinning broadly.

"That was a Sign and no mistake!" he laughed, "Hekla, you must have prayed some powerful prayers last night." Hekla preened as if she had singlehandedly summoned up the earthquake.

Overo's casual attitude to his rocky burial eased the tension, and they hastened to retrieve their belongings, shaking the dust and grit out of their furs. Fortunately the Firepot had been protected by the overhang, so they were able to cook breakfast before setting off again.

As before, Tom and Pedro walked in front to kick aside any loose rocks that might impede the sledges, and they made good progress, only pausing for ten minutes to snatch a noon meal. Several times the boys thought they saw water ahead only to discover as they got closer that they had been fooled by a mirage, but in the afternoon one seeming mirage developed into two figures – they were about to meet their first strangers on this trip.

Even from a distance Tom sensed the strangers' wariness, and when the men's spears identified them as hunters the boys stopped, waiting for them to approach. As soon as they were close enough the older man called out, "Have you come from beyond Cold River?"

"We have," Tom answered, "We're Guaza Clan and we've been on the trail for two weeks."

"Ah – Juncal's people," the younger man said, visibly relaxing, "We're Desert Clan – he's Kavir and I'm Sevier. We were out hunting and saw your dust-cloud. Did you feel the tremor this morning?"

Tom laughed. "I'll say we did – it demolished the shelter at the oasis and nearly buried us."

"The tremor was a Sign for us," Pedro added, "My parents are expecting a baby."

"So you'll be its big brother," smiled Sevier, touching the warthog tusk hanging on Pedro's chest. "And I see you're a hunter already – you'll be able to help your father provide food for it." The sledges had caught up while they were talking and Sevier hailed Juncal cheerfully. "What a surprise, cousin! We didn't expect to see you until the Festival next year. How is life treating you up on that cold mountain?"

"I have Etna to keep me warm," Juncal said, "And my daughter Kea." He lifted Kea from the sledge and sat her on his shoulder to show her off to his kinsmen.

"Greetings, Kea," Sevier said, "Your father and I were chasing lizards together when we were no bigger than you." Then, belatedly remembering their manners, the two men knuckled their foreheads to Overo.

"Where is your mate, Leader?" Kavir asked, "The Seer who performed Juncal's Mating ceremony?"

"The Mother took Maipu soon after we returned home," Overo replied, "The journey used up the last of her strength. Hekla is our Seer now."

The two Desert men were clearly taken aback by Hekla's blue quartz body – people of her colour were rare – and there was an awkward pause before they sketched a salute which Hekla acknowledged with the smallest of nods.

Sevier said, "We'll leave our hunting till tomorrow and help you with the sledges." The two men laid their spears on top of the clan's possessions. Overo was very glad to accept their offer, and with their assistance the travellers reached the Desert Clan's home well before sunset.

Grand Oasis was dominated by a huge outcrop of rock – a feature that Tom remembered well from the Festival three years previously. In front of this rock the Desert village fanned out from a main plaza, in the centre of which was a large sun-warmed pool and a communal hearth. At least forty sandstone houses lined the well-trodden paths which were shaded by tall palms and bustling with activity.

By the time the sledges drew to a halt in the plaza they were surrounded by a crowd of people – the buzz of excited talk only subsided when the Desert Leader Sonoran appeared to make the official greeting. Taking an ember from the central hearth, he clasped it between Overo's palm and his own, saying, "Our Fire is your Fire – your people are welcome at our hearth."

In response, Overo took a coal from their own Firepot and placed it in the Desert fire with the words, "May your Fire never die."

The formalities over, Sonoran said, "Sahra here will look after your people, Overo, while we share a drink and catch up on the news," and he took Overo off in the direction of his own hut.

Sahra led the others to some guest huts at the edge of the village and pushed open the door of the largest. "I swept this hut out when we spotted your dust-cloud, but I'm afraid it's a bit basic," she said apologetically, "We weren't expecting any large groups this year."

"Don't worry," Masaya assured her, "This is luxury after two weeks on the trail."

As she looked round approvingly, Sahra laughed. "I know what you mean – camping can be hard work." She peered into Masaya's face. "And I think I recognise you – didn't we meet at the Festival?"

"Of course, I remember you now – you'd just had a baby."

"Yes, a boy – he's about the same age as this little girl."

"Kea's mine," Etna said, lifting Kea onto her hip. "Juncal and I must take her to meet his parents. You can settle in without me, I'm sure." She had gone before Masaya could protest.

Sahra laughed, "She must be your sister."

"How did you guess?" Masaya said drily, and then Pedro tugged at her arm. "Is it all right for me and Tom to go and explore?"

"Go on then – there's not much to do if we're only staying one night."

"Can't you stay longer than that?" Sahra pleaded as the boys ran off, "You must meet my son, and I want to hear all your news."

"We've had a Call," replied Masaya, smiling at Flint as he handed her a bundle of blankets. "We will have a new baby to show you on our return."

"In that case any other news can wait," Sahra said, and hurried off to help organise a meal for their surprise guests.

When Tom and Pedro had met at Grand Oasis three years previously, the guest area had been crammed with clans that had congregated for the Festival, and the alleys had been ringing with strange accents. Today they found the terraced huts deserted – the only sounds were the trickle of the stream that sprang from the great rock to water the oasis, and the ever-present hiss of sand-grains shifting in the wind. The arena in the middle of the guest huts was now an abandoned space from which the wind brought to Tom's ears the ghosts of a thousand echoes. He could hear traders calling their wares, the shouts of children playing, groups of people chatting and arguing over prices, but behind that noise was another, familiar,

Voice. As he strained to hear, Pedro asked, "You all right, Tom? You've got that faraway look again."

"The Call is more from the south-west now," Tom said, "There's danger coming too."

Pedro shuddered. "Shut up, Tom, I'm sorry I asked – it's spooky enough in here as it is. Let's go and see what's for dinner."

The Desert Clan had set out an alfresco meal round the huge communal hearth, and the Guaza Clan shared a table with the Leader Sonoran, Donax the Desert Seer, and Juncal's parents – the plaza rang with the noise of a hundred people talking at once.

Confident they would not be overheard, Hekla quietly asked Donax, "Have you had any other Signs apart from this morning's tremor?"

Her question was not an unusual one for one Seer to ask another, and Donax answered readily. "Yes, I've noticed your Call for a couple of weeks – only faintly, of course, as it doesn't concern my clan. But I think you said you're going south-west?" When Hekla nodded, the Desert Seer shook his head. "That can't be right. There's nothing there but the Ocean, and certainly no volcanoes. To be honest, I thought the Sign felt more like a warning – are you sure you read the Call correctly?"

"Of course I'm sure," Hekla snapped, "The birth of a child always brings danger."

Overo leaned across the table to grip her wrist. "Hekla, remember we are guests at this table." He looked Donax in the eyes, saying firmly, "We would not have come this far unless we had confidence in our Seer." Hekla shot him a look of gratitude which changed to a scowl when Flint said, "Not only that, but Tom agrees with her."

"You have another Seer in your clan?" Donax exclaimed.

"He's not a Seer, he's just a boy who thinks he is," Hekla said dismissively, but Flint persisted. "Tom's got the direction right every time we've been hunting."

Hekla wouldn't let the matter to drop, particularly now that the Leader Sonoran was listening as well. "There's a huge difference between finding a herd of deer and knowing where a baby is to be born," she said, her voice rising.

Overo said quickly, "That's true, but two opinions are better than one. If Tom agrees with you then it must be a strong Call – we'll go south-west tomorrow."

After a beat of silence, Sonoran tactfully changed the subject. As the conversation became more general, Overo was overcome by a wish that Maipu was still alive – with all the conflict going on, he missed her wisdom more keenly than ever.

Noting Overo's expression, Juncal's father Mojave said, "The old man looks very weary – has he named his successor yet?"

"Etna thinks it should be me," Juncal answered reluctantly.

"But you don't agree with her?"

Etna slipped her arm through Juncal's. "He's only being modest – it's obvious who Overo should choose."

Juncal said sharply, "Leave it, Etna – this is not the time." He turned to his mother. "I've been meaning to ask you – where's Khali? I've not seen her anywhere."

His mother bit back a sob and hid her face in her hands as Mojave growled, "Your sister ran off with a hunter from down south. No proper Bonding ceremony or anything. We don't speak of it – it upsets your mother too much."

It was clear to Juncal that his mother wasn't the only one suffering – Khali's actions would have brought shame on the whole family. "She'll come back, Father, once she's got the wildness out of her system," he said, but Mojave's only reply was an emphatic, "Hmph!"

Tom slipped away before the party was over, his steps leading him back to the empty arena, where he sat on a sandstone block leaning against the wall of an animal pen. He was at a loss to understand what had got into Hekla. She was his mother – the woman who had lifted him from his birth-shell and held his newborn body next to her skin – who had spooned baby mush into his infant mouth, and shielded him all his life with a fierce protectiveness. Most other mothers would be proud of his new-found skill, and her sudden antagonism this year had come as a severe shock. It was some comfort that Flint and Overo believed in him, and Tom was determined to learn despite his mother's attitude, but her lack of empathy had cast a shadow over these past two weeks.

He straightened his back to shrug off the burden of Hekla's displeasure – he had more important things to think about. When he'd visited the arena earlier with Pedro he was certain he had heard ghosts, but his young friend had distracted him. Now he planned to find out if he could summon the ghost voices at will. With no-one to guide him he had no idea how to start but he was determined to give it a shot.

The blocks of stone arranged at intervals around the arena had been carved to represent the goods traded here – the one he was sitting on was decorated with a camel like those he had seen at the Festival. He traced the outline with his fingers, straining to summon the creature, and a sound made him look up. It had worked! To his astonished delight there was a camel being led across the arena by a fur-clad trader. He shook his head to make sure his imagination wasn't playing tricks, but when the whole arena filled with ghosts and voices he knew his wish had been granted. He froze, afraid to move in case he scared away his first real vision, and watched the scene for several minutes, spellbound by the sights and sounds of the busy marketplace.

He was smiling at a group of children playing five-stones when, without warning, the peaceful scene was shattered. The surface of the arena quivered like a pond beneath a breeze and then, in an endless moment of screaming terror, the sand devoured everything. Tom whipped his feet off the ground and clung to his stone seat as the group of children, scores of people, trade stalls and animals – everything before his eyes was swallowed by the formerly solid ground. Within less than a minute everything vanished, leaving the arena as smooth and empty as before, but now hiding a terrible secret.

He was still shaking with residual terror when another figure walked out of the shadows straight onto the arena. Tom called a warning, but the man crossed the sand unharmed and Tom stood up as he recognised the Desert Seer, Donax, who waved him back down. Sitting beside him on the sandstone block,

Donax asked, without any preamble, "What have you just seen?"

Tom was unsure whether to trust this man who had spent the whole evening talking to Hekla, so he simply described what he saw in front of him. "Sand and palm trees."

Donax tutted impatiently. "I'm not talking about what's in front of your eyes – you look as if you've seen a ghost."

Tom didn't think Donax would take him seriously if he said he'd seen a hundred screaming ghosts drowning in sand, but he had to say something. "I saw a trader with a camel – I think they passed this way recently, didn't they?"

Donax nodded. "Yes, the first trader of the season was here about a week ago." His expression was kind as he added, "But I believe you saw more than last week's visitors. You've seen something extraordinary, haven't you?"

"It was more like a nightmare," Tom admitted with a self-deprecating grimace, "I haven't had a proper vision before." Encouraged by the old man's interest, Tom described the horrific scene in the arena.

Donax's expression was untroubled. "What you've seen couldn't happen, of course – solid ground doesn't act that way – so it must be a metaphor for something else. You're only young – you will learn to read the hidden meanings in time." He smiled to take the sting out of his words. "Now tell me what you see of your own future."

Disappointed to have his disturbing vision dismissed so lightly, Tom thought back over the past few days. "I know my clan is right to be going south-west, and I see them coming back this way, but I don't believe I'll be with them." He raised troubled eyes to the old Seer's face. "Does that mean I'm going to die?"

"Shouldn't think so for a minute!" Donax said briskly, "A Seer always knows when the Mother is going to take him home – which can be a blessing or a curse, depending on your point of view."

Tom was unable to suppress a grin. "So you really believe I'm a Seer?"

"No doubt about it, lad. I'm a Seer, and we always know when we meet another one."

"Then why can't my mother see it?"

"Hekla's your mother? That explains a lot – she's probably blinded by mother-love."

"I don't think that's it," said Tom bitterly, "She puts me down every chance she gets."

"Then she's afraid of your power," Donax said without thinking.

Tom clenched his fists involuntarily. "Why would she be afraid? I'd never do anything to harm her."

Donax caught Tom's wrist and held it thoughtfully. "Your pulse has a strong beat, even for a Seer. I think your power is already greater than hers, and that must be hard to accept." Tom was taken aback, and Donax's next words came as a further surprise. "As your mother, Hekla wouldn't be your best teacher anyway. If you'd consider remaining here in the Desert, I would be happy to take you on as a pupil."

Tom summoned up a smile. "That's a kind offer, Donax, but I think my destiny lies further south-west. Besides, I must finish this journey with my clan before I decide."

"Of course, my boy – we'll discuss it when you return," Donax said, and laid a warning hand on Tom's. "It might be best not to tell your mother about our conversation."

"I agree with you about that," Tom said ruefully, and they shook hands and parted.

CHAPTER EIGHT – FOREST

First light found the Guaza Clan loaded up and ready to leave. A well-used trade route ran beside the stream which sprang from inside the huge sandstone outcrop. Juncal knew it well. His former clan traded regularly with their nearest neighbours, the Forest Clan, exchanging sandstone blocks from their quarry for timber and forest produce.

Flint and Juncal's massive bodies were already stronger for their two weeks of exercise, so as they marched along, harnessed together to the big sledge, they had energy to spare for talking – and for worrying. Flint looked over his shoulder to check Hekla was far enough away before asking Juncal, "Did you hear their Seer say there are no volcanoes south-west of here? We won't get a baby without a volcano – I hope Hekla knows what she's doing."

"It does seem strange," Juncal said, "I'd have thought the Coastal Range was a better bet." Catching sight of Flint's worried face, he tried to inject more confidence into his next remark. "Don't forget we've got a second opinion – Tom also thinks we're on the right track."

The frown eased on Flint's brow. "Yes, he does seem confident, doesn't he? Both of them can't be wrong." He leaned harder into his harness and increased his pace, forcing Juncal to do the same.

They made such good time that by midday they had reached the halfway point, where there was a small hut which had been constructed for traders and slower groups to use as an overnight stop. The clan simply ate a quick meal and moved on, keen to reach proper shelter for the night.

The stream on their right, fed by run-off from the Coastal Range that separated the desert from the Ocean, had now grown to a river, and the land around them was becoming more fertile with each mile they travelled. The desert sands here were mixed with silt washed down from the mountains, and the area was teeming with life. Insects buzzed, fish swam in the reeds, and tiny brown birds darted. Grassland had replaced desert on their left, and the men itched to hunt the cattle and deer that grazed there, but Hekla was constantly urging them to hurry. The hunters comforted themselves with the observation that the noise the little convoy was making kept the animals out of spear-range anyway.

By late afternoon a vast forest dominated the skyline, the damp scent of growing things filled the travellers' lungs, and the cries of unfamiliar birds and animals reached their ears. The contrast with the dry silence of the desert was startling, and its unfamiliarity caused most of the clan to close ranks, but Tom was entranced. In his three years of living on Guaza Mountain he hadn't realised how much he missed the forests of his early childhood. The lush greenery oozed mystery and excitement, and every instinct told him that his destiny would be revealed somewhere in this verdant mass of trees.

The clan had almost reached the outlying trees when several armed figures emerged from the forest and trotted to meet them, the thud of their approach vibrating through the ground. Ordering the sledges to halt, Overo planted his broad feet and Leader's staff in the long grass and waited calmly. Realising he was a clan Leader, the Forest group lowered their weapons to knuckle their foreheads in greeting.

"Have you come to trade?" their spokesman asked.

One of the other men peered into the nearest sledge and laughed, "You'll never believe this – they've brought coal! We've got more fuel than we can use."

Another man poked a meat pudding, asking, "What are these skin balls?"

Masaya slapped his hand away. "I'll thank you not to touch our food."

The man raised his hands in mock surrender and backed away. "At least you won't be hunting our aurochs if you've brought your own food."

"Your aurochs?" Tom exclaimed indignantly, "Food is for whoever can catch it."

"Not on our land."

The idea of ownership of land was a shock, and there was an awkward pause until Overo said, "We're not planning to hunt – we're here in response to a Call."

"Ah, that might explain the tremors," said the spokesman, visibly relaxing. "We wondered what they signified. Your Seer can talk to ours about them if you're coming our way."

Having established that the newcomers weren't after their livestock, the Forest men helped with the sledges as they walked on together, entering the true forest an hour later. A wide path followed the river, letting in plenty of sunlight, but the cool green darkness lurked only a few paces away, and there were strange calls and rustlings in the undergrowth. Pedro's hand hovered over his sling and he muttered to Tom, "Spooky here, isn't it?"

"You think everything's spooky. I like it, though it's a bit cold after the desert."

"You're right about that, Tom," said Juncal, "Get my tunic out of the sledge, will you? I've always said these Forest folk must have granite constitutions to live here."

After an hour the path opened out abruptly into a large clearing in which the smell of smoke and cooking food predominated, reminding the travellers that it was hours since they'd eaten. Shouts greeted the returning Forest men, ceasing abruptly when the Guaza Clan appeared – large numbers of visitors were rare. Silent groups of villagers trickled out of wooden huts – by the time the sledges drew to a halt the entire Forest Clan had assembled in the clearing.

The Forest Leader, Roca, was tall and black and, to Tom's astonishment, female. As she and Overo exchanged burning coals in the formal greeting, Overo failed to hide his own surprise, and Roca's black eyes danced with amusement. "Despite being a woman, I am the Forest Clan's Seer as well as its Leader," she said, "A forest is a very feminine place."

"Our Seer is female too," Overo said, hoping to cover his gaffe, and hastily moved on to explain their mission. Any group travelling for a baby was entitled to hospitality, and Roca ordered accommodation to be found for their unexpected guests.

The Forest village consisted of about twenty-five log huts grouped around a central hearth, in a clearing bounded on three sides by giant trees while the fourth side sloped gently to the river. The banks, though now green with new grass, showed signs of having been submerged by spring floods, and only weeks ago would have been a morass of mud. They reminded Tom of his vision in the arena at Grand

Oasis, and he shuddered – it would be so easy for rock bodies to sink into the muddy riverbank. A wooden structure jutted out into the water and what appeared to be several sledges were lying on the grass nearby.

"Those sledges look rather heavy," he remarked to a Forest man.

The man replied, "Those are rafts, not sledges, so they don't need to be light – they float on the river."

"What – you actually take them on the water?"

"And ride on them," the man said, grinning at Tom's horrified expression. "Once the floods have subsided the river's as calm as a pond."

Looking at the swift current, Tom suspected otherwise, but even as he said, "I wouldn't fancy trusting my life to one," he had an unsettling premonition he might soon have no choice.

Leaving the others to unpack their blankets in yet another borrowed hut, Tom slipped away alone to explore. Although tempted to follow one of the tracks that led into the forest, he could smell dinner cooking, so he confined himself to walking along a track that ran beside the river. As soon he was out of sight of the clearing, the village sounds were muffled. He sat on a log to watch the last of the daylight glinting on the river.

He was so weary after the long trek that in an instant his mind had flown, surfing the river just as he surfed the lava in his Sleep-dreams. His body seemed impervious to the cold as he swerved between the green banks, and he rode the river until there was water all the way to the horizon – he had reached the Ocean. Sitting on a rock, he watched the grey-green waves breaking over a reef into a calm lagoon.

Without warning the peaceful scene changed, and the entire ocean tilted as if the giant of Grandfather's story had stood on the edge of a stepping-stone. An enormous wave rose from the horizon and rushed towards him, looming closer and closer. Tom couldn't move, so mesmerised was he by its power. Then it reached the shore and the crest curled over menacingly far above his head. Certain he would be crushed, Tom recoiled so violently that he fell backwards – and returned to himself, jerked back to reality by the shock.

As he lay on the ground, still shaken by the vividness of his vision, he heard a giggle. His eyes snapped open and there, standing over him, was the most beautiful girl he had ever seen. Her body glowed green in the tree-filtered light, and in her brown tunic she resembled nothing so much as a sapling just emerged from the forest. As he gazed, afraid to move in case she vanished, she laughed, "You look as if you've seen a ghost!" and held out a hand to help him to his feet.

"For a moment I thought you were a forest spirit," Tom stammered.

She laughed again – a musical sound that pierced Tom's heart like a spear. "I'm no naiad – I'm real enough. My name's Verda. I was picking greens for supper when I nearly fell over you." She waved a handful of leaves as proof and continued, "You're one of those people from the east, aren't you? Tell me about the mountains there. The traders say you don't have any trees – I can't imagine a place without trees."

Mountains? Trees? Tom was so bemused by her beauty that he could scarcely remember what those were, but he brushed himself down and managed to answer, "We have a few trees, though they're not much taller than me – the ones round here look enormous."

"I could show you some that are even taller," Verda said, "But I can't stop now – Mother will be waiting for these greens – are you coming?" Tom followed her willingly, so entranced by her that his vision of a watery disaster faded from his mind.

Once again the Guaza Clan ate as guests at a strange hearth. Tom couldn't take his eyes off Verda, watching every move she made as she helped to serve the food. When she offered him a dish of greens he took a handful deliberately slowly to delay her and she flashed him a smile that said clearly, 'I know what you're up to'. She continued around the circle, but when the bowl was empty she sat down beside him and pointed at his untouched meal.

"That food will be cold by now – you need to heat it up," she said and picked an ember out of the fire. Her eyes teasing, she put it into Tom's palm and held it there.

The heat shot up his arm and set the lava bubbling right down to his toes – suddenly his body wasn't big enough to contain the life that surged through him. He gripped the ember between Verda's hand and his own, watching her lovely green eyes widen as the same tingling sensation coursed through her veins. The outside world disappeared and the buzz of talk faded – in that moment nothing else existed but the two of them. The tiny part of Tom's consciousness that was still active decided the Ocean wave vision must have been a premonition, because he was drowning now in a pair of deep green eyes.

An eternity later Verda eased her hand away and dropped the ember into Tom's food to heat it up. He stirred it with fingers that still trembled from her touch, looking round surreptitiously to see if anyone had noticed them, but the buzz of conversation continued unabated – it seemed that no-one else was even aware a miracle had occurred.

As at Grand Oasis, raised brows and puzzled frowns greeted the news of the Guaza Clan's intended destination, and once the meal was over Roca voiced her concern. "I am surprised at the distance you have travelled for this baby. I would expect you to get one from closer to home."

"That's what I thought," Masaya said, "But Hekla insists this is the right way."

"That's another thing," said one of the Forest men, "The only path south-west from here is beside the river and there's nothing that way but the Ocean."

"I am sick of having my Call questioned," Hekla snapped, her eyes icy in her blue face. "The Signs have grown stronger every day and I know I am right."

Roca made a placatory gesture. "I am not doubting you, Hekla," she said, "I too have felt the Signs, but I think you should head for the southern prairie. A volcano on the coast down there has been grumbling for a while. I wondered if the Call might be for the Shore Clan – they lost their Seer during the Sleep."

Overo sat up straighter and asked, "Why did you not offer them your services?"

Roca tensed at the implied criticism but answered calmly. "I was about to do so – I had even prepared a raft ready to go and see them – but I had such a strong warning of danger that I postponed my trip. This is another reason why I urge you to avoid the river and take the forest path to the prairie – some of my people can show you the way." She smiled at Verda, knowing she would be among the first to volunteer.

Overo said, "Thank you for the offer, and the advice, Roca, but we'll stick to the route chosen by our Seer." He heaved himself to his feet. "Now it's time we were in bed – we must make an early start tomorrow."

Tom, still engrossed in conversation with Verda, failed to move quickly enough for Hekla and she called impatiently, "Tomboro! It's bedtime."

He raised a hand in a half-wave. "I'll be there soon, Mother."

Hekla's face darkened. "You'll come now, Tom – this is not a holiday."

Tom glared but Verda whispered, "You'd better go – she's not going to give up."

"You're right," Tom sighed, "Once Mother's started she won't stop." He squeezed Verda's hand and walked over to their borrowed hut. The moment they were inside he confronted Hekla. "You did that deliberately to make me look small in front of everyone."

"You should have come the first time."

"I was talking to Verda, Mother."

"Is that what you call holding hands in public with a girl you've only just met?"

"Hekla, that's enough," Overo said wearily. "Tom, you should have obeyed your mother. It's time we were in bed – I have a feeling we're going to need all our strength tomorrow."

Tom let his breath out in a long sigh. Grandfather's word was law, and it was a waste of energy fighting with his mother when she was in this mood. He moved his blankets as far from Hekla as he could get, and fell asleep to dream of a girl who was half forest sapling and half naiad, and a tilting Ocean as vast as the sky.

CHAPTER NINE – RAFTS

In the dark hour before dawn Tomboro was still dreaming of Verda. He shifted in his sleep at the memory of her hand and his clasped together around the hot ember, but in the space of a heartbeat that dream was replaced by one much darker. He was by the Ocean again, sitting on that same rock, and again the water swelled into an enormous wave that curled over to engulf the land. This time Tom didn't retreat, because in the midst of the heaving water he had seen a baby, still glowing with the heat of its birth but cooling fast. Without hesitation, Tom's dream-self leapt in to save it, and as he clasped it to his chest the shock of the cold water jolted him awake.

He lay shivering in his warm bed, still disorientated by his dream, then a real tremor shook him fully alert. Throwing off his blankets, he dashed outside, where he found his mother, clutching her cape around her against the chilly night air. "Did you feel that tremor?" he asked.

"Of course – anyone can feel a tremor – but I was actually woken by a Sign."

"So was I," Tom said, "I dreamed about a huge wave and a baby coming from the Ocean."

As he spoke, Overo appeared in the doorway saying sleepily. "Something woke me – what were you saying about the Ocean?"

Brushing Tom aside, Hekla said, "There's been another Sign, and a vision of the Ocean itself, which means I've been leading us the right way – and now it's urgent!"

"That was my vision!" Tom protested, but Overo had already gone to rouse his clan.

As they scrambled to get ready, Juncal said to Flint, "Remember that Forest man Sasso we were talking to last night? He said a raft halves the time to get to the Ocean."

Flint's eyes widened – it was clear he was appalled by Juncal's implied suggestion – then Sasso and his father Chert appeared, saying, "We heard you talking – you're leaving earlier than we expected."

"Our Seer's had another Sign – an urgent one," Juncal told them, "I'm glad you're awake – we were thinking of asking to borrow a raft."

"You'd all end up in the river," Chert laughed, "You've got no idea how to use one."

"And we haven't got time to learn," Masaya said, shoving a bundle of blankets into Flint's arms. "If we don't hurry we'll be too late, and this track is too narrow for the sledges – we'll have to run!"

"You and Flint go ahead," Overo said, waving them away, "My running days are over."

As the pair disappeared along the riverbank, Chert looked at Overo's woebegone face and said, "I reckon we could get you there for the birth. It wouldn't take long to fix one of your sledges onto a raft, then the older ones can ride while the youngsters run."

"You're offering to take us?" Overo exclaimed.

Chert grinned boyishly. "Sasso's team was all set to take Roca to the Shore – seems a shame not to use them."

With the light of adventure in his eyes, Juncal unceremoniously tipped out the contents of the small sledge and hauled it down to the jetty, where the Forest carpenters made quick work of attaching it to a raft. In front of an amused crowd of villagers, the whole cumbersome craft was launched just as daylight seeped through the trees, and Overo and Hekla climbed gingerly on board. Etna passed over their blanket bundles, and Tom was about to throw his own pack in when Hekla said, "No, Tom – you children are staying here – we'll collect you on the way back."

Tom gasped, "I'm not a child!"

Hekla shrugged. "You're not a man yet, and you'd only be in the way."

"You're just jealous because I had a vision and you didn't," Tom cried.

Hekla's jaw tightened. "I am the Seer in this clan, not you, and you will do as you're told."

"Grandfather," Tom pleaded, "You can't leave me behind."

Overo shook his head. "I'm sorry, Tom, but I can't overrule your mother – you can keep an eye on the younger ones."

Tom's attempt to protest further was drowned by Chert singing out from the front of the raft, "You'd better sit down now because we're leaving."

Overo and Hekla hurried to opposite corners of the raft, Sasso untied the mooring ropes and pushed them off from the jetty, and a moment later the raft was gripped by the current. Tom was left standing on the bank, relegated to a child's place beside ten-year-old Pedro. He glared at Hekla's unyielding profile until the raft disappeared round the curve and then, unable to bear Verda's look of sympathy, he abandoned his pack where it lay and dashed off into the forest.

Pedro was debating whether to follow him when Mocha, a Forest boy, tugged his belt. "I've got my own raft – do you want to see?" he whispered, and Pedro nodded eagerly. He followed his new friend a hundred yards downstream where, out of sight of the village, Mocha dived into the undergrowth to drag out a little raft – three logs lashed together to create a raft roughly six feet by three – just the right size for a child to manage.

"Wow!" Pedro gasped, "Is that really yours?"

"Made it myself too," Mocha said, "Chert's my grandfather and he's the best carpenter in the Forest Clan – he taught me to work with wood."

"How does it work?" Pedro asked eagerly.

"I'll show you." Mocha pulled his raft onto the beach and sat astride it, holding its rope and swaying his body to demonstrate how he steered, "I'll probably take it out again soon," he said nonchalantly, "The river's warming up nicely – I might take you for a ride if you promise not to tell my mother."

"Aren't you allowed?"

"A boy drowned last year – they had to drag the river to get him out."

"That sounds a horribly cold way to die."

"Well, yes, but it *was* just after the spring floods. We told him not to but he always was a show-off. They burnt all our rafts, which wasn't fair, so I had to make another one."

"But how will we get away with it?"

"Simple – we'll just start from beyond the curve."

Pedro's face lit up at the thought of sharing such a dangerous adventure, and he slung his leg across the raft to sit behind Mocha, listening carefully to the Forest boy's instructions.

*

Verda had given Tom a few minutes to calm down before she went looking for him, but in those few minutes he had disappeared, and an hour had passed before she found him sitting on a tree stump. She kicked aside the broken branches by his feet that bore witness to his rage and sat beside him. "You've every right to be angry – your mother shouldn't have left you behind."

Tom squeezed her hand fiercely and said, as much to himself as to her, "I'm not sure who I'm the most angry with – her for stopping me or myself for letting her. That vision of the Ocean was mine – she had no right to steal it."

Verda held his cheeks in her soft hands and turned him to face her. "A vision? You didn't tell me you're a Seer!"

Tom smiled wanly. "I thought it might put you off."

"I can't think why it would," Verda said, "So tell me – what was this vision?"

Tom gazed into her beautiful dark green eyes and for a moment, with her pulse beating against his skin, he wished he wasn't a Seer, but it was too late for that – the Mother had chosen him. With a sigh that was half surrender and half relief, he launched into a vivid description of the Ocean creating a huge wave. He told her how it fell to crush him and everything around him, and how he rescued the baby from the water. Verda listened in silence until he finished with, "Perhaps it was only a vivid dream."

"Come on, Tom, you don't really believe that."

"My visions have already caused problems – Mother's furious because she doesn't have any. But you're right – I can't ignore them. It was the same vision of a wave that tipped me off that log yesterday."

"You did look funny!" Verda giggled.

She looked so lovely that Tom leaned in to kiss her, but as he did so the trees behind her blurred and towered over them like waves. Then they *were* waves – the same vision with one appalling difference. There were logs in the water – logs that Tom knew instantly were parts of the Guaza Clan's sledge and the raft – and then he saw tumbling head-stones, each bearing a face that he recognised. In total panic he jumped up and ran towards the village screaming, "They're all going to die!"

Verda ran after him panting, "Who are going to die?"

"My clan – I have to warn them – that giant wave is going to kill them!"

"This way's quicker," Verda said, dragging him along.

Just before the village they stumbled upon Pedro and Mocha playing with the little raft. Instantly Tom pounced on Mocha, demanding, "Does this thing float? Could it catch the other raft?"

"Of course it floats," Mocha said indignantly, "But you'll never catch them."

"I've got to try – my clan's in dreadful danger."

"They're my clan too," Pedro said, "And I know how to ride this thing." Before Mocha could stop him he snatched the rope from his hand, pushed the small raft into the water and slung his leg over it, yelling, "Come on!"

Tom didn't even hesitate – he simply jumped on behind Pedro and they let the current take them.

The speed was exhilarating and terrifying – with no rope team to hold it back, the little raft with the boys astride it shot down the river much faster than a man could run. Even when surfing the lava in his Sleep-dreams Tom had never moved at such a speed. Pedro held on desperately to the loop of rope, swaying his body as Mocha had taught him, while Tom held his waist and copied his movements. After a few seconds of breathless wonder he shouted in Pedro's ear, "I had a vision yesterday of riding the river like this."

"Well I wish you'd warned me," Pedro shouted back, "My arms are aching already!"

At the first curve the current swung them towards the bank and they only just avoided being beached, then the opposite curve flung them back. Each sudden manoeuvre threatened to overturn them, yet Tom still urged, "Hurry, make it go faster!"

"How can we go any faster?" Pedro asked, "The river makes the speed."

"I can feel it dragging at my legs," Tom said and lifted them out of the water to tuck alongside Pedro's body. The raft did move faster then, but when Pedro tried tucking his own feet up he nearly tipped them both into the river. After that he simply concentrated on steering the tiny craft while Tom balanced precariously behind him, clinging to his waist.

The banks became a blur, only the occasional streak of colour when a bird took flight to break the monotony. Tom yelled with the sheer thrill of speed, his voice bouncing from the green walls.

As they rounded one of the many bends, he caught a glimpse of movement and two creatures scrambled up the bank. They vanished in an instant, but the sight burned into Tom's brain – their mud-streaked bodies had been naked of fur, and they walked upright – just like the Humans in Grandfather's bedtime story.

The initial excitement soon wore off. The boys were colder than they had ever been before – even their plunge into Cold River to rescue Flint had been over quickly – and after an hour Pedro's legs were numb. They had been too intent on staying on the little raft to notice anything else, but as they leaned into yet another bend, a large crocodile slithered from the bank to intercept them. This wasn't anything like the lizards they had killed in the oasis, this was a real dragon! Pedro yanked his rope to steer them to the opposite bank, but the sudden move was too much for the little raft – it tilted beyond Pedro's powers to recover and threw both boys into the river.

Tom instinctively tightened his grip on Pedro's belt, but as they plummeted down in a panicky tangle of arms and legs he felt two rows of huge, sharp teeth close around his leg. For a few terrifying seconds the crocodile towed them along, but Tom kicked wildly with his free leg and when the solid weight of his foot connected with its scaly nose, the jaw opened and the crocodile let him go. Instantly he plunged to the riverbed, his muscles stiffening as the cold water sucked the heat from them, and his lungs screaming for air. For a dreadful moment he looked death in the face, but as his weight sank into the mud he felt rock beneath his feet – if he acted quickly he might still live. It wasn't just his life at stake, it was Pedro's too, and his friend was only here because of him. With a supreme effort he managed one step towards the bank, then another and another until, finally, his head broke the surface, his fingers frozen to Pedro's belt. Forcing his stiffened chest muscles to suck in a breath, he heaved Pedro up the bank and collapsed beside him in a patch of sunlight.

As the sun's warmth seeped into his body, Tom opened his eyes, hardly daring to believe they were still alive. Both of them were shivering violently, but there was no sign of the crocodile and, miraculously, Pedro was still holding the rope! He nudged Pedro. "Come on, you – get yourself moving!"

"Leave me alone," Pedro mumbled, "Are we dead?"

"No we're not – but we've got to get warm quickly or we will be."

Hurting all over, they sat up, stripped, and wrung what seemed like half the river from their tunics. They rubbed their legs in a rough massage to get the lava flowing, and after a few minutes dragged their damp tunics back on. Pedro stared at the beached raft with something approaching hatred. “I’m done for, Tom – my legs will only go numb again.”

“I don’t want to go back in the water either,” Tom admitted, “But we can’t give up now – there’s no-one else to warn the others.”

“Couldn’t we run from here?” Pedro pleaded, “We must be close to the other raft now.”

Tom shook his head. “They had too much of a start on us, and with my feet on solid ground I can feel the warning even more strongly. There’s hardly any time left – we’ll have to use the raft.”

“Come on, then, if we’re going,” Pedro said, touching his tusk necklace for courage, so they waded back into the water, remounted the raft, and pushed out once more into the current.

*

The Guaza Clan’s air of urgency had infected the Forest men, and the rope teams had run along the towpath at the mile-consuming speed of a band of hunters chasing a herd of deer. The sledge-raft was rounding the final curve when Overo spotted movement behind them. He nudged Chert so hard that he nearly lost his footing. “Chert! Look – there’s another raft!" He narrowed his eyes to peer upstream. "By the stars – it's Tom and Pedro!"

Chert stared and then laughed. "I wonder where they got the raft. They didn't like being left behind, did they? Young dare-devils – even I never rode this far at their age."

Overo bit back a grin to warn, "They'll crash into us in a minute – we'd better get ready to rescue them."

Pedro was struggling to control the raft as it bounced in the wake of the larger one, but Tom ignored the danger and let go of Pedro's belt to shout through his cupped hands, "Get away from the river! Danger's coming!"

Masaya and Etna, who were on the towpath a few yards behind the others, were first to hear him. Masaya, seeing Pedro in danger, was too stunned to move, but Etna grabbed her wrist and dragged her up the steep grass bank. "They're both going to die!" Masaya wailed but Etna said, "The men will catch them," and refused to let her go – Tom's warning had the ring of truth.

Having watched them scramble up the bank, Tom looked away to see the raft was running out of room. "We're going to crash!" he yelled, and they both leaned hard left to steer into the bank, missing the big raft by a whisker.

Flint waded into the shallows to grab Pedro, but Tom shook off Juncal attempts to help him, shouting, "Get away from the river – it's coming now!" He tugged frantically on the huge raft, as if he could pull it ashore single-handed.

Juncal grabbed his arm. "Tom – calm down – we know the child's coming."

"We can't stop now – we're nearly there!" Hekla shrieked, but this time Tom would not be silenced.

"I had a vision! The Ocean rose up like a wall and crushed everything. You must get off the river and up into the trees, and you must do it now!"

Sasso immediately ordered his team to pull the raft into the bank. The Forest men weren't nearly as nonchalant as they pretended about the perils of rafting, and Tom's warning reminded them that their own Seer had foreseen danger.

"I should have guessed that it was Tom who had that vision," Overo said to Hekla, picking up the clan's precious Firepot to follow Chert to land.

"Mother – get off!" Tom yelled.

Overo bellowed, "Hekla – if you don't move now I'll come back and carry you!"

For long seconds she glared at them both, until a sudden surge of foreboding told her Tom was right, and sheer terror catapulted her ashore.

CHAPTER TEN – ERUPTION

A few hundred yards downstream, from their village on the bluff, the Shore Clan watched the action on the far bank uncomprehendingly. The odd-looking raft was a surprise in itself – in fact any raft was unexpected this early in the year – but then several things this spring had been worrying.

The strangeness had begun when they were shaken roughly from their winter Sleep by a strong tremor, and emerged from their caves on a cliff-side plateau to see steam rising from the rocky islet in the lagoon that separated them from the Ocean. That islet was two hundred yards offshore, but each summer some of the more daring youths would paddle over to it on small rafts to collect shellfish. Last year one boy had even claimed he'd found a crab already cooked, although no-one had believed such a wild tale. On the first day of spring, however, when the clan members saw the steam, they wondered if the story had been true after all.

Since then they had gone about their daily routine with a wary eye on the small cloud that hovered over the islet, but no-one had been brave enough to take a raft over and investigate. To add to their unease, the air had a sulphurous smell, the water in the lagoon was a strange green colour, and intermittent underground rumblings kept the whole clan on edge.

Their old Seer, Cho, had died during the Sleep, and the Shore Leader, Yakan, had been considering going upriver to consult Roca when this strange raft appeared. Unexpected visitors were not always welcome, so Yakan sent two hunters to the ford to investigate while the rest of the clan watched from the trees, armed with piles of loose rocks to use as missiles. Then Yakan recognized his old friend Chert, and he was about to go down to meet him when the visitors pulled their raft ashore and scrambled up the steep bank into the trees, evidently in haste.

Yakan raised his considerable voice to shout, "Chert! What's happening?"

Chert waved his arm, shouting back, "Later!"

Any further attempts at communication were drowned by a great coughing roar and the rocky islet in the lagoon exploded.

The two Shore men at the ford stood frozen in disbelief as the river disappeared from beside their feet and then, far too late, they turned to flee. A solid mass of water rushed back upstream from the lagoon, engulfing them in an instant, and their women's horrified screams from the plateau above were lost in a wall of noise. The disaster was so sudden and overwhelming that for a long moment nobody moved, mesmerised by the heaving water. They only came to their senses when red-hot stones began falling from the slate-grey sky. A rain of super-heated stones was dangerous, especially for children, so Yakan turned his back on the chaotic scene below and, spreading his arms wide, herded his people into the relative safety of their caves.

The great wave – first twenty, then thirty feet high – roared upriver with unbelievable speed, stripping everything in its path. The Guaza and Forest people had acted in the nick of time – if they'd spent another minute arguing they would all have been lost.

The tow-ropes were ripped from their hands as the raft Hekla had been on moments before was swept away. Churning water swept by within inches of their feet, so they scrambled even further up the wooded slope, coughing in the ash-laden air and clinging to trees. Flint held Mocha's small raft over his head and they crowded beneath its inadequate shelter – even their rock skulls were vulnerable when the sky was raining hot stone.

Tom watched the fulfilment of his vision with grim satisfaction, thankful that his warning had saved his clan, but his self-congratulatory calm was shattered when Pedro screamed, "Where is she – where's Mother?" In the panic they had forgotten the two women who'd been behind them on the towpath – Masaya and Etna weren't with them.

Leaving Overo to hold the little raft shelter aloft, Flint, Juncal and Pedro dived into the painful shower of debris calling Masaya and Etna's names. Through the deafening cacophony of rushing water, crashing rocks and falling branches their chances of hearing any answering call were minimal, but they still shouted. Zigzagging up and down the slippery bank, they searched from the thick undergrowth between the trees right down to the edge of the foaming water, horribly afraid that the huge wave had swept the women to their deaths.

They might never have found them in the murk if Pedro hadn't literally stumbled over them. His mother and aunt were huddled under a tree, clutching each other and sobbing in the awful certainty that their entire clan had just been wiped out. Flint hauled Masaya to her feet and wrapped her in a fierce hug. "By the Sun, woman, I was sure I'd lost you," he said, while Pedro clung to her hand, incoherent with relief.

Etna flung herself into Juncal's arms sobbing, "We saw bits of the sledge go past – we thought the Ocean had killed you all!"

"And *we* thought *you* were dead."

"The boys warned us in time," Masaya said, scooping Pedro up into her arms. He wrapped himself around her as if he would never let her go, and she looked over his head at Flint. "We could have lost Pedro – that's too high a price to pay for another baby."

"You're right," Flint said, "But we didn't lose him." He rubbed Pedro's head affectionately. "Our son's a brave boy – he and Tom saved everyone's lives." He shot out his hand to catch a large flaming rock before it could land on their heads and added, "Let's get back to the others before this gets any worse."

The Forest carpenters had cobbled together a bigger shelter out of fallen branches, but when the rescue party returned it was still a tight squeeze under its roof. Everyone there was torn between fear of the falling debris and fascination with the eruption – the shelter was in constant danger of collapse as they jostled for the best view of this once-in-a-lifetime event.

Hekla raised her voice over the booming roar of the eruption to brag, "I knew all along we were going the right way."

Throwing her a disgusted look, Overo burst her self-congratulatory bubble. "I agree you led us to the right place, but you didn't foresee that giant wave. If Tom hadn't seen it coming we would all have been killed."

Hekla glowered at Tom, who avoided her eyes and pointed across the river where, through the mist of spray, they could see the Shore Clan flinging rocks at the heaving water. "They look really angry – I wonder why?"

"Etna and I saw some bodies," Masaya said, "They must have lost someone."

Chert waved his arms to catch the Shore Leader's attention and spread his hands in silent query, learning that two men had been swept from the ford. He shook his head sorrowfully – danger was the price everyone paid for being the children of a volcanic Mother, but he and Sasso knew every man in the Shore Clan – the dead men would have been their friends.

The salt water surged upstream for several more minutes before it stilled briefly then returned seawards, bringing with it a soup of chopped vegetation and dead animals. The eruption continued fiercely for another hour before it began to subside. When the shower of hot stones eased off, the Guaza Clan and their Forest friends abandoned their shelter and moved to the low bluff for a better view.

In the centre of the lagoon, where formerly there had only been the tiny rock islet, was a cone, spitting fire in a shower of red-hot cinders that was setting the trees alight on both sides of the river-mouth. It was a truly spectacular sight, and every member of this volcanic race watched the emerging volcano with awe. The intense heat held no terrors for them – it was how they had all been born – and everyone took deep breaths of the intoxicatingly sulphurous fumes.

Then Overo remembered why they were here. Gesturing at the cone he said to Flint, "Well, there's your volcano, small though it is, but how are you going to get there? We've lost the raft."

Flint looked down the bank. Although the tsunami had spent most of its fury, the backwash still heaved in the river below them, and the waters of the lagoon under the rain of hissing rocks looked even more dangerous. Between them and the volcano from which their baby would be born lay a hundred and fifty yards of turbulent water. His shoulders slumped as he admitted, "It would be suicide to attempt that crossing."

Masaya covered her face and sobbed – after coming all this way it looked as if she wasn't going to get her long-awaited baby.

As the volcano grew in size, the debris fell further away, leaving a relatively calm central area, so they abandoned the bluff to slide down through the grit and cinders to the beach. Yakan and a few Shore men did the same on their side, but there was no hope of conversation over the noise of the eruption. Although they could communicate with gestures it made no difference – neither group had any idea what to do next.

Pedro tugged Tom's tunic and asked, "Did you see all this back in the Forest village?"

"I saw the wave," Tom said, but he really didn't want to talk, even to Pedro. For him the eruption was much more than a spectacle – he felt a strong personal connection with this infant volcano. He moved away from the crowd to an isolated outcrop where he sat simply staring at the exploding lava.

As the child of a travelling Seer he had been present at a few births, but never in his wildest dreams had he imagined actually witnessing the birth of a volcano. Deep down he was aware that it was this volcano, rather than Flint and Masaya's baby, which had summoned him from their distant mountain.

His own heart beat in time with the throb of the volcano's pulse, and his conviction was growing that after the baby was born – the baby that might somehow come from the water – he would not be able to leave. Young as he was, he knew he must find a way to stay here.

Hekla's voice broke into his thoughts. "I suppose you expect me to be grateful you disobeyed my orders? Well, I'll admit your warning was useful – I was too intent on the baby to see that wave coming – but I did see a volcano where there wasn't one."

"Yes you did," Tom agreed, "From hundreds of miles away. Did you also see the baby coming from the water?"

As Hekla snorted contemptuously, "Babies and water don't mix," Masaya and Flint joined them.

"We can't settle back there," Masaya said, "It must be nearly time, surely?"

"A few more hours," Hekla told her, "The eruption's too fierce at the moment."

"Hours or minutes – it's all the same if we can only watch our baby die," Flint said bitterly, "And what is Tom saying about water?"

"I can't see it clearly yet," Tom said, "Looking at this mess, it might just mean that you'll have to go through the water to get your baby."

"If that's the only way, we'll manage somehow," Masaya said.

Flint gestured hopelessly at the wide gap between them and the new volcano. "How the hell does the Mother expect us to get across there? Tom – you should know how if you're really a Seer."

Tom flinched as if Flint had struck him, and motherly Masaya tried to take the sting out of his words by pointing out, "Hekla can't tell us either."

Hekla snapped, "The Mother Called us here, so She will show you how – you should have more faith."

Flint threw her a hostile glance. "Well, I wish She'd get on with it – I can't see why She was in such a hurry to get us here if all we can do is sit and wait."

"Because if you'd left the Forest any later that wave would have caught you on the towpath," Tom reminded him, but he could understand their fears. At every birth he'd witnessed, the parents had been able to run beside the lava-flow and pick their moment to grab their baby-shell. If Flint and Masaya's shell rolled into the water it would solidify, and their baby would die before it was even born.

For the rest of the day the Guaza Clan and their Forest friends remained on the beach by the lagoon, keeping vigil with the expectant parents, but still nobody could work out how to reach the volcano. When evening approached and the light faded, they began to think about shelter for the night.

The eruption was throwing out enough heat, but for the children's sake the men braved the rain of debris to gather some fallen trees and construct a rough bivouac on the beach.

Their store of food had been lost with the raft, but the forest also provided a meal. They found a number of animals killed by the eruption – monkeys, pigs and some other, unidentifiable chunks of meat. After they had chopped it into pieces and completed its cooking over an open fire, everyone was too hungry to care what their makeshift meal looked like.

CHAPTER ELEVEN – TSUNAMI

Watching from the Forest beach as Tomboro and Pedro were whisked away by the river, Verda and Mocha were transfixed with horror – Mocha because the secret of his raft was out, Verda because she was sure the two Guaza boys were riding to their deaths.

"We have to tell Roca," Verda said, "She might be able to help them." Mocha pulled a face but nodded reluctantly and followed Verda back to the village.

The central area was very peaceful after the bustle of the departure, and there were only a few people about when the two scared youngsters got there. Mocha went home to confess before his mother heard the story from someone else, while Verda ran straight to Roca's hut, hoping the Seer could somehow protect Tom and Pedro. Roca, who was deep in conversation with the Elders, frowned at the interruption. "This is a serious discussion, Verda – can't it wait?"

"I'm afraid not," said Verda, "Tom had an awful vision, so he and Pedro have gone after the others."

Seeing her evident distress Roca asked more gently, "What kind of vision, child? And when did they go?"

"Just now – Tom said his clan were in dreadful danger." Her lip quivered. "They took Mocha's raft."

There was a stunned silence – everyone present knew that for a tiny raft to survive such a trip was almost impossible – and Roca put an arm around Verda. "Tell me exactly what Tom told you. I called this meeting because I sense an eruption coming, though I can't see where it will be." After Verda had described Tom's vision of a huge wave, Roca said, "That could be the result of an eruption beneath the Ocean – both rafts could be swamped."

"I've seen the Ocean in a storm, which was bad enough," said one Elder, "How big would this wave be?"

"Tom said it was as tall as the trees," Verda sobbed, "They're all going to die, aren't they?"

"What worries me more," said another Elder, "Is whether it could reach our village."

Roca nodded. "I think we'd be wise to prepare for the worst," she said, and the Elders dispersed rapidly to issue instructions to the villagers.

For the remainder of that morning the Forest Clan carried babies and belongings to higher ground. Mocha's mother Galena loaded his small arms with furs, her face grimmer than he had ever seen it. "I will deal with you later," she promised, but when Mocha escaped to the impromptu camp he found his friends were treating the whole thing as an adventure, and he was the hero of the day.

After erecting makeshift tents for shelter, the villagers were just hauling their remaining rafts away from the river when an eerie silence descended on the forest and the ground began to shudder. Women huddled together clutching their children and their Firepots – even the strongest men couldn't stand upright without holding onto a tree. One man, attempting to rescue the last raft from the beach, noticed that the river had stopped flowing and ran for his life. Not a thing moved – even the birds had stopped singing – they were all convinced their last moment had come. Then a distant rumble swelled to a roar and their river, which had always flowed to the Ocean, raced round the bend and surged upstream. Roca and her people clung to trees praying for deliverance as the great wave roared past, and watched in superstitious horror as enormous logs somersaulted in the water, their bridge and jetty were demolished, and their beach vanished.

It was several long minutes before the tumult subsided and the ground stopped shaking. The clan stared at each other in stunned silence – even Roca didn't know what to say. Everyone had seen the river rush inland so there was no denying what had happened, but their belief in the natural order of things had been severely shaken. Verda wept in her mother's arms, convinced Tom was dead, and Mocha buried his face in Galena's tunic, afraid to look at her.

Eventually, after the current had swirled uneasily for a while, the river began to flow west again – it was still overflowing its banks but to their relief it was at least going in the right direction. Even so, Roca kept her clan in the forest for another hour before leading a wary group down to investigate the damage. They kept their distance from the river, which was still a turbulent mess of torn undergrowth, and the litter of debris on their beach included dead animals and fish. As well as the jetty and the bridge, they had lost two rafts, and a few of the huts had been damaged, but the decision to move away from the river had prevented any loss of life in the village.

For the sledge-raft and its passengers and crew it was another matter entirely – no-one believed any of them could have survived. Galena spoke for all the families of the rafters when she said, "We have to find out what happened to them. My son's father and grandfather could be lying out there injured."

"I'll take a team downstream tomorrow," Roca promised, although privately she feared she would discover only bodies.

Verda said at once, "I'm coming with you – I have to find out what's happened to Tom."

"You've only just met the boy," her father objected, "It's not fitting for you to go," but her mother looked at Verda's determined face and, knowing she would go with or without permission, persuaded Zircon to let her join the expedition.

Reluctantly, Roca agreed to take her, saying only, "We leave at dawn – you can come as long as you can keep up."

CHAPTER TWELVE – BABIES

With the sun obscured by the cloud of volcanic ash, nightfall came early by the Ocean. After the scratch meal, the new arrivals could do nothing but sit beside their beach fire, watching the slowly growing volcano and wracking their brains for a way to reach it. On the north side of the river mouth the Shore Clan could be seen going about their normal activities outside their cliff-side caves before, eventually they retired to bed. Soon afterwards, worn out by the excitement of the day, the Guaza and Forest people were also lulled to sleep by the constant vibration. Even Hekla dozed off, leaving Tom, Flint and Masaya to share a sleepless vigil, sitting on the beach lit only by the strange orange glow of the eruption.

At dawn a sudden increase in sound brought everyone fully awake. First Hekla and then everyone else scrambled out of the little shelter just as one edge of the infant volcano collapsed and fell into the lagoon. When a tongue of lava peeped over the lip of the broken cone Flint cried, "Here it comes!" and he and Masaya actually ran into the water, obviously prepared to wade out despite the danger until Tom yelled, "Wait! The lava will come to you!"

"Don't listen to him," Hekla countered, "Go on – you're wasting time!"

Flint and Masaya took a few more steps but Tom repeated, "Wait – I promise it will happen any minute now." His voice carried such conviction that they stopped again, chest-deep in the lagoon. For the first time the pair became fully aware of their precarious position – the volcano-heated water was warmer than usual, but if they fell into an unexpected dip they could drown. Holding hands, they froze where they stood, waiting for further instructions.

With agonising slowness the tongue of lava swelled to bursting point and overflowed the lip of the cone. A thick stream of red-hot rock coiled with ponderous inevitability towards the shore, and now Flint and Masaya were in danger of being trapped by it. As the seawater boiled into steam around them they splashed hastily back to the beach and stood poised on an outcrop, swaying with the effort of holding themselves back. The instant the lava touched their outcrop they raced up the moving flow, searching for the shell of fragile rock that would contain their child.

Masaya zigzagged from side to side, peering into the hissing spray, terrified that the water would kill her baby. She had good reason to be fearful – the edges of the lava were already hardening where they met the lagoon. Meanwhile Flint raced ahead and clambered up the side of the cone, flailing his arms to disperse the steam that was obscuring his vision. They were both in constant danger of being caught by the lava-flow, and watchers on both sides of the river-mouth held their breath as the drama unfolded before their eyes.

Then there was one brief moment of clarity when the curtain of steam wafted aside, and Flint saw a globe of incandescent rock rolling down the centre of the blazing stream. "Masaya!" he screamed – even though he was nearer, it was the mother's place to catch the shell. Masaya raced to his side and leaned out precariously over the flow, her arms outstretched towards the shell while Flint held her hips to steady her. The shell was a hand's-breadth from the far side – a second away from rolling into the lagoon – when

Masaya made a desperate lunge and caught it. Only Flint's hold prevented her from toppling into the lava-stream, but he dragged her safely back with her arms around the glowing shell and carried them both to the beach.

The shell was still red-hot when Flint brought it hard down onto the outcrop of rock, and it cracked into three pieces. Masaya plunged her hands inside to lift her baby from its cradle of liquid lava, and the Guaza Clan crowded round them to watch as the golden baby cooled to a soft brown colour against Masaya's chest.

"A beautiful little girl," Overo said, smiling at his new grandchild as her hot little hand closed on his finger.

"Just what I wanted," Masaya said, "A sister for Pedro."

"I wanted a boy to play football with," Pedro muttered, but only Tom heard him.

"I'm glad it's a girl – she'll be company for Kea," Etna said, stroking the baby's head, "And the next baby is bound to be a boy."

Tom stared at her, wondering if she had heard him mention another baby, but Overo said, "Let's celebrate this one's arrival before we talk about any more."

Hekla bustled forward to welcome the new arrival. After tipping the clan's Firepot to shower the baby with embers, she relit it with a piece of glowing lava, thus linking the baby and its volcanic mother with the clan's Home Fire. Once the simple ceremony was over, Flint took Masaya and their baby back to the temporary shelter while Juncal and Etna climbed up into the ruined forest in search of more food.

Tom remained on the bluff above the cooling remnants of birth-shell. The pull of the volcano was still very strong, and he was haunted by his image of a baby coming from the water. Instinct told him to stay alert, and he stood watching the rolling waves of lava that were slowly narrowing the river-mouth.

Overo and Pedro joined him there, the old man sitting on Mocha's little raft which had somehow survived the eruption. "I've seen many wonders in my life," he said to Tom, "But watching a volcano being born beats the lot. Was this what you saw in your vision?"

"I didn't see the volcano," Tom admitted, "But I did see the giant wave, which is why we came after you. If it hadn't been for Pedro we'd have been too late."

Pedro grinned, "We weren't too late, so why are you still all jumpy?"

"Because I think there's going to be another baby – the one I saw coming out of the water – but I can't tell when."

"Have you asked your mother what she thinks?" Overo asked.

"She'd only say I'm…" Tom began, but then suddenly he was sliding pell-mell to the water's edge – he had spotted another shell rolling down the side of the lava-flow.

With dawning horror Overo saw disaster racing to meet him, because Tom was too slightly-built to withstand the heaving cauldron where the river met the lagoon. He leapt down the bank with the agility of a much younger man, shouting, "Tom! I'll get it," and plunged into the water, grabbing the shell just as it slipped beneath the surface. Lifting it above his head he turned round, but the effort had drained his last reserves of strength – he couldn't carry it back to dry land.

Overo's dilemma was clear from his agonised expression, and there was no time to waste. The boys launched Mocha's raft into the foaming water and, with Tom in the shallows holding the trailing rope, Pedro paddled furiously with his hands to reach Overo. He had just got there when Overo staggered, but with last a desperate lunge the old man thrust the precious shell into Pedro's arms. Tom dragged the raft to shore where other hands pulled them to safety.

The shell had only been in the water for a minute but the surface was already dull. Knowing time was running out for the baby, Tom snatched up a rock and drove it with all his strength onto the last red patch he could see. He had to hit it three times before anything happened, but then to his intense relief the shell cracked in half. Lava spilled out to form a boiling puddle in the centre of which lay a baby, glowing with heat and kicking vigorously. Tom picked it up, and for a moment he and the baby could have been the only two people in the world. The little boy seemed to have wave-images flowing over his amazing sea-green body, and had been born from water, just as he had foreseen.

Belatedly remembering Overo, Tom tore his gaze away from the baby's dark green eyes and shouted across the river, "Grandfather – he's safe!" but Overo wasn't there – the Shore Clan had formed a chain of men to rescue the old man and taken him to be nursed in their caves.

Turning back, Tom found his entire clan and the Forest men clustered around him. The circumstances were so unique that no-one knew who was meant to be the baby's parents. "I think Grandfather should decide whose baby this is," Tom said eventually, "He and Pedro caught the shell between them."

"I can't be its mother!" Pedro protested.

Tom laughed. "Of course not – the same as I'm too young to be his father although I cracked the shell."

"And you have no mate," Hekla said, pushing nearer, "You'd better give him to me."

Tom almost obeyed her out of habit, but he recoiled from the acquisitive expression on her face. His reply lashed like a whip. "You have no mate either, and you're too busy being a Seer to be a proper a mother." Shoving her aside, he gave the baby to Etna. "I had a vision weeks ago of you holding a baby, so I think he must be yours."

As Etna took her new son with a little sob of joy, Hekla said furiously, "That's not your decision to make, Tom."

"It isn't yours either, but Grandfather will confirm if I've made the right choice."

"If he's still alive."

"Of course he's alive – what kind of Seer are you if you can't tell?"

Mother and son stood nose to nose, glowering, neither of them prepared to back down, until finally Hekla drew her bearskin around her shoulders with an angry shrug and stomped off to fetch the Firepot. Repeating the ritual of welcoming this second baby into the clan restored some measure of her authority, but it was clear to everyone that she was still seething with fury.

Moments later the volcano's roar sank to a murmur, as if the effort of giving birth to two children had exhausted its strength, and the lava-stream eased to a standstill. Their thoughts turned now to Overo, but they couldn't reach him – what had once been a broad river-mouth was now a daunting bottleneck of deep, churning water. On the far side of this barrier they could see the Shore Clan's plateau, where women were stirring cooking pots as if nothing extraordinary had happened.

"They'd have told us if Overo was dead, wouldn't they?" Flint said anxiously.

Chert reassured him. "Of course they would. As soon as possible we'll go over and check on him."

"How?" Flint asked. "We can't cross this."

Chert laughed. "My men have been looking at the old ford – it should be possible to ferry us over with a raft, and it won't take me long to knock together another one."

Although the river had dropped almost to its former level, the stepping-stones that were the usual method of crossing the ford had become clogged with a mass of debris. A team of Shore men began working to clear it from their own side while the Forest men attacked the mess from theirs, dragging out a tangle of vines and timber that contained whole trees as well as the torn carcasses of animals. Both teams kept a wary eye on the spitting volcano – this destruction brought home the savage power of the tsunami and no-one wanted to be caught by another one.

Meanwhile Overo was being nursed in Yakan's own cave, where the Shore Leader's mate Tarifa had put him close to the fire, piled hot rocks around him and swathed him in blankets. Several chunks had been gouged from his body and lava was oozing from his wounds, but he was still breathing. Until his clan could cross the river this brave old man was Tarifa's responsibility, and she worked desperately to keep him alive under the watchful eye of her mate.

After what seemed to her like an eternity, Overo stirred and groaned, "Hekla?"

Tarifa patted his hand and assured him, "Hekla will come soon – go to sleep now." As Overo lapsed back into unconsciousness, she told Yakan, "Even with all these blankets he's still cold – I'm not sure he'll last the day. You'd better tell his clan."

Grim-faced, Yakan hurried down to the ford, but the water level was still too high for safety. He cupped his hands round his mouth and bellowed, "The old man's fading fast – he's asking for someone called Hekla."

"We're making a raft for a ferry," Flint shouted back, "Tell Overo we'll be there soon."

Chert and Sasso's hastily-constructed raft was a simple affair of fallen trees lashed together with vines, but it served the purpose. Yakan's men tossed a weighted rope over the river and, with the Forest men paying out another rope from the south bank, Flint and Hekla were ferried across.

At the sound of their voices Overo roused himself, but they were dismayed by his appearance – the big man seemed to have shrunk and his black skin had paled to a sickly grey. Hekla began barking orders for hot water and medicinal clay but Overo stopped her. "There's no point, woman – I'm past saving," he said and Hekla knew he was right – he was beyond anyone's power to heal. He turned his head painfully to locate Flint and asked, "Did the second child live?"

"He did – Tom broke the shell and gave him to Etna."

"Good decision – bring them here – I want to see the child before I die," Overo said, and his eyes drooped shut.

Flint told Hekla, "Do whatever you must to keep him alive," and ran back to the ford, where Tom and Pedro had just landed, but Masaya and Etna were dithering on the far bank, refusing to trust the new raft. Flint rode it back to tell them bluntly, "You won't see your father alive again unless you come now," and so, clutching their babies, they boarded the raft and were ferried across.

Hekla had brewed Overo a restorative drink and his daughters found him sitting propped against the wall. His breathing was laboured, but his eyes shone with delight when Masaya and Etna knelt beside him and put their new babies in his arms.

"Do you remember Flint and I had a girl?" Masaya said.

"Of course I remember! And I see Etna has a boy – that green is an unusual colour."

"So he *is* mine!" Etna said. "I wasn't sure, because you and Pedro caught the shell."

It was rare for Etna to be uncertain about anything, and Overo smiled at his normally fiery daughter. "Hekla brought us here for Flint and Masaya, but there was no Sign that the Mother meant them to have twins." He looked past Hekla to locate Tom. "It was Tom who foresaw this water-baby – and he also foresaw that Etna would be its mother." Tom held Grandfather's gaze in silent thanks, and Overo managed a nod in response. Then, with an obvious effort, he returned the babies to his daughters and leaned back against the wall. "Flint, you must lead the clan home – I will die here."

"No – you can't die!" Pedro cried, flinging himself across the old man's chest.

Overo stroked his smooth young head and said gently, "It is my time, lad, so don't grieve too much – you must teach Etna's little boy how to be a man." He caught Tom's eye over Pedro's head. "It is your time, too, Tom – time to break free." Tom nodded wordlessly and Overo issued his final order, saying simply, "Build my cairn next to Maipu," before his head fell back and he was gone.

Masaya and Etna sobbed quietly while Flint and Juncal straightened Overo's limbs and rolled him in his own bearskin robe. Pedro and Kea were crying too, but Tom stood silently in a shadowed corner, watching in awe as Grandfather's spirit lifted free of his body. In spirit the old man was strong and vigorous again and, as he followed his body to a secluded corner of the plateau, Tom saw his spirit-hand brush each member of his family in farewell. Only vaguely aware of Hekla praying, Tom's mind was filled with Overo's final words of advice: "It is your time to break free."

CHAPTER THIRTEEN – CHO

Yakan offered the Guaza Clan the use of an empty cave, which they accepted gratefully. Tomorrow they would have to work out how to take Overo's body home without their big sledge, but what the women needed now was a place to rest with their babies. Leaving them to settle into the borrowed cave, Flint and Juncal welcomed Yakan's invitation to join a hunting party. For once Tom was happy to let them go without him. He had seen a narrow track winding further up the cliff-face and felt compelled to explore it.

As he climbed, his feet fitted so perfectly into each hollow that the footpath could have been made for him, and he had a strong impression that he wasn't alone. At one point he even stopped to call out, "Who's there?" but all he heard was the rustle of leaves, the low rumble of the volcano, and the splash of waves breaking on the reef. If anyone *was* watching him, Tom sensed they meant him no harm.

He continued climbing, catching tantalising glimpses of the smoking cone at every turn, until the path ended abruptly on a broad ledge from which the cliff-face dropped sheer for two hundred feet to the lagoon. He was nearly at the top of the cliff, level with the rim of the small volcano which lay directly opposite the river-mouth. The tongue of lava that had delivered the babies linked the volcano to the far bank, effectively cutting the river-mouth down to half its former size. The remaining narrow channel, directly beneath the Shore Clan's home plateau, churned with white water, and Tom realised it was a miracle they had been able to rescue the second baby.

The volcano itself was shrouded in smoke that reflected a red glow, hinting at more fireworks to come – Tom simply gazed at it in wonder. This was *his* volcano. He had sensed it calling him from Guaza Mountain, and had heard the warning that saved his clan from the fury of its birth. He looked up at the seagulls wheeling over the Ocean and wished he could fly like them – he wanted to soar over the volcano and peer into its glowing heart. His desire was so strong that he spread his arms and leaned out over the cliff edge, mesmerised by the sun glinting off the slow ripples of the lagoon below. He was on the verge of losing his balance when he felt something pulling him back and came to his senses just in time. His heart pounding, he turned round to thank his rescuer, but there was no-one in sight. "Strange – I could have sworn…" he muttered, but apart from him the ledge was empty. Shaking his head to clear any more imaginary thoughts, he began belatedly to take in his immediate surroundings.

The ledge, roughly a hundred feet by fifty, was edged by a low parapet of pale rock, like a dish that had been broken in half and stuck to the cliff. The surface was dry and smooth under its scattering of volcanic fallout, and in the vegetation-covered cliff-face at the rear was the dark triangle of a cave. As Tom moved towards the entrance he caught sight of a figure and paused. "Hello," he called, "Am I intruding?" but there was no reply, and when he moved closer, the figure had vanished. Slightly unnerved, he approached the cave warily and ducked inside, but it was empty. On the walls, streaks of green rock caught the light and drew his gaze towards the darkness at the back, but then he spotted a hearth and a battered pot. Afraid he had, after all, invaded someone's privacy, he backed out, too embarrassed to notice the figure that materialised by the hearth, and as he retreated down the winding path he didn't hear the faint voice pleading with him to come back.

The voice that greeted him when he re-entered the village was impossible to ignore. "That damned volcano has ruined my ford!" Yakan the Shore Leader had returned from hunting, and the damage wreaked by the tsunami had put him in a foul mood.

Tom hurried past to his clan's temporary cave and asked Sasso, "What's all that fuss about?"

"The Shore people make a good profit out of their ford – the north-south trade route goes through here," Sasso informed him, "But Yakan isn't a man to be defeated for long, you'll see."

Sasso was quickly proved right. After scowling for a while at the river as if it had done him a personal injury, Yakan announced, "I'm not going to let it beat me – we'll build another ford," and took some men upstream to explore. Before long they found a spot where the tsunami had scoured and widened a formerly fast-flowing stretch of river. Yakan, in his mercurial fashion, declared it was a vast improvement on the old ford, and when Chert was summoned to give his opinion, he approved the choice.

"Those shelving beaches will make landing rafts much easier," he said. "The place only needs stepping-stones to be perfect."

Yakan beamed. "You're right, and the sooner we get started the better."

His men knew him well enough to interpret that as an order, and waded in immediately to collect the larger rocks from the riverbed and pile them in heaps to create stepping-stones. To counteract the chill of the water they worked their ten-minute shifts rapidly, and the little islands were growing fast until one man held aloft a battered rock, saying shakily, "This one looks like Fogo!" All work stopped while Yakan inspected the find before nodding grimly – they had found the head of one of the men killed by the tsunami.

Following that reminder of the tragedy the Shore men worked more carefully, and before long someone found the second man's head, then they continued scouring the riverbed until the cold forced them to stop. Meanwhile Yakan personally sorted through the rocks they collected, meticulously picking out every stone that could be part of their dead comrades, smashed to pieces by a power too strong even for a Rockman to withstand.

It was early evening when the sad procession returned to the village, where Yakan sought out Flint. "It's lucky you brought your Seer with you," he said, "We'll need her to cairn these two men – or what's left of them."

"What happened to your own Seer?" Flint asked.

"Oh, Cho died last winter," Yakan said airily, "We've got his body stored at the cairn site, so your Seer can cairn him at the same time as these two men."

"What ailed him?" Tom asked.

"We don't know – old age, I suppose. He was dead when we went up to his cave after the Sleep." Yakan saw Tom's scandalised expression and added hastily, "We were going to send for Roca to cairn him but the volcano erupted."

"Send for Roca?" Hekla's tone was icy. "You don't send for a Seer, you ask politely." She folded her arms and glared at Yakan until he asked her more respectfully to officiate.

Hekla issued instructions for the two widows and their families to carry the stones of their dead through the forest to the cairn site – a large clearing studded with scores of cairns that bore witness to the many years the Shore Clan had lived in this remote spot. Two of the Elders brought the leather-shrouded body of the deceased Seer from a secluded corner of the site and unwrapped it. Yakan told Hekla, "The old Seer had no sons so I will do the honours."

Tom edged closer. The still form of the old Seer seemed tiny and the features were fixed in a peaceful expression, confirming Yakan's theory that he had simply passed away during the Sleep. Yakan fetched an enormous hammer from behind a rock and, with a few well-aimed blows, reduced the body to its component parts. Even though Cho had long been dead and cold, Tom winced, and at that moment he heard a giggle and a voice said, "Didn't feel a thing!"

He looked round, startled by the irreverent remark, but there was no-one near him.

The families of the two drowned men wielded their own hammers and then the Shore Clan built the three cairns, adding rocks from the outcrop that overhung the site. This was customary to link the dead with their home ground – people tactfully refrained from mentioning they had to use more rocks than usual to bring these cairns up to size. The two widows placed their men's headstones on top of their cairns and Yakan placed Cho's, after which Hekla recited the prayer for the dead and poured hot fat over all three cairns. With a taper she ignited the fat to speed the fire-born souls on their way back to Mother Earth.

Tom clearly saw all three spirits. While all other eyes were on the flaming cairns, he watched the two dead Shore men brush their mates with a final kiss before they faded from his view. The old Seer's spirit took longer, weaving a trail of light through the entire Shore Clan before pausing to hover in front of Tom. Grinning like a naughty child, the old Seer said, "I'll see you later," and then shot off towards the volcano, leaving Tom to turn back to the ceremony just as the last flame flickered out on the cairns.

"Right, that's done," Yakan said briskly, "Time to eat," and the assembled crowd obediently trooped back to the plateau for supper.

After the solemnity of the Cairning ceremony, the meal rapidly turned into a rowdy wake for Cho and the two tsunami casualties, but Tom couldn't relax and enjoy it. Now that he knew the little cave had belonged to the dead Seer he wanted to explore all the way inside before he had to leave the Shore. As soon as he decently could, he took a torch and slipped away from the party to the little ledge under the stars, where he entered the cave to find the old Seer sitting on the bed, rubbing his face and complaining, "That hot fat leaves grease all over you!"

Tom laughed. "You're the old Seer, aren't you?"

"The very same, lad – and you're the new one." The ghost chuckled at Tom's startled expression. "I would have thought it was obvious – I died, you were Called here – the Mother wants you to stay." As a slow grin of realisation worked its way up from Tom's heart and spread over his face, the old man nodded. "Right – now that's settled, let's get acquainted. I'm Cho and I know you're Tomboro – follow me and I'll show you our Sanctum."

As he moved towards the rear of his cave, Tom said, "Just a minute – why are you still here? Your soul should have gone back to the Mother after you were cairned."

Cho pulled a sheepish face. "Normally that would be true, but there's a bit of me still here, and that's enough to keep a Seer grounded."

Tom looked round the small cave but he could see nothing out of place. "There are dozens of stones here – which one is yours?"

"That would be telling," Cho said smugly. "I've stayed to show you the ropes, so you're stuck with me until I decide to go. Now – do you want to see this Sanctum or not?"

Yielding to the inevitable with a shrug, Tom followed the sprightly ghost along the passageway which led further into the cliff, where the torchlight revealed a tiny chamber just high enough for him to stand upright.

"It's a good job the Mother didn't send a taller man," Cho observed.

For the first time in his life Tom was pleased he was short. If Cho was right and this was his Sanctum, he was staying here – Hekla and the Guaza Clan could go home without him. Then an awful thought struck him. "What if Yakan won't have me? We've hardly even met."

"Don't worry about that – he'll want you," Cho laughed, "The Shore Clan will need their own Seer now they have a volcano on their doorstep."

"But I haven't got any experience!" The enormity of what he was contemplating almost overwhelmed Tom until he remembered Roca, the Forest Seer, lived only a day's journey away. "I suppose I could ask Roca to teach me."

"Oh, you won't need to bother her," Cho said airily, "I'll be here for a while. I saw this volcano born and I'm not leaving yet. Just don't tell Yakan I'm here – he's a big man but he's afraid of ghosts." He spread his arms, looking surprisingly substantial for a ghost. "Now – what do you think of the place?"

Tom stuck his torch in a handy niche and gazed around. It was clear that Cho and his predecessors had levelled the floor, but the walls and roof undulated in torch-lit waves, their resemblance to the Ocean emphasised by a broad seam of green rock that flowed all the way in from the outer cave. It was a truly beautiful Sanctum, and at the thought that it was going be his, Tom's heart soared like a bird. Suddenly he couldn't keep still. Every cell in his body bubbled with the thrill and terror of his decision to stay here, and he ran outside to race round the ledge with his arms spread as if he really could fly.

Cho, watching from the cave entrance, said drily, "You should behave more like an adult if you want to be taken seriously," but Tom felt he would erupt if he didn't talk to someone – preferably someone living. Abandoning Cho with a wave, he ran headlong down the track, only to pull up short on the home plateau, uncertain who to tell. It would be sensible to find out if Yakan would have him before informing his own clan, so he couldn't burst in with his news yet. On top of that, he should tell his mother first – in fact he supposed he ought to ask her permission, though his insides clenched at the thought. Then he remembered Pedro, who was sure to be pleased for him, and went to track him down. But he found Pedro holding his baby sister, gazing at her with a besotted expression as if he couldn't quite believe yet that she was real. There was clearly no point in trying to gain his attention, so Tom decided to leave his announcement until the morning, and rejoined the wake.

*

Having mulled things over in the small hours, after breakfast Tom went in search of Yakan, who was supervising the construction work at the new ford. Tom was a hundred yards away when he heard a shout and saw Verda sliding down the muddy riverbank into the arms of one of the ford builders. For a moment he feared she was only a figment of his imagination, until he saw Roca and a couple of other Foresters behind her. With a yell of sheer joy he dashed to the ford and across the new stepping-stone islands to meet her. Oblivious to the amused onlookers, he took her face between his hands and kissed her.

"Oh Tom," Verda cried, "I was so afraid you were dead."

"It was a close thing," Tom admitted, "But Pedro steered that little raft like a demon and the wave missed us all by a minute – the Mother obviously meant us to get here in time."

"Did your clan get their baby?"

"We got two, and I cracked open one of the shells – come and see." Tom took her hand to lead her down to the river-mouth, where the pieces of shell were still where he had dropped them. Verda stroked the smooth interior with her finger. "It's green! Is the baby green too, like me?"

"He's sea-green," Tom said, touching her cheek, "You are green like the forest."

Verda caught his wrist, scolding, "People will see!"

"You didn't worry about that when I kissed you just now," Tom grinned.

"I was happy you were alive," Verda said, flushing, and stood up. "We ought to get back to the others now."

"Not till I've shown you the other shell," Tom said, and took her over the lava-flow to the lagoon side where Masaya's baby's shell still lay in its puddle of solidified lava. "These shells should be in my cave," he said, levering it free. "You carry this while I get the green one."

"What cave?" Verda asked.

"Let me show you," Tom answered, so they carried their prizes across the ford and up to Tom's ledge on the clifftop where, with a proprietary air, he invited her to inspect the small cave.

Verda looked around with a woman's eye. "It's sweet but a bit bare. It could do with a blanket or two – but why do you say it's yours?"

"Because this was the old Seer's cave, and I'm going to be the new one."

"You mean you're going to stay here?" Verda gasped, "Oh, Tom – that's wonderful!" Her eyes shone with an emerald glow and Tom gazed into them, mesmerised by love. Certain that Destiny had brought them together, he stroked her cheek and said, "Verda – will you…" but she put her fingers swiftly over his lips. "Don't ask me yet," she said, but she was smiling.

Tom laughed. "All right," he agreed, "I'll wait, but not for long," and he pulled her close. A moment later he sensed a warning. The volcano looked no different from five minutes earlier, but he knew something was about to happen. "Here we go again!" he exclaimed, pushing Verda into the safety of the cave before yelling down to the plateau below, "Get under cover – the volcano's about to blow again!"

This time nobody argued. Flint relayed Tom's warning upstream, Yakan repeated it at his usual bellow, and the men working on the ford dashed up the bank to the trees, the memory of the fate of two of their comrades fresh in their minds. Everyone else headed for shelter just as the first sparks shot skywards. Tom and Verda stood in the entrance of his cave and watched as one side of the cone collapsed, releasing a new stream of lava. This one headed outwards to the reef, and the backwash that swept over the new ford was small, but Tom's ledge and the village plateau were once again bombarded by a rain of pumice.

After a while the novelty of the solid rain began to wear thin. Each individual pebble weighed very little, but collectively they were sharp reminders that even a Rockman's tough skin was not impervious to pain. Merely going outside for water or to stir a pot on a fire was done reluctantly, and Yakan was loudest in his complaints. The Shore Clan were accustomed to living in the open and fretted at their enforced confinement – even the splendour of the show on their doorstep had already begun to pall.

When Tom and Verda appeared for the midday meal, Roca scolded, "I promised Verda's parents I'd look after her." Then she saw their expressions. "What have you two been plotting?"

Tom gripped Verda's hand for courage. "I'm going to be the Shore Clan's Seer."

He heard a sharp intake of breath from Hekla but it was Roca who exclaimed, "Yakan didn't waste any time!"

Tom's ochre skin flushed a darker shade. "I haven't actually spoken to him yet."

"You're very young," Roca said gently, "What does your mother have to say about it?"

His heart pounding, Tom turned to Hekla, whose face was a mask. She stared at him for an eternity before finally saying, "If Tom wants to stay then he has my blessing."

Relief washed over Tom with such force that he failed to read her true motives, but Roca saw with devastating clarity that Tom's mother would be glad to see the back of him. If he went back east with the Guaza Clan, his Sight would be a constant reminder of her failure to foresee the tsunami or the second baby. Catching sight of Roca's sardonic expression, Hekla cut short Tom's stammered thanks, and Flint stepped quickly into the tense pause.

"We'd better see if Yakan will agree to take you on," he said, and accompanied Tom and Hekla to talk to the Shore Leader.

Yakan was initially doubtful when presented with such a youthful candidate for the vacancy, but when Flint cited the many examples of Tom's abilities, Yakan asked him, "Are you sure about this? Letting a Seer leave your clan is a big decision."

Giving Flint no time to answer, Hekla said, "I am the Guaza Clan's Seer – we don't need another one."

"And we're only a small clan," Flint added quickly, to cover her lack of grace, but Yakan was not deceived.

Winking at Tom, he said, "You're welcome to a place with us, my boy. With our own volcano producing babies in pairs, our clan will soon double in size."

Tom gasped, "You can't expect all the babies to be for your clan!"

"Of course not – the first two weren't," said Yakan, clamping his big hand on Tom's shoulder, "But you'll see all the others before anyone else, won't you?"

Yakan's sheer size and arrogance threw Tom momentarily off balance, but he knew his life here would be intolerable if he let him get the upper hand. Fixing Yakan with the steeliest look he could manage, he said, "The Mother tells a Seer who a child's parents should be."

There were several beats of silence before Yakan blustered, "Yes, yes, of course She does." After a moment he added, "Mind you, there are bound to be some parents who don't get here in time. Being on the spot, as it were, we'll get any spares." He rubbed his hands to indicate the subject was closed. "Right – now we have to decide where you'll live."

Tom said quickly, "I've already decided that – I'm going to use the cave up on that small ledge."

"Good choice, my boy, good choice! Our last Seer – may the Mother rest his soul – lived up there, but you'll need to be fed and you're too young to take a mate." Yakan dismissed Verda with a glance. "Banca will look after you. She lost her mate Fogo to the tsunami – and she has a son already, so she knows what boys like."

Tom decided now was not the time to object to being called a boy and merely said, "Are you sure she won't mind?"

"Why should she mind?" Yakan laughed, "It'll take her mind off things. Besides, everyone around here does what I tell them, as you'll discover. Now –

there are a few cuts to patch up after that fall of rocks, so let's see what you're like as a healer."

Tom's heart sank – he hadn't even considered that a Seer was expected to be a Healer as well, but to his surprise Hekla came to his rescue. "I'll help you, Tom – I could do with a bit of peace after being crammed in that cave with two babies."

*

Growing up with Hekla, Tom had learned enough about medicine to get by, but when he had smoothed off the last patch of clay that afternoon and dismissed his patient, Hekla asked, "How will you manage if you have to deal with something more serious?"

Tom sat back on his heels, pleased that she was concerned for him. He briefly considered telling her about Cho but caution prevailed. "If I get really stuck I'll ask Roca to help me."

"Make sure you do – if you make any dreadful mistakes they'll blame me for not teaching you properly." She brushed dried clay from her hands and stood up. "Now you'd better show me this cave of yours before I go."

So Tom took Hekla up the winding track to his ledge, where she took in the view of the volcano and lagoon in one sweeping glance. "You are a lucky boy – fancy waking up every day to this view," she said and then, without warning, marched into the small cave and prodded the rushes with her toe. "These will have to be thrown out before you sleep here – they're filthy." Tom heard a sharp intake of breath and realised they weren't alone, and while he was distracted Hekla took the torch from his hand and moved towards the passageway. "I assume the Sanctum is through here?"

Briefly, Tom the son wrestled with Tom the Seer, but the Seer won and Tom shot past her to bar the way. "You can't go in there – it's my Sanctum."

"But I'm your mother," Hekla said, trying to push him aside.

Tom stood firm. "You wouldn't let anyone else into *your* Sanctum," he reminded her, and then the torch guttered in a sudden puff of air and went out. Hekla glared at Tom suspiciously as he said, "I think it must be supper-time now," and shooed her out of his cave. As he ushered her away from his ledge and down to join the others, he distinctly heard the old Seer cackle gleefully.

*

Roca's rescue party had brought the Guaza Clan's small sledge, expecting to be transporting bodies back home, and Flint was very relieved to see it. The problem of carrying Overo's body thus resolved, he planned to leave first thing in the morning, and that night's supper was a farewell to Tom and their new Shore friends.

After the meal, Yakan asked Flint, "What will you call your babies? They must have names before you leave."

Flint smiled fondly at the baby asleep in Masaya's arms. "It would have been bad luck to share their Naming ceremonies with last night's funeral feast, but Masaya and I have decided to call our daughter Riva."

"And the little green boy?" Yakan asked, looking at Juncal, who said immediately, "We think your new Seer should choose his name," and Etna placed the baby in Tom's lap.

"Me?" gasped Tom.

"Yes, you – we wouldn't have a son at all if you hadn't been watching out for him."

Tom cradled the baby, wondering what name to give this child with the extraordinary deep green eyes. The little fist gripped his finger and he felt a pang of regret that he wouldn't see him growing up – if he had been a few years older he might even have been this child's father. He imagined Pedro playing with the little boy, and the thought of Pedro's cache of coloured marbles gave him the inspiration he needed. "Call him Onyx, like the green stone," he said, and handed back to its mother the first child whose birth he had foreseen.

Juncal nodded approval. "Onyx – a good strong name."

Yakan raised his cup in a toast. "Mother Earth – we give you Onyx and Riva – the first twins from Your new volcano." And as the assembly drank to the babies' Naming, the volcano spat a burst of fireworks into the night sky.

CHAPTER FOURTEEN – ENDINGS AND BEGINNINGS

They left at dawn – all the Forest people and the Guaza Clan, and Tomboro went with them.

"I'll be back within the week," he promised Yakan. "If I'm needed any sooner, I can always ride Mocha's raft down again!"

Yakan's hand tightened on Tom's shoulder in a painful reminder that life under his Leadership wasn't going to be easy. "Your sense of humour leaves a lot to be desired, my boy."

Tom said he was going to see his old clan safely on the first leg of their journey home, but Yakan guessed the young Seer also wanted to spend more time with Verda. Tom was content for him to believe that, for it hid his true motive – Roca had offered to teach him the basics of his art, and during the coming week he planned to cram in as much learning as possible.

Overo's body in its bearskin shroud weighed the sledge down as Flint and Juncal pulled it through the wrecked forest. It was tough going, as they frequently had to lift it over debris or circumnavigate fallen trees, and the group spent one night in the open, warmed by a fire of fallen branches. With their toes almost touching the burning logs, Tom and Verda snuggled together under one blanket.

Hekla pursed her lips disapprovingly, but Roca was unconcerned. "With so many people around it's hardly likely they'll get up to any mischief," she said. "Besides, I suspect there's a betrothal in the air."

"They're far too young!" Hekla exclaimed.

Roca fixed her with a cold stare. "If Tom's old enough to leave his mother and his clan, he's old enough to take a mate," she said and, unable to think of a suitable retort, Hekla subsided into stony silence.

They were on the move again at first light, and arrived at the Forest village late in the afternoon to a rapturous reception, only slightly modified by the presence of Overo's shrouded body. Everyone in the village had been so certain their clansmen were lost that Chert, Sasso and the rope team were fêted far into the night, and Mocha, the little boy who had built the raft that saved them all, was again the hero of the hour.

The next day it rained – a real tropical downpour that kept everyone indoors – and Flint decided to delay their departure until it stopped. Tom spent the day with Hekla, sketching notes on a length of bark while she described which plants she considered most effective for various ills. She was generous with her knowledge now that Tom no longer posed a threat, and he was reminded of the hours they used to spend preparing medicines together. When the light began to fade, Hekla sat back on her heels saying, "That's about all I can tell you in a few hours."

"What about the sparkle powder you used back at home?" Tom asked, but she said cagily, "Sparkle rocks are difficult to describe – and I haven't seen any around here."

Tom didn't press the point – if his mother wouldn't tell him he was sure Cho would.

*

In the freshly-washed morning of the next day the Guaza Clan left for home. Overo's body lay in the sledge packed round with their remaining provisions, and Masaya and Etna tucked their babies carefully into a nest of furs by his feet.

Assuming the place that had been Overo's the previous week, Flint led the clan north out of the village, and Tom walked with them. He was reluctant to say that final goodbye, but Pedro plodded along beside him in such reproachful silence that at the edge of the forest Tom stopped and said, "I think I'd better turn back now."

Flint halted the sledge immediately and gripped Tom's hand. "Good luck, Tom – I'm going to miss your help in the hunt."

"With two more mouths to feed you'll have to teach Pedro instead."

"I've already decided to do that, but we will never forget that we owe you our lives."

"Couldn't have put it better myself," said Juncal, pumping Tom's hand vigorously.

When it was Pedro's turn, Tom stood uncertainly, not sure how to approach him, but Pedro threw both arms round him in a fierce hug and said, "Don't forget me, will you?"

Tom swallowed a lump in his throat. "How could I? I'll remember you every time I see a raft – that's a ride I'll never forget." He pushed Pedro gently away and leaned over the sledge to place a reverent hand on Overo's fur shroud. "Protect them on their journey, Grandfather," he whispered before kissing Onyx and Riva. "Look at them holding hands," he laughed, "You'll have a hard job separating them!"

"They say twins are double trouble," Etna said cheerfully, "They'll be getting up to all sorts of mischief soon." She gave Tom a quick kiss and Masaya hugged him with the promise, "We'll see you at the Festival next year."

Finally Tom turned to Hekla, and all the things he had planned to say flew straight out of his head. For eighteen years they had never been apart – it was only over the past month they had fallen out – and she *was* his mother. Conscious of the others trying not to listen, he blurted out the first thing that came into his mind. "Thanks for your help with the medicines, Mother."

"You can always ask Roca if you get stuck," Hekla answered coolly, "She seems competent enough." There seemed nothing else to say. Tom was just wondering whether he should hug her when Flint glanced at the sun and said apologetically, "We'd better get moving." A moment later the sledge was sliding away over the prairie grass.

For a long time Tom stood where they had left him, watching their figures dwindle until they wavered and faded in the heat-haze – the only family he had known had gone. He rubbed his hands over his face, feeling very young and alone, then straightened up and walked back to the forest where Verda and his new life awaited him.

Verda's father's attitude had softened once he realised that Tom was going to hold a respected position as the Shore Clan's Seer, and he accepted their romance, even allowing Tom to sleep in their hut, although he moved his own bed to the middle to keep the sweethearts apart.

Each morning Tom studied with Roca, learning the skills necessary to a Seer, but in the afternoons he and Verda roamed the forest tracks, gathering herbs and getting to know each other like any young couple in the first days of a relationship.

Tom was envious of the calm environment in which Verda had grown up, while she was enthralled by Tom's stories and begged for every exciting detail. He had forgotten most of the early years with his father's clan, but he had vivid memories of his nomadic years with Hekla.

"Looking back, I'm surprised we survived," he told Verda. "I remember once hiding in a cave while Mother fought a sabre-toothed tiger for its kill – she still bears the scars."

"It all sounds very thrilling," Verda said, "I've never been further than Grand Oasis." She fiddled with her basket of herbs as if checking she had enough, but there was a catch in her voice when she asked, "What if you get the urge to travel again?"

"It's a lonely life being a nomad," Tom said, capturing her hand to lace his fingers through hers, "Now I've found where I belong I'm not going anywhere."

*

On Tom's fourth day with the Forest Clan, he was collecting mushrooms with Verda when he felt his volcano calling him. He dropped the large bracket-fungus he had just picked into Verda's basket and told her, "I've had a Sign that a baby's coming – I've got to go back to the Shore."

Verda put on a brave face – she had known the idyll couldn't last forever – and asked, "Who's having a baby?"

Tom's mouth fell open in dismay. "I don't know! I haven't learned how to identify the parents. I'll have to ask Roca right now!" Grabbing Verda's hand, he hurried back, to find the village buzzing with the news that a group of people had been spotted on the far side of the river, heading for the Shore.

"I recognized one of them," Sasso told Tom, "They're from Twin Lake – north of the desert." So perhaps this baby wasn't for the Shore Clan either, Tom thought, but he had to be there. While Verda took the mushrooms home to her mother he went straight to Roca's hut, where he found her trying to heal an axe-cut on a woodman's thigh.

She greeted him with obvious relief. "Tom, I'm so glad you're here. I can't hold this wound closed and mix clay at the same time."

Tom knelt beside the man to pinch the edges of the deep wound together. "We ought to seal off that vein first – clay won't be enough," he said and Roca agreed. "I'm afraid it won't, but I've tried everything to stem the flow."

The woodsman was pale and shivering as his lava leaked away between Tom's fingers, and they knew it was possible they could lose him. Then Tom remembered how quickly the volcanic lava had solidified in the lagoon. "Have you thought of using water to seal it?"

Roca pursed her lips. "D'you know, I think that might actually work." She reached for a jug of water. "Hold him still – he's not going to like this." She was right – when the stream of water hit his bubbling vein her patient hissed with pain, and it took all of Tom's strength to keep him still, but in moments the leak was sealed. After they had packed the wound with clay, Roca eased the woodsman back against his pillows and mixed a poppy draught while Tom piled embers round the injured leg to restore the circulation.

"He'll need constant nursing for a couple of days," Roca said, "I'll have to stay with him. But I've had a Sign that Jargo and Amber are to have a baby from your volcano – will you escort them there? It'll be good practice – the sooner you start using your gifts the better."

"How can you tell the baby is for them?" Tom asked, but Roca waved him away. "I'm too busy with this patient, but the Mother will show you when the time comes. You know the rituals already – you watched your mother perform them only last week."

"It's different if I've got to do it," Tom said, "How long have we got before it's born?"

"Three or four days." She grinned at her young pupil. "Sasso's getting a raft ready for tomorrow – go and enjoy your last few hours with Verda."

The next morning the whole of Verda's family trooped down to the landing-stage to see Tom off. Inspired by the sledge-raft which had taken them to the Shore the previous week, Chert and Sasso had built their latest raft with protective sides, and Chert was standing in the stern holding a rudder – another innovation. "What do you think of our design, Tom?"

he asked proudly, "This should be a more comfortable ride than your last one!"

Tom shuddered. "Thanks, but I'd rather walk."

"Suit yourself," Chert laughed. "Give your things to Amber's mother."

As Tom passed his blanket-roll to the elderly woman passenger, her daughter appeared at his shoulder. "Roca says she can't come but you'll be able to help us." Amber's face clearly expressed her doubts.

Her mate Jargo gripped Tom's arm with the calloused hand of a woodsman. "Roca says you know what to do – I hope she's right."

"Don't worry – you will get your baby," Tom said, assuming a confident tone.

Then Sasso called, "Time to go!"

The rope teams took up the strain, and there was only time for Tom to drop a quick kiss on Verda's cheek before he had to leave her and follow them.

A work team had spent the last few days clearing tons of tsunami-borne debris from the riverbank. The fallen trees had provided logs to shore up the softer edges of the towpath, so there were few obstacles to overcome – the group travelled at a pace that rapidly ate up the miles. Tom jogged behind the rope team with Jargo and Amber, and as the steady rhythm calmed his anxiety he began to look at the scenery he had shot past with Pedro a week earlier.

About an hour into their journey another river joined theirs from the north, the new water a murky brown, with a distinct line between that and the clear green of their own river. Instead of brown water, Tom saw thick mud and heard screams, reminding him of his frightening vision in the arena at Desert Oasis, but then he tripped over a root and the nightmare dissolved. He shook his head to clear the last vestiges of it and asked Sasso, "Where does that river come from?"

"That brown muck? That flows through the Coastal Range from Twin Lake. Those people we saw yesterday will have followed it down."

At the midday halt Amber's parents produced a pot of hot food which they had been balancing on top of a Firepot all morning, and after the long morning's run it was very welcome.

"This is much better than cold sausage," Sasso said, scooping out a handful of the hot, thick stew, and as everyone took their share the old couple beamed with pride.

Tom ate as hungrily as the others, but he didn't dare to sit down for fear of not being able to get up again – his legs ached badly. He was beginning to wish he'd taken up Chert's offer of a ride after all, but Amber was keeping pace without any sign of tiring, so pride forced him to continue running for the second half of the journey.

The sun was beginning to set when Sasso said, "Only a few more miles to go," and everyone dug into their reserves to increase the pace. They reached their goal just as the brief tropical twilight gave way to darkness, and the volcano welcomed them by spitting a shower of sparks into the night sky. Weariness forgotten, they stood watching the show until men with torches came to lead them across the stepping-stones. On the newly-scoured beach by the ford a group of people was congregated around a fire in front of a small cave.

"They must be those Lake people," Chert muttered, "Is Yakan making them camp down here? That's not very hospitable."

While his rope team hauled the raft ashore, a man approached and asked, "Are you Forest people? I'm Bala, the Seer from Twin Lake."

Chert took his outstretched hand. "Chert – Forest Clan – have you come for a baby too?"

"Yes, I heard a Call a week ago. There's going to be one child for my clan, possibly two."

Hearing the uncertainty in Bala's voice, Tom frowned. What chance had he of getting it right if an experienced Seer wasn't sure how many babies were coming for his own clan? Despite the long day he suddenly felt too sick to eat. Lighting a torch, he slipped away towards the cliff path, trudging up to the small ledge on legs that were almost too weary to carry him. When he discovered that someone had left a pile of firewood and a blanket in his cave, he almost wept with gratitude, and was just lighting the fire when Cho appeared.

"So you decided to come back," the ghost said, "About time too."

"Roca says there's a baby for a couple from the Forest Clan," Tom said wearily, "Why are you so peeved – is there one for the Shore too?"

"What sort of Seer are you, not to know who they're for?"

"A very inexperienced one, and no-one's had the time to teach me everything."

"Well, you'd better learn fast." The old Seer patted the bed and said more kindly, "Lie down – when you've had a rest I'll show you how." In that moment Cho sounded so much like Overo that Tom almost wept again. Obediently he pulled his blanket round him and lay down – he was asleep in seconds.

He woke to moonlight shining on his face, and as soon as he'd refuelled the fire, Cho appeared. "Time for your lesson, Tom."

"I hope I can learn quickly," Tom said, "I don't think there's much time."

"Time enough," Cho assured him. "First thing you have to do is switch off the outside world, which is easy – just relax and look deep into the fire."

Tom did as he was told, hoping it would work – he had never gone deliberately into a trance. His last conscious thought was surprise at how quickly it was happening. At first, when he felt Cho's mind tugging at his, he instinctively put up a barrier, but, reminding his subconscious that this wasn't one of Hekla's invasions, he surrendered to Cho.

A moment later he was floating on a current of sulphur-scented air over the lagoon, laughing with delight as his dream of flying became a reality. Together he and Cho soared high above the night-dark water to hover in the gases belching from the mouth of the crater. Tom was mesmerized by the shifting colours in the lava lake and could have stayed up there, but Cho pulled him down. When Tom realised they were heading straight into the fierce heat of the lava, he faltered until Cho reminded him, "You can't melt – you left your body in the cave." Tom visualised himself lying safely in his bed and threw himself into the adventure.

As they dived through the liquid rock he could feel it flowing past him, like the river had flowed past Mocha's raft, but infinitely hotter. There was a subtle change in texture when the lava-stream they were following plunged below the Ocean through a gash in the earth's crust, and then they were in the hot heart of Mother Earth Herself. Here, where the lava seethed like a cauldron, Tom saw five babies, their shapes gradually blurring as birth-shells formed around them. He had the irreverent thought that they were bobbing like dumplings on the surface of a stew, but then he noticed something else. "Two of them have sparks of light in their chests," he exclaimed.

"Those are fragments of the Mother's soul," Cho told him, "When you see that light you'll know a baby is nearing its birth-time."

"But how do you tell who their parents are?"

Cho sighed. "Use your eyes, young man!"

Then Tom saw that one baby was flanked by faint images of Jargo and Amber, and the other one was for a couple he had glimpsed in the Lake group. "Right – I understand now," he said, and instantly he was in the grip of a strong current that thrust him up through the volcano to the surface.

Conscious again, and feeling more alive than ever before, he sat up in bed in his own cave. He ran his hands over his body just to make sure it was actually there before he asked Cho, "That upward rush – is that what babies experience when they're born?"

"It's possible, but no-one remembers being born," Cho replied, "And let me tell you – you were lucky to see the parents' faces – some Seers only hear their names." He patted Tom's pillow paternally. "Now go back to sleep – nothing's going to happen for a day or two." As Tom lay back, the old Seer's ghost dived into his little fire and was gone.

CHAPTER FIFTEEN – LAKE CLAN

Early the next morning Tom walked down the cliff path to be hailed by Banca, the widow to whom Yakan had delegated the task of feeding him. Somewhat diffidently he entered her hut to find her small son Aran tucking into a bowl of porridge.

"Sit down and eat, you must be starving," Banca said, filling another bowl to the brim and giving it to Tom. "I cooked a meal for you last night but you disappeared."

"I'm sorry," Tom said, "I just had to be alone."

"Did you find your firewood all right?" Aran asked.

Tom smiled at the little boy. "Was that your doing? It was just what I needed, and thank you for the blanket too – I was very comfortable."

"Yakan says you need a woman to look after you," Banca said, refilling Aran's bowl. "I'm happy to do it – it will help fill the days now Fogo's gone."

Aran's spoon stopped halfway to his mouth at the mention of his father, and Tom said swiftly, "Does everyone do what Yakan tells them?"

Banca returned his smile with genuine amusement. "Most of the time. It's easier, though he can be a bit overbearing at times – just don't let him bully you."

"I'll try not to." Tom put down his bowl and refused a second helping. "That was just what I needed, thank you. Now I ought to talk to Yakan, but where is he? The plateau is very quiet this morning."

"He's got everyone working on the new village."

"What new village?" Tom asked and Aran jumped up immediately. "I'll show you."

Yakan greeted Tom with a hearty slap on the back, booming, "There you are, lad! It obviously didn't occur to you to pay your respects last night."

Aware that everyone had stopped work to listen, Tom spoke clearly enough for them all to hear. "I went straight to the volcano – there are more babies on the way."

Yakan's scowl vanished. "Why didn't you say so? They're bound to be for us this time."

"I'm afraid they're not," Tom said with a barely-suppressed sigh. "One is for the Forest couple I arrived with and one for the Lake people on the beach."

As Tom had feared, Yakan wasn't happy. "Are you telling me that our very own volcano won't give us babies? I expect our Seer to do better than that."

There was a mutter of agreement from some of the workmen but Tom, bolstered by Banca's advice, stood firm. "We discussed this last week, Yakan – the Mother decides whose children they are, not me or you."

The Leader glared at his new young Seer, clearly about to argue further, but Tarifa broke the tension by yelling across the compound, "Yakan! You'll have to go hunting today – with all those people on the beach we've got extra mouths to feed."

At the mention of hunting, Yakan's mood altered in a heartbeat. "Anything you say, Tarifa, my pebble!" he replied cheerfully and raised his voice to a bellow, "Who's coming hunting today? We leave in five minutes!" and his men scattered to collect their weapons.

When the hunting party had gone, Tom made his way down to the ford, where the visitors had turned the small crescent of beach into a temporary home.

"You're looking a bit stressed," Sasso greeted him, "Is Yakan giving you a hard time?"

"He thinks all the babies should be his," Tom replied ruefully, "I haven't yet learned how to handle him."

"He's always been an awkward customer," Sasso laughed, "Don't worry – you'll work it out in time. We're staying down here out of the way."

Tom looked round admiringly. The two small caves beneath the over-hanging bank would be a tight squeeze with all the Forest people plus five from Twin Lake, but the men had begun extending the caves with rock walls and the women had built a fireplace. Bala the Lake Seer was watching the proceedings from a convenient rock. Tom went across to introduce himself. "I see your people know how to make themselves comfortable," he said to the older man.

"We wouldn't normally go to this much trouble," Bala replied, "But we're a couple of days early. We left home in good time because we didn't know what damage the eruption had done."

"I see the expectant parents have brought some friends along." Tom was merely making conversation but his remark drew a frowning response from Bala.

"How would you know who they are? A Seer should only see the children for his own clan."

"I can't help what the Mother shows me," Tom said, "But it is possible I'm here because the volcano is new, not just because the Shore Clan needs a Seer."

"If that's the case, parents could just turn up and ask you which baby is theirs."

Tom did his best to calm the Lake Seer's agitation. "Don't forget your people wouldn't be here at all if you hadn't brought them."

Bala nodded slowly. "That's true. And there's another thing you haven't seen, young man – the second couple is here because I know the Lake Clan will be taking two babies home, and these two are due for one soon."

Tom opened his mouth to argue but shut it again. Bala clearly held his youth against him, as Yakan did, and protesting would only make matters worse.

He collected his belongings from the raft, and on an impulse he stopped by Banca's hut to ask if Aran would like to help him. The little boy's face lit up and, as he ran off with one of Tom's bundles, Banca said, "I'm delighted you offered. He's been brooding about his father and it will do him good – just don't let him be a nuisance."

"I'll be glad of his company," Tom replied, "At least he believes I'm a Seer."

"Is Yakan giving you trouble already?"

"Him and the Lake Seer – neither of them thinks I'm old enough to know what I'm doing."

"Well, you'll just have to prove them wrong, won't you?" Banca said briskly. "Now run along before Aran wrecks your place." Tom followed Aran up the cliff path, ruefully aware that Banca regarded him in the same way as she did her eight-year-old son.

Tom and Aran spent the day arranging his possessions. They collected fresh brushwood for Tom's bed, and Aran expended some of his surplus energy by chopping up Cho's old bedding for kindling. Tom hung his collection of forest herbs up to dry and pounded roots to mix with oil for ointments. Banca provided them with pottery jars, and after a busy day the space beneath Tom's bed had begun to fill up with medicines.

The following day they took an axe into the forest and cut up a fallen tree for firewood. After they had stacked their logs outside the cave, Aran swept a patch of ground smooth and pleaded for a game of marbles. Tom didn't need much persuading – Aran had begun to fill the Pedro-shaped space in his heart, and his undemanding presence eased the tension of waiting.

Each time Tom entered the village he could feel Yakan watching him, and in the camp by the ford the nervous anticipation was so strong it clouded his instincts. He was more comfortable on his ledge, and each night before sleep he took a torch into his Sanctum, hoping it would clear his mind to deal with this first real test of his powers. The broad swathe of green rock along one wall of the Sanctum rolled like the Ocean in the wavering light of his torch, and he would stare at the flickering colours praying for guidance.

At last the help he sought came. In the early hours of the third morning he had a vision of the two babies with the spark of soul pulsing in their breasts, their shells now fully formed. They were ready to be born – one baby for Jargo and Amber and the other for the Lake Clan couple. He dashed outside just as the volcano roared into life and the night sky turned to flame.

He hurtled down to the beach camp to find the place buzzing with excitement. Bala had woken everyone and several torches were already bobbing down the opposite bank towards the lagoon. Tom ran over the stepping-stones to catch up with Jargo and Amber, who were hovering with the Lake couple beside the lava flow which now formed a solid causeway to the volcano.

"What do we have to do?" Jargo asked him agitatedly, "Where's the fresh lava-flow?"

"Round the other side," Tom told him, "I saw it from my ledge – yours is the first baby and the Lake one the second – don't mix them up!"

The causeway of folded rock was brightly illuminated by the eruption and the four young people sped across – in less than a minute they had disappeared into the murk on the other side of the cone. The Forest and Lake clansmen spread out along the shingle beach, Amber's parents in their midst clinging to each other, and their anxiety was so strong that Tom saw it as a gold thread linking them to Amber. He let his spirit follow the thread and was just in time to see Jargo breaking the birth-shell, but it was several more minutes before Amber emerged from the ash-cloud holding her baby. Her mother seized her grandchild and inspected him minutely before informing the world at large, "He's perfect, and his eyes are green – definitely a Forest child."

Tom sagged with relief that Roca's trust in him had been vindicated. After all that worry the birth had gone as smoothly as honey. He had seen the baby coming and matched it with its parents, and there had been no explosion, no real danger, and definitely no water.

A few minutes later the scene was repeated when the Lake couple stepped ashore with their daughter. Bala scurried forward to lay his hand on the baby's chest. "This is a Lake Clan child," he said, granting Tom a half-smile, "You got that right, at least."

Amber's father handed Tom the Firepot they had brought from home. "You'll have to perform the ritual – do you know how?"

"Of course," Tom assured him, immensely relieved that he had watched Hekla do one last week, and he accompanied Bala around the flank of the active volcano. The beat of the eruption pulsed through his body so strongly that he was in a daze of delight as he emptied the Firepot and relit it from the glowing lava. Bala followed suit and they returned together to the beach, but beneath his feet Tom could feel the pressure rebuilding and knew it wasn't over yet. Only two babies had been born so far – he and Cho had seen five.

They celebrated the births over an early breakfast in the camp, after which Tom wandered upstream to see how the new village was progressing. On the site just above the new ford he found a busy scene – half a dozen huts were already standing and the ground was cleared for several more. The sounds of hammering ceased as Yakan strode over to confront Tom. "So the Forest and Lake people got their babies. That's four so far but none for us."

Tom's euphoria over the births evaporated. In some ways the Leader's resentment was understandable – all the volcano had done for his clan was to bombard them out of their homes. The Shore Clan wanted someone to blame and, with Yakan's attitude affecting them all, their new Seer was the obvious target. Looking at the set faces ranged behind their Leader, Tom threw diplomacy to the winds. "Listen to me, all of you!" he said, his voice cutting like a blade through their muttering, "The Shore Clan will have children when the Mother decides – not when I do." In the shocked silence which ensued he added, "And of course, She might consider that a clan which resents the good fortune of others doesn't deserve any." From Yakan's stunned expression it was clear he had made his point so he spun on his heel and walked away, not stopping for anything until he reached his eyrie.

Cho was sitting on the pallet bed, beaming all over his face. "That was more like it, Tom! I heard you from here. They've got so used to Yakan's bluster that you have to yell sometimes to get through their thick skulls."

"I just hope it doesn't backfire on me," Tom said, blowing on the embers of his fire to build it up to a comforting blaze. "I'm glad you're here, Cho – could you tell me the names of the Shore Clan's young couples? If a baby does come it would be embarrassing not to know who to tell."

"You should have stayed here and learned their names instead of going off with that Forest girl," Cho growled, "But I can't help you anyway – I can't get off this ledge, let alone down to the village!"

"Tell me where your stone is and I'll take you with me," Tom offered.

Cho refused. "For all I know you might drop it – I don't want to haunt the riverbed for all eternity."

"I wouldn't lose it," Tom protested laughingly, but then there were footsteps on the path and Cho vanished as Aran appeared.

The boy flung himself down on Tom's bed. "Wow – you stirred up a storm just now, but you told 'em good!"

Tom tried to look stern but failed. "I didn't know you were there."

"Course I was there – I'm helping my uncle build our new house," Aran said proudly. "You were brilliant – even Yakan didn't know what to say!"

Tom looked at Aran's laughing face and it dawned on him that here was the solution to one of his problems. "Aran – you know everyone in the clan – can you teach me their names?"

"No problem – we'll start tomorrow."

*

Before the Forest group left for home the next morning, Jargo shook Tom's hand. "We were really worried when Roca couldn't come with us, but you did your job well, Seer!"

Tom flushed with pleasure and watched the rope team begin to haul the raft upstream, then he turned and bumped into Chert. "Aren't you going with them?"

Chert grinned happily. "Most of these Shore men don't know how to nail two planks together, let alone make a decent dovetail joint, so I'm staying on to keep an eye on them. Yakan wouldn't be happy if his log cabin collapsed around his ears!"

Tom was grateful for old woodsman's friendly presence – he might need some support. Before the raft was out of sight the Lake people had spread out to occupy both caves, and Bala was sitting by the fire as immovable as the rock wall behind him. The Lake Seer obviously still believed his clan were getting another baby and he wasn't going to leave until it appeared.

CHAPTER SIXTEEN – ACCIDENT

Tom spent the next few days with Aran, walking round the Shore Clan plateau and the site of the new village that was growing upstream, memorising names. The babies still waiting to be born weighed heavily on his mind, as he had not yet seen their parents' faces. Added to that was Bala's accusatory presence on the beach by the ford, and Tom's sleep was haunted by nightmares. In one dream he was paddling furiously across the lagoon on Mocha's little raft to reach some floating birth-shells, but each time he got within touching distance of one it sank – lost to the water because he had been unable to find the parents.

The tension built with every uneventful day. The waiting had stretched as thin as a spider-web by the fourth morning when Tom woke from a vision of two birth-shells rising with the lava-stream towards daylight – two of the babies were going to be born today. He had seen their parents clearly, but they weren't Shore people. Something further north had delayed them – he could see them, running desperately to reach the volcano in time.

By the time he had crossed the ford and reached the causeway, Bala was there with the second Lake couple. Tom actually heard him say, "I know it's a Lake baby so it must be yours – go and claim it."

"No!" Tom cried, "The parents are on their way." He saw a shifty look cross Bala's face and said, "You've seen them too, haven't you? You know there are two babies – and that their parents are coming."

"But they're not here yet, are they?" Bala retorted belligerently, "If someone doesn't go right now both shells will be lost!"

"Both shells?" Yakan had arrived. "Two babies – and no sign of the people Tom claims are coming?" He glared at the young couple. "Two babies will end up in the lagoon while you're wasting time. I'll catch them both myself!" Pushing everyone aside he leapt onto the causeway, and he had just disappeared round the far side when a yell came from the ford. Four strangers raced over the stepping-stones, past Tom and the others, and straight into the volcanic murk.

Ashen-faced, Bala apologised to Tom. "I should have listened to you. With Yakan in this mood those four are heading for trouble."

The newcomers had almost given up hope of reaching the volcano in time, but when they found Yakan standing beside the burning stream, clearly waiting for the shells, they were horrified.

"Those babies are ours," one man shouted over the roar of the eruption, grabbing Yakan's arm, "What are you doing here?"

Yakan shook him off. "You're too late – I got here first – and who said they're yours anyway?"

"Our Seer sent us."

"If your Seer's not with you then I've only got your word for it."

The two younger men were so enraged that in another second they'd have come to blows, but then one girl cried, "Tabor – here comes our shell – stop fighting or we'll lose it!" and the other girl said, "Ours is over there," before jumping across the lava-flow to reach it from the far side.

By this time Yakan had lost all sense of proportion – in his view this was his volcano and these should be Shore babies. Just as Tabor's mate caught the shell, Yakan made a lunge for it, but he trod on a loose rock and his foot slipped into the red-hot stream. The thick, viscous lava coiled around his ankle, and as he began to slide off the solid rock his scream ripped through the thunder of the eruption. Reacting instinctively, Tabor caught one of Yakan's flailing arms and pulled him back onto firmer ground, leaving his mate to crack their shell open. The lava poured out so rapidly that she only just saved her baby from being washed back into the lava-stream.

"Jura!" Tabor dropped Yakan unceremoniously on the rocks, and helped his trembling mate away from danger as their friends rejoined them carrying their own baby.

When Yakan didn't respond to Tabor's terse order to stand up, they tried to heave him upright, and it was only then that they discovered how badly he was hurt – the boiling lava had taken his foot clean off. What should have been a joyous occasion was marred by the horrific accident, and while the two girls carried their babies back to the waiting crowd, the men bore Yakan's semi-conscious body.

Yakan's temper was like the man himself – larger than life and as volatile as a volcano. When he came round to discover he was crippled, he roared, "Those stupid interfering lumps should have left me to die! How can I hunt with only one foot?" What infuriated him most was the knowledge that he had no-one to blame but himself, and that his humiliation had been witnessed by everyone, including a bunch of strangers who would spread the tale far and wide.

Two of those strangers would actually be going home to Twin Lake with Bala. Tabor and his mate Jura had joined the Lake Clan two days after Bala's party left for the Shore. As soon as he heard this, Bala said to Tom, "That explains why I thought there would be another Lake baby, but I still owe you an apology."

"The Signs must have been confusing," Tom said, "And they did only just get here in time. But I have another problem now – can you think of anything I can do to help Yakan?"

Anxious as he was to make up for his earlier attitude, Bala had to admit that he could think of nothing. "I saw a similar injury once when a mother lost a hand while catching a shell, but once a limb's gone, it's gone."

"So all I can do is treat the stump and administer poppy juice," Tom said.

Bala gave him a curious look. "Why would you want to help him anyway? He doesn't treat you with much respect."

Tom gestured at the volcano that was still spitting fire downstream. "This is my volcano. If I want to stay here I must live with the Shore Clan, and Yakan has the final say on that. Besides, he treats everyone just as badly."

Bala chuckled. "That's true enough, but how long will a cripple remain Leader before someone ousts him?"

"Long enough to throw me out if he feels like it." Tom gestured at Bala's walking stick and said, "Maybe what he needs is a carpenter – we could make him a crutch."

"Yakan's too proud to use one," Bala said.

Tom knew that was probably true. "Then I've got an even better idea, and the man to help me is Chert."

Chert took some convincing, but eventually he agreed and went with Tom to the Leader's hut, where they found Tarifa ferociously scrubbing some already spotless cooking pots. Chert put a comforting hand on her arm. "Still in a bad mood, is he?"

Tarifa sniffed and brushed an angry hand across her cheek. "A filthy temper is more like it, and he won't see you – he's refusing to see anyone."

"I'm not giving him a choice," Chert said, "I'll go in first, Tom." He ducked through the doorway to find Yakan lying on his bed in a dark corner of the hut, nursing his pain and humiliation in equal measures and refusing to meet his visitor's eyes.

"Sulking won't work with me," Chert said briskly, "So you can stop behaving like a child and listen." Taken aback by Chert's uncompromising tone Yakan lifted his gaze from the floor, and when Chert saw the fear in the Leader's eyes his voice softened. "I'm going to get you upright again, old friend – and before you start shouting at me, I'm not talking about a crutch."

Yakan's face creased into a sneer. "Going to make me a new foot, are you?"

"That's exactly what I am going to do," said Chert, "A wooden one you can strap on after that stump has been treated. Your Seer will take care of that."

"I'm not letting that boy near me!" Yakan bellowed.

"Yes you are, and with a good grace," Chert countered. "He's the best Seer around these parts, and if you'd listened to him in the first place you wouldn't be in this mess."

"I know that, you don't have to tell me," Yakan moaned, "That's why I can't..."

Chert cut across his protests. "I'm not listening to any more arguments. You'll do as you're told because you've got no choice." Without giving the Shore Leader a chance to raise any further objections he called Tom into the hut.

The moment Tom saw the oozing veins on Yakan's stump he remembered the woodsman he had helped Roca to treat. He asked Tarifa for a bowl of water, and while she fetched it he brewed up a poppy draught.

"I don't need that sissy stuff," Yakan protested, but Chert forced it down his throat. Even so, when Tom plunged his stump into the water the big Leader hissed with pain. "Rut it, boy!" he snarled, "Are you trying to get your own back?"

Noting Yakan's clenched jaw and deeply creased face, Tom tempered his reply. "I don't need to take revenge – I think the Mother has punished you enough." Yakan merely grunted in response, so Tom applied some salve and left his patient to the ministrations of Tarifa while he went in search of food.

Tired out by the dramas of the day, Tom retired to his quiet cave straight after supper. The Mother still hadn't shown him the parents for the final baby, but he also hoped to see Verda in his dreams. It was a whole week since that snatched farewell kiss, and he missed her dreadfully. As he closed his eyes he tried to fix the image of her in his mind, but his subconscious refused to cooperate, returning instead to its recurring theme of water.

The moment he fell asleep he found himself hovering over water, as he had with Cho, but the lake below him was far larger than the Shore lagoon, and it was covered with ice. Once in his youth he had seen a film of ice on a bucket of water, but this vast lake of freezing water was the stuff of nightmares. Ice stretched almost as far as he could see, some whitened by snow, other areas almost black with menace. Tom saw a huge iceberg topple in slow motion from a glacier, to fall with a crash that sent shock-waves of sound booming across the lake. He watched the ice-blue water surge back and forth, bouncing the enormous floes like autumn leaves on a river, and he shuddered so violently that he shook himself awake.

Throwing an armful of logs onto the fire he sat with his feet in the hot embers, shivering while he tried to interpret the dream. He supposed it was possible he was just visualising the Knowledge legend of the Sun and the Cold, but he was convinced the dream was a warning. The trouble was, he couldn't imagine any Rockman being near enough to a frozen lake to be in danger. He mulled it over until he had warmed up enough to take his feet out of the fire, and this time when he fell asleep, the Mother let him dream about Verda.

When he went to treat Yakan's stump the next morning, the Leader endured the application of herbal salve without protest, then lay back on his bed, grinning almost like his old self. "I'll admit you have the healing touch, young man, but I still maintain that if those people had arrived a minute later, two babies would have been lost." He glanced at Tom and laughed mirthlessly. "We'll agree to disagree on that, shall we? And talking of babies, when is that crowd on the beach going home? We've fed them for long enough."

"They're as keen to leave as you are to get rid of them," Tom said, "Only their route back to Twin Lake is blocked by a landslide."

"Bala's group came that way without a problem."

"It only happened two days ago – that's what delayed Tabor and his friends. The whole group will have to take the longer Ridge Path, and they didn't come prepared for such a journey."

Tom didn't need to say any more – guilt made Yakan unusually generous. He sent Tarifa to round up provisions, and the beach caves hummed with activity for the remainder of the day, as the women roasted meat for the long trek while the men sharpened their spears for hunting en route.

That evening Yakan left his bed to preside over the farewell party, and as a way of apologising for trying to steal the babies he asked Tabor for the story behind his change of clans. Tabor made his catalogue of disasters sound like an exciting adventure, but what caught Tom's attention was his description of their previous clan's home. Tabor and Jura came from a range of mountains so far north that they were snowbound in winter. The mere thought of snow made his audience of southerners shudder, but Tom asked eagerly, "Is there a frozen lake up there?"

To his disappointment, Tabor answered, "None that I've heard of – and nobody could live further north than the Wolf Clan." It was clear he still missed his lost clan.

Tom would have dropped the subject if Bala hadn't asked, "What's your interest in a frozen lake, Tom? Twin Lake can be very cold but it never freezes."

"It was just a dream I had," Tom replied, and would have elaborated, but then Tarifa asked Jura how the Wolf Clan had managed to keep warm so far north and the moment had gone. Tom slid back into his seat, still convinced the Mother was sending him a warning. He was determined to keep asking. He would question every visitor to the Shore until he had discovered the location of the huge, frozen, dangerous lake of his dream.

CHAPTER SEVENTEEN – DEATH AND BIRTH

Chert made Yakan the promised foot, using soft pine to spare his stump. He advised the Leader to take things gently at first, but his words fell on impatient ears. From the moment he strapped on his wooden foot, Yakan was clumping around, although from his expression it was clearly painful. He wore the first one out in a day – the base shredded by rough ground and the top scorched by the heat of his truncated ankle.

When Tom saw the state of the stump that evening he was furious. "I said you could try it out, not dance around on the damn thing!"

"I was bored." Yakan pouted, but instantly replaced his pout with a wolfish grin. "Besides, if I hadn't shown my face quickly, my clansmen might have got the idea you were in charge!"

"Well, now you've made your point, you can stay put until that stump heals," Tom said severely, throwing the wooden foot into the fire. "I shall tell Chert not to make any more for a while." He took Yakan's silence as assent, though he doubted Chert would be able to hold out for long against his old friend's blandishments.

A few days later Sasso made a return trip to the Shore bringing a raft-load of ready-trimmed roof-beams, a few sacks of early grassland wheat, and Verda. Tom was ecstatic, and in front of the delighted Foresters he wrapped her in his arms and kissed her thoroughly. When she could draw breath again, Verda said, "I'm only here until Sasso goes home tomorrow, and Mother insists I stay with Banca – we mustn't be alone after dark." She giggled, her green eyes sparkling with mischief. "She's convinced we'd misbehave! Now, let's go up to your ledge – I want to see how much your volcano has grown."

From Tom's ledge the volcano was spectacular – they had an aerial view of the lava spilling over the lip of the crater, and could hear the hiss as it rolled into the water two hundred feet below them. Verda clutched Tom's hand to lean as far out as she could. "It's incredible," she exclaimed, "That tongue of lava has almost reached the reef."

"I think it will break right through eventually," Tom said, "But there'll be another eruption before that happens." Knowing he mustn't tell her about the fifth baby before he told its parents, he closed the subject by pulling her close and kissing her. After a long moment he drew back and trailed a finger down her cheek. "If we've only got till tomorrow I'm taking today off."

"Yakan won't like that," Verda said.

Tom grinned. "That's why I'm not going to tell him, and if anyone sees us, we'll say we're hunting for herbs." Fetching a basket from his cave, he slipped away into the forest with his girl.

Tom hadn't left the Shore in over a week, and after the constant noise of the village the peace of the forest was blissful. He and Verda rapidly filled the basket with herbs, then found a sun-warmed hollow and lay entwined, kissing and murmuring nonsense. Lulled by the swish of leaves and the humming of bees, their talk gradually faded to nothing, and they were almost asleep when a harsh bird-call startled them back to consciousness.

Still dozy, Tom leaned up on one elbow and gazed into Verda's emerald green eyes, lazily caressing her throat where the pulse beat hot. Verda lifted a hand to cup his cheek, stroking his lips with her thumb, and he caught her wrist and bit her. Holding her arm trapped, he trailed the fingers of his free hand up the soft suede of her skin to the bend of her elbow and pressed down hard on her pulse. Verda's eyes darkened and she made a feeble effort to break free, her heart beating so hard that Tom heard it, and he growled with fierce delight in his power to arouse her.

Suddenly neither of them could bear the suspense any longer. Releasing the fiery savagery that lurks beneath the surface of every Rockman, they lunged at each other, their bodies meeting with a crash that scattered the birds from the branches. With tangled limbs and panting breath, their hunger for each other exploded into a frenzy. They rolled around the hollow with the ferocity of fighting tigers, kissing and biting, the heat in their bodies escalating more swiftly than they had thought possible. Tom was on the verge of tearing off Verda's tunic when he felt a Call and sat up abruptly, his hand still on Verda's thigh.

"What's the matter, Tom?" Verda cried, trying to pull him back, but he stood up and hauled her to her feet. "There's a big eruption coming – I have to go and warn people."

"I never expected a volcano to play chaperone," Verda said with a shaky little laugh as she tugged her tunic straight, "But it's probably just as well we stopped – Mother would guess what I'd done as soon as I got home."

The moment he heard Tom's warning Yakan ordered the clan to take cover in their homes, but Tom and Verda headed for his eyrie. They had just reached it when the volcano spat a huge ball of golden rock hundreds of feet into the air in an impressive show of strength. Tom and Verda stood on his ledge with their mouths open in awe, and the Shore Clan's caves and huts emptied immediately – no-one wanted to miss a moment of the show. Even Yakan stood clinging to his doorpost to watch the fiery ball, which hung briefly suspended like a second sun before curving over and plunging into the Ocean with a spectacular hiss and an enormous spout of spray. This ball of rock must have been plugging the cone because once it had been expelled, a stream of lava spilled over the edge towards the cliff, narrowing the gap through which the river entered the lagoon.

Yakan had already persuaded Chert to carve him another foot, and now he took some of his men down to the strip of beach that ran from the ford to the lagoon. Tom wondered why they had abandoned the better view from the plateau, but he soon discovered the reason. When the space between lava and the cliff had shrunk to a few yards, some of the younger men waded into the water that was rampaging through the gap. Tom, struck by an awful premonition, raced down to the beach, grabbed Yakan's arm and demanded, "What on earth are they doing? Leave it alone!"

Yakan shrugged him off. "We can't let that gap close – the river will flood everything."

"But closing the gap is part of the Mother's plan," Tom said, "You can't stop a volcano."

But Yakan wouldn't listen. "We're Rockmen – we can have a damn good try," he retorted, and Tom could do nothing but watch as the young men – roped together in a pathetic nod to safety precautions – put their backs against the leading edge of the lava and pushed. It was unbelievable – Yakan had sent all the young men of his clan into appalling danger in a futile attempt to divert thousands of tons of liquid rock. Tom tried to protest again but Yakan feigned deafness, and Tom was left standing, his mouth open in horror as the disaster unfolded.

He wasn't the only one aghast at the sight – everyone could see it was hopeless. The men's parents and mates shouted from the plateau above that they should give up and come back. Women were screaming and small children were crying, but it was only when the gap had shrunk even further and the water was up to the men's chins that Yakan finally gave the order to retreat. Only just in time, too. The young men's bodies had been cooled to danger-point by their immersion in the water, and extreme exertion had sapped their strength. Perhaps this was why, as they staggered back to safety, no-one noticed that two men had been left behind.

Tom was never certain afterwards whether he heard a yell for help or if the Mother alerted him, but when the shivering Shore men had passed him and hurried home to their fires, he knew there were two men still out there. There was nobody left on the beach but him and Sasso, and he knew he wasn't strong enough to rescue them.

Sasso offered instantly, "I'm used to water so I'll get them – you go and tell Yakan."

While Tom sped off for help, Sasso roped himself to a tree and waded along the cliff edge, with the river pummelling him every step of the way and trying to sweep him off his feet. Using every handhold to resist the force of the water, he reached the nearest man and slid an arm round his waist. "We can make it if we move now!" he yelled in his ear, "Grab your friend and let's go!"

The man turned frightened eyes on his rescuer and said through his clenched jaw, "We can't move – we're stuck to the lava."

In one horrified glance Sasso saw that the man's shoulder had become welded to the super-heated rock. "Then I'm going to have to pull you off, and it'll hurt like hell."

"Don't waste time talking – just do it!" the man begged, so Sasso, ignoring his scream of agony, tore him free and slung him over his shoulder. He couldn't carry them both, but he had seen two Shore men coming to the rescue, so he hefted his now unconscious burden and forced his way against the current back to the beach, where Tom was one of the group hauling on his rope.

"Keil is stuck even worse than this one was," Sasso told them. "I don't think he's going to make it."

Tom's spirit raced out to the stricken youth. Knowing the death was coming made it no easier to bear. Keil was only eighteen, the same age as Tom, and far too young to die. Tom held his own breath in sympathy as Keil fought to keep his head above water, trying not to swallow the waves that splashed his face. Feeling the pain of others was the curse of a Seer, and Tom suffered with Keil the agony of knowing the odds were stacked against him. His back burned with Keil's as the volcano slowly subsumed him, his own chest heaved with the effort of moving chilled muscles enough to breathe, and through his mind flashed Keil's short lifetime of memories.

He knew when the rescuers stopped, defeated. The volcano and the causeway that joined it to the southern bank had created a swirling pool, and the water was now too deep for them to reach the trapped youth. The people on the plateau watched in appalled silence as Keil made one final desperate effort to breathe, inhaling instead a lungful of water. That was the end – the inrush of cold water extinguished the fire that burned inside every Rockman, and a moment later his heart stopped. Tom doubled over with the agony of it and for a moment he feared he would die too, but suddenly it hurt no more. The young Shore man was dead, and Tom experienced one of a Seer's blessings. He saw Keil's soul lift free from his cold body and hover briefly over his home, before a gentle spirit hand emerged from the volcano that had taken his life and drew him back into Mother Earth.

And then, as if to mock Yakan's desire to halt its progress, the lava stopped moving. There was still a gap a couple of yards wide and the river was still flowing, but Keil was dead, his body stuck fast to the rock. The entire clan stood in shocked silence, and Tom was so angry he didn't trust himself to speak. Only days ago Yakan had lost a foot to the volcano, yet he had sent his men to confront it, with the result that a young man was dead and another seriously injured. Tom turned on his heel and left the scene.

Having treated the latest victim's oozing back with the same salve he had used on Yakan, Tom stormed outside and berated the Leader in front of a crowd of shocked villagers. "What could you possibly hope to achieve – ten men against a volcano?" he yelled. Turning on the men who had made it back unscathed, he added, "And you bunch of idiots should have known better than to listen to his hare-brained scheme."

One brave man interrupted Tom's tirade to say, "We were trying to push it sideways so it would leave a gap for the river to get through."

"For heaven's sake! Did none of you hear me say it should be left alone? It's *supposed* to close. The lava will make a bridge by tomorrow, and without that bridge a child will be lost."

"Whose child?" the man asked.

"Zan and Crystal's," Tom said, scanning the crowd to find the right pair. "I saw it last night – you're going to have a baby tomorrow."

As Zan and Crystal dashed off to tell their families the good news, a lad ran up and tugged at Yakan's tunic. "Chert says the little beach is flooded and soon the ford will flood too – what should we do?" Yakan seized on the message as a welcome distraction and limped off upstream to the ford, where the newly-built stepping-stones were already covered by an inch of water.

The sunset that evening was a splendid display of orange and purple through the cloud of volcanic dust, but there was no time to admire its beauty. Keil's parents insisted his body must be retrieved so they could build him a cairn, without which his spirit would wander forever. Tom forbade anyone to venture back into the water, so after a furious debate, two of Keil's friends climbed down the cliff, secured by ropes. With hammer and chisel they managed to detach his head and arms before dusk made it impossible to see, and Tom cairned him by torchlight.

The lava recommenced its slow crawl towards the cliff shortly after the Cairning ceremony, and Tom's Call came an hour after midnight. Knowing a baby was finally coming for the Shore Clan, no-one had slept, and within minutes Zan and Crystal were standing on the riverbank. Tom felt compelled to go against tradition and accompany them, desperate to ensure the safe arrival of their baby for his own sake as much as for theirs.

The beach was now knee-deep in water, and they had to edge past Chert's latest raft which was tethered to the bank. Together they crept along the narrow strip of submerged gravel at the foot of the bluff, grasping at every handhold, until they reached the lava-flow which was inching closer to the cliff. White water seethed through the shrinking gap.

"We can't go through there," Crystal whimpered.

Tom reassured her, "We won't have to – the gap's going to close any minute now." Then without warning his legs were swept from under him, water closed over his head and his recurring nightmare became awful reality. The current rolled him across the river-bed as if he weighed no more than a pebble, and he was convinced he was going to be swept through the gap to die in the cold waters of the lagoon. He was running out of air when his body slammed against the lava, and instantly he dug his fingers into the soft rock to claw his way to the surface. Dragging in a deep breath, he felt the lava burning his fingers and knew he must keep moving or suffer the same fate as Keil. Digging hand- and toe-holds into the malleable rock, he clambered up the vertical face of the lava, not stopping until he was well above the river. There he perched on the thin rippling crust of the lava like a seagull riding a wave, while below him Zan and Crystal still clung to the cliff-face.

"Hold steady!" he shouted, and Zan held Crystal firmly to his side as the leading edge of the flow slammed against the land with enough force to send liquid rock splashing up towards the crowd on the plateau. The gap between volcano and land had closed and the flow was diverted seawards, but the crust was cooling rapidly – there wasn't much time.

"Quickly!" Tom yelled to the young couple, "Come the way I did." Their expressions scared but determined, they pushed through the warm water towards the side of the lava-flow, but in those few minutes Tom's footholds had smoothed out and the lava had begun to harden. They couldn't climb up the side of the lava, and with the dammed-up pool filling rapidly they were in imminent danger of drowning. Custom dictated that nobody should assist the parents at a birth, but Tom shouted, "Help them, someone!"

Immediately Yakan waded to the rescue, determined not to lose the Shore Clan's first baby, and Sasso followed him. Both were tall men, heavily muscled from a lifetime of work, and Sasso stood on Yakan's shoulders to make a ladder for the youngsters to climb. A moment later, their bodies steaming as the water evaporated from them, Zan and Crystal were standing beside Tom.

The leading edge of the lava was now flowing into the lagoon, and for a fleeting moment of panic they feared their baby was already in the water, but then Tom saw the shell rolling towards them. "Here it comes!" he cried. The couple braced themselves, but on the steep slope it took three of them to catch the heavy shell. Zan broke it open for Crystal to lift out their baby, and as she did so, drops of lava splattered down onto Yakan and Sasso.

"Watch what you're doing!" Yakan yelled, "And if you're coming back this way, get a move on – I'm drowning down here!"

Crystal peered past Sasso at Yakan's upturned face, but she was afraid to climb down the man-ladder with her baby, and while she dithered, the water closed over Yakan's head. He jumped up to take a breath, dislodging Sasso in the process, and they both fell into the water. The watching crowd gasped, but the two men simply walked across the riverbed until their heads emerged into fresh air. As they pushed upstream in the swirling water, a cheerful voice came out of the murk asking, "Want a ride?" and there, bobbing at the end of its rope, was the raft with Chert on board. Sasso and Yakan clambered up, and a score of willing hands hauled the raft back to the beach.

Meanwhile the rest of the clan dropped knotted ropes from the plateau and helped the new parents to scramble up the cliff-face with their baby. Crystal's father passed down a Firepot for the ritual relighting, after which Tom was finally able to leave the still-moving lava and climb up to join them.

All thoughts of sleep were forgotten as the ecstatic Shore Clan celebrated the birth around a roaring fire outside their old familiar caves. Yakan made a speech to welcome the newest clan member but also, with an apologetic grimace at Tom, spoke of the tragic loss of Keil. His words took his audience from joy to tears and back again, and Tom began to understand why the man was such a popular Leader despite his mercurial temper.

Later, when everyone was mellow on wood-spirit, Yakan hobbled over to join Tom and Verda, bringing a jug with him. For a while they shared it in companionable silence, watching the volcano's reflection in the night-dark sea. Tom waited, sensing the Leader had something weighing on his mind, and finally Yakan said, "You showed more courage tonight than I expected from someone your size."

Tom smiled at the backhanded compliment and replied, "I knew they would need help, and I wanted to make sure our clan got its baby."

"That's the first time you've called it your clan," Yakan said shrewdly, "But I think it's time I left you two lovebirds alone." Topping up their cups, he hauled himself painfully upright and returned to sit with his family.

"That man's moods swing like a monkey on a vine," Tom observed when he'd gone. "Life with the Shore Clan is never going to be easy. I wish you weren't going home tomorrow."

Verda squeezed his hand. "We've still got the rest of tonight – let's go up to your ledge and watch the volcano from there."

Tom and Verda weren't the only ones to leave the party early, and Yakan finally gave up trying to keep his clan away from the Mother's show. Despite the danger, it was impossible for anyone to resist the sight of the liquid rock rolling into the lagoon. They watched, mesmerised, as the bulbous leading edge crusted over in the cooler water, only to split open again as more lava swelled each bulge. To the background sound and smell of hot lava hissing into salt water, the Shore Clan on the plateau and the couple on Tomboro's ledge viewed the spectacle through swirling curtains of steam – steam that changed colour constantly in the volcanic glow.

Dawn wasn't far off when Aran came up to the ledge with a message from Banca. "Mother says Verda's bed's ready and we should all get some sleep."

Tom made a little sound of protest but Verda said, "I'll be there right away," and kissed Tom goodnight. He didn't need any special powers to read her mind clearly – this afternoon's tryst had shown how easily they could get carried away, and to spend the remainder of this night together would be asking for trouble.

CHAPTER EIGHTEEN – TUNNEL

The new lava-flow had completed the job of damming the river and by the following morning the ford was impassable. The towpath was also flooded for such a distance upstream that the Forest group, together with Verda, had to abandon the raft; instead they crossed the dam to take a higher path home.

Tomboro watched until Verda's green body was no longer visible through the trees, and then squared his shoulders and returned to his cave to collect a pot of salve to treat his latest patient. Ness, the young man who had been stuck to the lava, had lost half the skin from his back – without frequent applications of hot salve, the new skin would set rock-hard and he'd be crippled for life.

Several mornings after Verda had gone home, Tom had a vision which sent him looking for Yakan. He found him standing, as he did every day, glumly surveying the flooded ford. The islands which the Shore men had so laboriously built to act as stepping-stones were now under six feet of water, and between the islands the water swirled ten feet deep. They had fixed a guide-rope across the submerged islands so that Sasso's abandoned raft could be used as a ferry, but it was a poor substitute for the ford that had hitherto been a very profitable link between the north and south.

"We could build those islands up higher, I suppose," Yakan said when Tom appeared. "At least the traders could get across, although their camels would have to swim."

"The current would sweep them off their feet," Tom said, remembering what happened to Flint when they crossed Cold River, "But I see help coming soon which will solve the problem."

"I hope you're right," Yakan said miserably, "We've already had two traders turn back. When they spread the word that our ford is out of commission, no-one else will come this way." Even as he spoke, two men came out of the trees on the far bank and stood waving to attract attention. "Oh stars!" Yakan groaned, "It's that old Desert Seer Donax – that's all I need."

"He might actually be just what you need," Tom said, "I think the younger man is the help we've been waiting for."

"Really? Well, in that case…" Yakan's face lit up like a torch, and when the newcomers had been ferried across the ford he shook the Seer's hand enthusiastically. "Donax, old friend – it's good to see you!"

"And you, Yakan," Donax replied. "I've brought my son Scapa along – we couldn't wait any longer to see your volcano." He greeted Tom with a nod. "I knew you were a Seer from the moment we met, young man. Glad to see Yakan's taken you on." He eased a pack off his shoulders and dumped it at his son's feet, saying, "Take care of this, Scapa, while Tomboro and I have a chat," and he set off for the Seer's ledge so fast that Tom had to run to catch up with him.

Donax surveyed Tom's domain with approval. "It wasn't this tidy in Cho's day," he said, "All right if I have a look round?" and he was inside the cave before Tom could react.

"Damn cheek!" Cho exclaimed. "After him, Tom!"

Swiftly following his uninvited guest, Tom made an effort to control his irritation. "I believe you wanted a chat, Donax – is something on your mind?"

Donax smiled paternally and gestured at the volcanic cone outside. "I came as soon as I could be spared, my boy. Your mother said you were now the Shore Seer, but I'm sure you could use some instruction. I thought I might stay here for a while."

"Tell him to sod off," Cho growled, "You don't need him – you've got me."

"Stop pestering me!" Tom hissed.

Donax bristled visibly. "Are you talking to me?"

"No," Tom sighed, "I was talking to Cho."

Donax was momentarily thrown off balance but he recovered quickly. "Cho and I were good friends," he said, "He'll be pleased I am able to help you."

"He was no friend of mine!" Cho snorted.

"It's good of you to offer," Tom said to Donax, "But Cho himself will be teaching me."

"I suppose he can teach you enough for this backwater of a place," Donax said, forgetting he was supposed to be Cho's friend, "Have you changed his Sanctum at all?" and, in an appalling breach of good manners, he walked straight through to the inner cave.

As Tom hurried after him, Cho said, "I certainly never invited him in here. Watch him, Tom – I don't trust him an inch."

Tom found Donax stroking the streak of green rock on the wall. "This explains the colour of the Guaza Clan's baby," he said, "And you've got his shell!" He bent to pick up a smooth green pebble. "This is more of the same rock – where did you find it?"

"It's a lava drop from baby Onyx's shell," Tom said, "And it belongs in here," he added, catching Donax's wrist, "Not in your pocket – please put it back where you found it."

Donax stared at the pebble as if surprised to find he was holding it. "Sorry, my boy – wasn't thinking," he said breezily. "Now – I'm sure there must be some things you need to know that old Cho hasn't covered – ask me anything."

Reluctantly, Tom raised the issue that still disturbed his rest. "I have had a warning vision that I can't make sense of – perhaps you can throw some light on it."

"Always happy to oblige, my boy – tell me all about it."

Tom steered the light-fingered old Seer back to the outer cave, where he treated him to a vivid description of his vision of freezing water and floating ice. Donax shivered at the images Tom painted, but he didn't give Tom's concern much credence. "A lake that cold must be way up in the north – much too far away to concern you," he said, smiling indulgently. "You might be picking up another Seer's warning – after all, you're very young and you're bound to get things wrong on occasions." He slung a heavy arm round Tom's neck and dragged him out into the sunshine. "Now, I'm hungry after that long walk – shall we go and see what's for dinner?"

From the plateau Yakan and Scapa were surveying the dam. "You were right about help arriving, Tom," Yakan said. "This splendid young man is a quarryman – he thinks we can cut a tunnel and release the water from the pool!"

"A tunnel through solid lava?" Tom asked doubtfully.

"It's not all solid," Scapa told him. "I think there's a layer of gravel in that far bank, beneath the lava, that you could excavate. It would take some hard work, but it's possible."

"Hard work never hurt anyone," said Yakan, "When can you start?"

"Me?" Scapa gasped, "That's not what I meant…"

But Yakan turned on the full force of his charm. "My clansmen haven't got the skills for this – and I'll make it worth your while to stay."

Tom smiled inwardly as he read Scapa's thoughts. The quarryman didn't need any extra inducements to stay – he simply couldn't resist the challenge to dig a tunnel beside an active volcano and release a river from confinement.

Scapa put on a show of reluctance but finally said, "I suppose I could spare a few weeks."

"Weeks?" Yakan groaned.

"There's at least twenty yards to get through – and that pool is a major problem. We could drive most of the tunnel through from the lagoon beach, where it's dry, but some of the work will have to be done from this side."

They stood in silence, watching the deep pool that swirled like oil below them, murky with debris, and Tom wondered aloud, "Could the pool-side work be done from a raft?"

Scapa pursed his lips. "I suppose it's possible – if we can keep a raft steady enough."

"You'll have so many ropes it'll look like a spider in its web," Yakan assured him before clapping Tom heavily on the back. "Brilliant idea, Tom – what would we do without you?" and he limped off to the village to muster a team of workmen.

Donax watched him go. "You seem to have Yakan under your spell, Tomboro," he remarked sourly, "And as you've got Cho's ghost for advice you obviously don't need me. If Yakan can provide me with an escort, I shall go home."

Tom said nothing to dissuade him, and the next day Donax returned to the Desert, escorted by a

Shore trader who was taking a pack of smoked fish inland.

The moment he had gone, work began on the tunnel. As Scapa had guessed, there was a gravel layer beneath the bank at the southern end of the dam. They would dig a tunnel through this, twelve feet in diameter, which Scapa said was the right height for a grown man to swing a pick comfortably. Most of the work would be done from the lagoon beach, but some had to be tackled from the dam pool – a much more daunting prospect.

Every member of the Shore Clan knew that without the outlet of this tunnel they would lose their trade route, but they loathed the work. Rock bodies need heat – usually the clan members spent as much time as possible in full sunlight – but the beach they were working from faced west and was in shade for half the day. To make matters worse, water spilled over the dam continuously, and the first picks had to be swung beneath the resulting waterfall. Each man could only manage five minutes before he was too cold to continue and had to hand over to another.

The women kept a huge bonfire burning on the beach – each shivering miner in turn would stand in the flames to restore his circulation before stoically returning to work another shift. As the tunnel grew longer it was slightly less arduous, as they could duck through the waterfall and work inside the tunnel, but half an hour was still the most any man could bear. Even so, with Yakan, wooden foot notwithstanding, taking his turn with the pick, it became a matter of pride for every fit man to work several shifts a day.

Meanwhile a group of older boys tethered the raft on the pool side of the dam and attacked the gravel from this floating platform. The previous year the same boys had got their thrills by paddling tiny rafts out to the islet that was now their volcano – some had even gone as far as the reef – but now they had another way of proving their manhood. Each boy in turn would simply drop over the side of the raft into the warm pool and sink like a stone to the bottom, scrape out a bucketful of gravel and then carry it up a ladder back to the raft, their only concession to safety a rope tied round their waists.

Even the women, children and elders worked, carrying the tunnel spoil half a mile upstream, where they spread it on the riverbed to strengthen the ford in anticipation of the lowering of the water-level.

During the late summer evenings around the village fire, the rival gangs of miners, divers and ford-builders traded tales of prowess, but to a Seer's sensitivity the underlying tension was acutely painful. Tom spent every daylight hour with the divers, counting the boys out and back. The raft had been his idea and he dreaded the prospect of having to drag the deep pool if one boy failed to surface. His sleep was haunted by nightmares. In one the warm waters of the lagoon froze over, trapping him beneath the ice; in another he was wading through the mud of the lagoon-bed searching for a lost boy. As the tunnel grew, so did his sense of approaching disaster.

When the tunnel reached thirty feet – about half the length Scapa had estimated – water from the pool began seeping through the workface. Inside the dark, humid tube, every pickaxe-wielding man was horribly conscious of the thousands of gallons of water straining to escape from the dam-pool. Each bucketful of gravel he dug out – each rock he prised away – could be the one that caused a catastrophic collapse. Now Tom wasn't the only one with nightmares – a steady trickle of tunnellers visited his cave in the mornings before work to ask for his blessing, each man searching Tom's face for a sign that he had foreseen their death.

One morning Tom awoke trembling from a dream in which the entire workface gave way, and he sped down to the village to tell Yakan and Scapa they would have to find another method of finishing the work. He met none of the opposition he had anticipated.

"I couldn't agree more," Yakan said. "I was in the tunnel myself yesterday and it was an un-nerving experience."

"So what's our next move?" Tom asked. "We can't give up now."

"I've been thinking about this for a couple of days," Scapa said. "What I reckon we need is a good solid battering ram."

Yakan loved the idea of bashing through the final yards of the obstruction, and once he had set his mind to something it happened quickly. Within a day his men had felled an ironwood tree – one of the few trees that was heavier than water – and hauled it to the river. Two groups of men stood on the dam holding a massive hawser to jerk the tree downstream and batter the tunnel beneath their feet, after which men on either bank would haul the tree back upstream ready for another blow. Every daylight hour echoed with the sound of the Shore men battering away at the last few yards of their tunnel, and the constant pounding set everyone's nerves on edge.

No longer needed on the raft, Tom still kept an eye on the workers from his ledge, but one afternoon he heard Yakan screaming, "Tomboro!" and he shot down the track to find the whole village in uproar.

"What's happened?" he asked urgently, "Has there been an accident?"

"Worse than that," Yakan growled, "It's my daughter Sima – she must be Bonded immediately." He dragged Sima forward. "She's disgraced us all – she and that damned boy Ness have been mating!"

"Ness?" Tom queried, "With his back I'm surprised he was fit enough."

"You've done too good a job of fixing him up," Yakan said, "His mother caught them in the act." He shook Sima roughly. "This daughter of mine and her lover will be on your ledge first thing in the morning to be Bonded," he ordered and stomped away, his wooden foot beating its now familiar rhythm on the tightly packed earth.

Tom heard the whole story in detail over supper with Banca and Aran.

"The first thing we knew about it was Ness's mother screaming," Banca told him, her eyes alive with merriment. "She found Ness and Sima mating in her hut, *and* they were using her very own Bondstone!"

"What's a Bondstone, Mother?" Aran asked.

"I'll tell you when you're older," Banca said hurriedly. "Tom – you should have heard her – she called Sima a shameless little hussy and accused her of taking advantage of a sick boy. Then Tarifa burst through the door yelling, 'How dare you speak to Sima like that? Might I remind you she *is* the Leader's daughter.'"

Bianca had difficulty getting the next words out. "Thori screamed, 'We're not likely to forget that – she throws her weight around just like her father.'"

"I heard a slap too – it was brilliant!" Aran said. "I was hoping they'd come out and fight where we could see them, but Yakan came along and stopped them."

Tom clapped his hand over his mouth to smother a snort of laughter. For Ness to have used his parents' Bondstone was appalling, but he was sorry he'd missed all the excitement. "What did Yakan do?" he asked.

"He crashed through the door roaring like a bear, then everyone was yelling at once, and then there was a thud. Yakan must have punched Ness because Thori screamed, 'Don't hit him – he's too ill to fight.' Yakan yelled back, 'He wasn't too ill to rut, was he?' then he exploded out of the hut shouting for you."

"What's rutting, Mother?" Aran asked, his eyes wide and innocent.

Tom interjected swiftly, "Yakan says Sima and Ness must be Bonded tomorrow."

Banca picked up on the hesitation in his voice. “Do you know how to perform a Bonding?” she asked.

Tom almost told her about Cho, but the last thing he needed was for Aran to spread the news of his ghost, so he just said, “Roca taught me what to do, so I must go and prepare,” and he escaped to his ledge, where Cho calmed his nerves and described the Bonding ritual.

“You don’t need to worry,” he assured Tom. “They make a big production out of Bonding at the Festivals but there’s nothing to it really. I’ll stick around to make sure you get it right.”

*

Sima looked as if she’d been crying all night when her father marched her up to Tom’s ledge the next morning. There had been no time to make her a new outfit, but her best tunic was freshly brushed and she had found time to paint her face. She stood sullenly between her parents while they waited for Ness, who arrived leaning heavily on a friend’s shoulder.

Catching sight of Ness’s father behind him, Tom’s subconscious picked up echoes of a conversation from the previous night – 'Becoming Yakan's son-in-law is more than you could have hoped for with that back,' the older man had said. That could explain why Ness looked so cheerful for a young man about to be forced into Bondage – Tom saw him squeeze Sima's hand when his friend left him at her side.

Swallowing the nervous lump in his throat, Tom called on the assembly to witness the Bonding, using the words Cho had taught him.

Then he waited while their parents removed the couple's clothes. Tying one of Sima's wrists to one of Ness's with a cord, he smeared their cupped palms with wet clay. When he picked up the ceremonial knife from the makeshift altar, Sima tensed visibly but, following Cho's advice – 'Do it quick and clean and they'll hardly feel it' – Tom cut a swift nick in each belly. Catching the lava that welled out of the cuts in a bowl, he poured it into their joined hands and instructed them, "Mix it quickly."

The young couple moulded their own lava with the clay already in their hands while the crowd watched intently – the level of success was considered to be a sign of how well a Bondage would work. Working their tied hands as a pair wasn't easy – Sima giggled as they both fumbled nervously – but before the lava cooled they had combined Sima's creamy stone with Ness's grey into a lovely marbled tablet. When they held it up for inspection there was a murmur of approval from the crowd, and their parents smiled for the first time since the previous afternoon.

Ness and Sima were so pleased with themselves that Tom had to ask them twice before they would stand still enough for him to scrape the residue from their palms and smear it on their bellies – when their cuts healed, the scars would each hold a trace of the other's lava, linking them for life.

Finally Tom held their joined hands over the brazier until the leather cord that bound them had burned through.

Lifting their newly formed Bondstone aloft, he repeated the words he had learned from Cho:

"I declare to the Shore Clan and any others here present that Ness and Sima are now Bonded. May the Mother bless their union and make it fruitful."

Almost before Tom had finished speaking, Yakan took charge. "Right – now that's done, everyone back to the village – this is as good an excuse as any for a party."

The newly Bonded pair's mothers Tarifa and Thori had put their fight behind them and arranged a very creditable Bondage feast. The atmosphere was so cordial that no outsider could have guessed that a day earlier Yakan had been ready to reduce Ness to a pile of rubble.

When he raised his cup to toast the happy couple, he spoke of Sima with love and pride, and referred to his new son-in-law as 'a splendid young man'.

The party had been going for some hours before Ness and Sima's friends started the chant, "Bondstone, Bondstone!" Flushing prettily, Sima took the disc of lava from her pocket and pushed it into the embers of the fire.

When it was red-hot she pulled it out and Ness stood up, a little wobbly but unaided, to lead his mate through a barrage of ribald remarks to the hut that had been prepared for them. When the door had shut behind the couple, Tarifa and Thori dabbed their eyes, Yakan poured a hefty drink into Ness's father's cup, and the party continued loudly enough to cover the crashing sounds of two rock bodies making love in the bridal hut.

*

"It went surprisingly well," Tom told Cho much later that night, "I expected more fireworks from Yakan."

"That man could squeeze a diamond out of a lump of coal," Cho said.

But Tom didn't answer – he was staring intently at the volcano. "What's wrong?" Cho asked sharply.

"Nothing's wrong, but the Mother's taken me by surprise this time – they're having a baby."

"Sweet merciful heavens, not another one! Who are – and when?"

"Ness and Sima – tonight." Tom answered, and left the old Seer gaping while he ran down the track to the village. "Ness and Sima – where are they?" he asked the crowd.

"Still in bed, of course," someone called out amid laughter, but Yakan had seen Tom's expression and demanded, "What's the matter – did you get their Bonding wrong?"

"No, they're Bonded all right – and they've got a baby coming, right now."

In a second Yakan was hammering on the hut door. "Sima! Stop what you're doing and get out here!"

The door creaked open and Sima's flushed face appeared in a narrow gap. "Leave us alone, Father – this is our Bonding night."

"I know that, girl, but rutting will have to wait – Tom says you're having a baby."

"What – now?" Sima gasped.

"Right now."

"But I'm too young for a baby!" Sima wailed.

"You'll grow up quickly enough with a baby to look after," Yakan snapped.

Tarifa pushed him aside and said more quietly, "Hush, child – I'll help you – and besides, a grandchild might make your father forget the disgrace."

Sima slumped, realising she had no choice, and as she pulled the door to, everyone heard her say, "Ness – come here now," in a peremptory tone very like her father's.

Ness appeared promptly, struggling to pull his tunic over his sore back and scowling when he saw the crowd gathered outside the hut. "What's so urgent that you have to disturb us tonight?" he grumbled, but when Sima explained what was happening his next question was fired at Tom. "Are you sure it's for us? We haven't even got our own hut."

"And whose fault is that?" Yakan snapped, "You'd have had plenty of time to build one if you'd exercised more self-control."

Ness's voice was resigned as he looked downstream at the volcano. "It seems quiet enough at the moment – when's the baby coming?"

"Very soon," Tom said, and to back up his statement the volcano groaned, rumbled, spat out a red-hot plug of phlegm and erupted.

Sima seemed frozen with shock, but Ness grabbed her hand and pulled her along to the dam. Gripping the rope handrail tightly, they edged across its wet and slippery surface until they reached safer footing on the rough rock of the volcano itself. This time no help was needed – the shell rolled into Sima's arms as if it had been carefully aimed, Ness broke it open without mishap, and the entire birth went as smoothly as the oily salve that still smothered Ness's back. Tom joined them on the volcano to perform the ritual blessing, and the fading remnants of the Bonding party burst into renewed life to celebrate the arrival of the second Shore baby – Yakan's grandson.

Sima sat spooning hot broth into her son's little mouth under the watchful eyes of both his grandmothers, while Ness and their friends passed a jar of wine from hand to hand. The older generation reminisced about the scores of other such celebrations they had shared over the years.

Catching sight of Yakan drop an ember into his cup to heat his wine just as Overo used to, Tom was overcome by a wave of loneliness. These people had known each other all their lives, but they were just his clan by adoption – his only real friends here were a small boy and a ghost.

Hoping to leave unnoticed, he stood up, but Yakan called out jovially, "Going to bed, Tom? No more babies tonight, I trust?" He waited for the murmur of laughter he considered his due before tapping his leg. "There's another foot I've worn out!

Perhaps you could send a message to Chert that I need some more. Sweet dreams, my boy."

Tom replied with a withering look intended to indicate that his gift wasn't to be used for ordering feet, but Yakan had already forgotten him, so he waved one arm in a general 'goodnight' gesture and headed for bed. As he left the circle of firelight he stumbled slightly and heard Ness say, "Our little Seer's had a drop too much." The group of young clansmen around the newlyweds laughed and, burning with embarrassment and misery, Tom hurried off to the comforting seclusion of his own cave.

While he waited for the embers of his fire to catch the fresh fuel he sat hunched on his bed, miserably aware that his lack of height was making him the butt of jokes. Images of the night's birth brought back memories of a green baby that could have been his if he'd had a mate; thinking of the Bonding ceremony he had performed only this morning reminded him of Verda, and of the lovemaking that the volcano had interrupted; even the Guaza babies' shell fragments made him wonder where Cho had left his toe-stone, which brought him full circle back to

Yakan's request for more feet. He supposed he'd better try sending a message to Chert.

He smiled then – if he really could send his thoughts to the Forest village with such a mundane message, maybe he could also visit Verda in her dreams – it was worth a try.

CHAPTER NINETEEN – MOCHA AND ARAN

Verda had been dreaming of Tom, and woke with such an ache of longing in her breast that she felt she would burst. Unable to face even the thought of breakfast, she refused the bowl of porridge her mother offered and left the hut. In an irrational hope that Tom might be there, she headed for the place where she had first met him, but instead of Tom she found Mocha.

"What's the rush, Verda?" he asked, raising a forlorn face. "Where are you going?"

"Nowhere really," she replied. "I'm just fed up."

"Me too," Mocha said. "I'm not allowed to make another raft. Anyway, why are you miserable?"

"I miss Tom," Verda said, finding it strangely easy to confide in the little boy.

Mocha shifted over on his log seat to make room for her. "When are you going to see him again?"

"Your father said I could go on the next raft, but I don't know when he's going."

Mocha's small face lit up. "Do you think I could come too and see the volcano?"

Verda smiled at his eagerness. "I could ask him if you like," she offered.

Mocha flung his arms round her. "Let's go and ask him now."

They found Sasso assembling a pile of cut timber on the riverbank. "We're going to build a hut at the halfway jetty," he told them. "A rope team can rough it for a night in a tent, but older people need their comfort, and that volcano is bound to attract visitors."

"How long is that going to take?" Verda cried. "I thought you'd be going to the Shore soon – I haven't seen Tom for ages."

"Well," Sasso said, "First we'll need to take stone blocks down to make a proper fireplace for the hut, and then…"

"Sasso! Stop tormenting the girl." Zircon had strolled over to see what was happening. "I'll take her myself if you're not going yet. I've a mind to see this volcano erupting."

"Oh Father – you're a darling!" cried Verda, hugging him. "Can Mocha come too?"

"I can't see any reason why not," Sasso said, winking at his ecstatic little son, "The hut shouldn't take us more than a week." Once Sasso set his mind to something he moved quickly. By the end of the week there was not only a proper night shelter at the halfway point, the other stopping-places also had jetties for passengers to step ashore.

Both Verda's parents had decided to go, ostensibly to chaperone their daughter, but their real motive was simple curiosity – the new-born volcano was an irresistible attraction. Sasso warned them only to bring one small bag, and when they arrived at the jetty on the morning of departure it was clear why. The raft was half-filled with trade goods – pots of honey, a stack of leather and several sides of beef from the grassland cattle, and a lumpy sack full of wooden feet that Chert had made for Yakan.

Verda's mother Noyau boarded the raft nervously and sat on the pile of leather, balancing a Firepot on her knees, but Zircon stood confidently next to Chert at the tiller, his eyes sparkling with excitement as he relived the rafting days of his youth.

Chert had expected his grandson Mocha to ride beside him, taking a turn at steering on the easy stretches, but Mocha had chosen to walk with Verda – the girl who kept her promises.

It was high summer – the air buzzed with insect life and the trees were raucous with birdsong. To begin with the passengers were too excited to pay much attention to the damage around them, but when they stopped at midday to heat a pot of soup they noticed evidence of the giant wave everywhere. Debris was caught high up in the forks of trees, and there were long stretches of exposed earth where chunks had been torn from the banks. The salt water had killed off much of the vegetation which was only just beginning to recover, and underlying the smell of growing things lurked the slimy stink of decay.

After a night at the newly built cabin, which everyone declared to be the height of luxury, they set off on the second leg of their trip with mounting excitement.

By mid-morning the smell of sulphur was very strong, and a cloud of fine ash drifted down like grey snowflakes – proof that they were getting close.

A low background hum increased throughout the morning to a muted roar, and when the raft rounded the last bend, the entire group stopped to stare.

Tom, of course, had known they were coming, and met them at the ferry, where Verda leapt ashore directly into his arms and kissed him passionately, totally oblivious to her parents' presence. Chert was the second to disembark, and hurried up to the village with his sack of newly-made feet for Yakan, leaving Zircon and Noyau to enjoy their first sight of the volcano in the company of the awestruck Mocha. After they had had their fill of staring, Banca and Aran escorted them to the guest hut which Tom had asked her to prepare.

*

Introducing Mocha and Aran was like lighting a fire too near a pile of straw. Aran and his friends Farr and Naze had been listening enviously for weeks to the young men's stories of rafting to the islet that had sprouted their volcano. Now that was no longer possible, they'd been itching for similar adventures, and Mocha, the boy carpenter, was the spark that set them ablaze.

As soon as he and Mocha were alone, Aran said, "Tom rode all the way from the Forest on the raft you made – will you show me how to make one?"

"I'm not really allowed," Mocha said, looking round furtively, but his father had gone to inspect progress on the tunnel, Verda had disappeared with Tom, and the older ones were settling into the guest hut.

When Aran said, "We've got a secret place so nobody will know," the scene was set.

Many of the women had joined the work teams, leaving their children to their own devices, so the four youngsters – Mocha and Aran, Farr and Naze – were free to spend hours unsupervised in a tiny cove they had found facing the Ocean, building their own raft with wood scavenged from the fuel pile.

Following the simple design of Mocha's original raft, they lashed three logs together with vines – a base of two with one on top to make it easy to straddle. The lagoon was now divided in two by a lava flow from the volcano to the reef, and they planned to float their raft on the northern half, nearer to home.

A narrow strip of beach ran along the base of the cliff from their cove to the lagoon, but it was only usable at low tide and they were nervous about going that way. Mocha hadn't admitted to his new friends that up till now he had only ridden a short distance along the riverbank, but bravado prompted him to volunteer to tow the new raft to the lagoon.

With the other three children watching from the cove, he took a tow rope in his mouth and edged along the narrow beach. The shingle shifted alarmingly beneath his feet but he dug his fingers into cracks in the cliff-face and soldiered on. He had managed several yards before the entire beach sloped so suddenly that he slipped, gasped in fright, and the rope dropped from his mouth. He let go of the cliff to grab the trailing rope and was lucky not to end up in the Ocean. Shivering with cold and terror, he scrambled back to the cove and told the little gang, "We can't reach it that way – we'll have to use the south half of the lagoon."

"But someone will see us," Farr pointed out, "The tunnel starts there."

"Not if we go at night," Aran said.

Naze stared at him aghast. "After dark?"

"It won't be really dark, stupid!" scoffed Farr, "There's a full moon."

"We'll go after supper," Aran decided. "Everybody meet by the ford."

"I can't come," said Naze, "I have to go to bed straight after supper."

"You can pretend to go to sleep quickly and then sneak out after."

"That's settled then," said Mocha, and the young adventurers hauled the raft up the cliff to conceal it among the trees near the ford.

*

Tom and Verda had spent the morning in the forest picking herbs, and the afternoon sitting on the bed in his cave sorting through them. It was nearly time to return to Banca's for supper when Tom held up a flower and said, "I don't recognise this one."

Before he could throw it in the fire Verda snatched it and held it on top of her head. "Don't burn it – I think it's pretty."

"It's not nearly as pretty as the face under it," Tom said and, despite their agreement not to get carried away again, he leaned close and kissed her.

That one kiss was enough to make Verda's eyes flare with desire. Pulling a stick from the fire she held the glowing tip to the pulse in his wrist, then drew it slowly up to the stronger pulse-point beneath his jaw, pressing it there until it faded to ash.

Heat raced through Tom's body and he gasped, "What are you doing?"

"It's called the Firegame – do you like it?"

Verda smiled and Tom croaked, "Like it is an understatement," and slid his hands inside Verda's tunic.

"No, Tom – we mustn't," she protested, pushing them away.

"But you set me on fire!" Tom replied, twisting suddenly to straddle her. Verda squirmed to get free but he held her down with more strength than she had expected. For a split second she was afraid, but when he murmured in her ear, "Trust me," she stopped struggling. "Now it's my turn," Tom said with a wicked smile, and pulled a burning stick from the ever-present fire.

Verda had heard the older Forest girls whispering about the Firegame and imagined it would be fun to try, but she hadn't realised the danger of playing with fire. She shuddered as Tom traced a slow line on her body with the glowing tip of the stick, her lava seeming to follow the fiery path from her ankle up to her thigh.

Tom held the flame there while he kissed her, and when she wrapped her legs around him they were almost lost, until a cough brought Tom to his senses – Cho had intervened just in time.

Tom untangled himself carefully, stroking Verda's face with a gentle hand. He kissed her nose, trembling with the knowledge of how close they'd come to mating, and not sure whether he was grateful or sorry that Cho had stopped them.

Verda's eyes came slowly back into focus as she sat up. "We shouldn't have done that."

"You started it," Tom replied childishly.

Verda looked away, rubbing at a burnt patch on the hem of her tunic. "I didn't realize what a powerful game it was – let's go outside and cool off."

Out on the ledge they sat a little apart in strained silence. Both of them were alarmed by the intensity of the feelings the game had aroused but too embarrassed to talk about it, and neither knew how to recapture the former ease of their relationship. After a while Tom cleared his throat and asked, "The Firegame – who taught you that?"

Verda stared at him. "Nobody taught me – I just heard the older girls talking."

"Seemed to me you knew what you were doing."

"I've never done it before – and don't pretend you didn't like it."

"You know I liked it, but that's not the point."

"So what is the point? Just because you enjoyed it you accuse me of doing it with someone else?" Verda's voice rose on a sob. "It was obviously a mistake to come and see you – the sooner I go home the better!"

Horribly afraid that Tom would see her crying, she ran away down the track, and in her anger she punched a tree so hard that a chunk of bark fell off.

The Forest-bred girl was horrified at having hurt a tree and she was trying to stick the bark back on when Mocha appeared.

"Why are you trying to mend that tree, Verda?"

"Don't jump out at me like that!" Verda snapped, "I thought you were a ghost."

Mocha giggled and flexed his muscles. "Me – a ghost? I'm too solid for that."

"Too dirty as well," said Verda, "Where on earth have you been?"

"Oh – just playing," Mocha replied airily, "Me and some Shore kids."

"It's good you've made some friends," Verda said dully, "I wish I'd gone with you."

"You've got Tom to play with," said Mocha, and was appalled when Verda burst into tears. He patted her arm awkwardly and tore up a fistful of leaves to wipe her face.

"What did I say wrong? Have you had a fight?" When she nodded miserably he threw his arms round her waist. "Never mind, Verda – I love you – I'll be your boyfriend."

He was thrilled to his hot little core when she hugged him fiercely and said, "Mocha, you're a darling – I love you too."

*

Tom remained slumped on his bed in a foul temper. How dare Verda speak to him like that – he was a Seer, and should be respected. Maybe by getting involved with Verda he was tying himself down too young. She'd probably done him a favour by opening his eyes in time, so why was he so miserable? He stared into the fire, hoping for some spiritual comfort, but the flames only reminded him of the game that had caused the argument. Clenching his jaw, he closed his eyes, fighting back the impulse to weep, and dropped like a stone into sleep.

"Tom! Supper-time!" Aran's familiar voice roused him later and he followed the little boy down to Banca's hut for his meal. Verda deliberately avoided catching his eye, and Tom was too miserable to notice the simmering excitement of a small group of children.

When Scapa announced that he expected the battering-ram to break through the final stretch of tunnel the next day, all other thoughts flew away in a buzz of excitement.

Naze's mother was surprised when he clung to her at bedtime, pleading, "Tell me a story, Mother – you haven't done that for ages." It was true, she thought with a pang of guilt, she'd been too tired from her work on the ford, so she made two mugs of his favourite drink and settled beside his bed to tell him a story.

Mocha, Aran and Farr waited in the shadows by the ford for ten minutes, jumping at every rustle, before Farr went to look for Naze. She reported back, "I could hear his mother telling him a story, and it's a really long one – he'll never get away in time."

"Then we'll have to go without him," Mocha said, "If we wait here any longer someone will catch us."

No-one spotted the little gang jumping from island to island across the ford, towing their raft behind them. No-one saw them either when they hauled it ashore and dragged it through the trees, or when they slid down the bluff onto the beach beside the south lagoon. The air was full of fumes and quite warm, but Aran shivered. "It looks bigger from down here – and the water will be cold."

Even Mocha was daunted, but when a wavelet splashed their feet he grinned. "Feel that – it's as warm as a bath. Come on, Farr – we'll let you go first as you're a girl."

Farr put on a brave face. "All right, but promise you won't let go of the rope."

"We'll hold really tight," Aran promised, so Farr straddled the raft, clinging on with one hand to the vines that held it together, and Aran passed her the paddle.

The swell in the lagoon was nothing compared with the big ocean waves of their little cove, Farr told herself, and she paddled away bravely.

Mocha was right – the water really was warm – but when she'd just got the hang of balancing on the waves, Aran called, "There's no more rope," and she had to go back. Turning round was trickier than she'd expected, and she nearly fell off when a wave caught her sideways, but with the boys hauling on the rope she landed safely on the beach. Her face glowing with achievement, she said, "Wow! That was fun – I want another go."

"Not till I've been," Aran said, "The raft was my idea." So she took the rope from him reluctantly and told him to watch out for the waves when he turned round.

Mocha looked at her admiringly. "The Forest girls are too scared to go rafting – you did really well," he said, and Farr was glad the darkness hid the dark flush that raced up her neck.

Aran paddled out as far as the rope would allow and turned round with a flourish that nearly toppled him, but he was beaming with pride when he landed. "We made a good raft, didn't we?"

"Almost as good as mine," Mocha conceded, "Now I'll show you how it should be done."

He swung his leg nonchalantly across the logs and dug his paddle into the water. The raft surged forward and hit a wave head-on. It was only a small wave, but it reminded him that this lagoon was very different from the calm river back home. Carefully he shifted his weight until he was more evenly balanced and paddled sedately, but even so he reached the end of the rope far too soon.

He knew if he went back for a longer rope the others would want a second go, and he wasn't ready to give up the raft yet. Looking along the shining path of moonlight on the water, he thought that if he paddled really hard he might be able to reach the reef. "Let go of the rope," he called softly, his voice carrying clearly across the water.

Aran called back, "You can't – it's not safe!"

But Mocha insisted, "I know what I'm doing – let it go!" so they let go and he was free.

He balanced easily, enjoying the sensation of lifting and falling on the swell, and he thought this was probably the best raft he had ever made. Cutting the front to a point had been a good idea, and putting a bigger log in the middle made it really comfortable to sit on.

He paddled steadily – left side, right side – heading for the dark silhouette of the reef where the surf was breaking into brilliant white foam. Ignoring the distant pleading of Aran and Farr, he let the moon pull him, imagining his little raft could follow that silver path all the way to the edge of the world.

In a trance of wonder he paddled on, warm water lapping at his legs and the others' voices fading – all he could hear was the intoxicating rumble of the volcano and the pounding of the waves as he got closer and closer to the reef.

He was just thinking it would be exciting to paddle right through the rocks and keep going for ever when an extra large wave hit the reef and splashed him all over with cold spray. That woke him up with a jolt – the Ocean wasn't nice and warm like the lagoon – he would die of cold out there.

Turning round with an expert dip and push of the paddle he started back, but the raft wasn't as easy to manoeuvre as it had been. Each pull on the paddle only took him a foot or two nearer the beach. In fact, now he looked at it properly, the two bottom logs were awash, which meant they'd soaked up too much water and he was sinking. Throwing a look of sheer terror at Farr and Aran, he paddled furiously, trying to reach the safety of the beach before the raft gave up completely.

*

Tom was sitting on his ledge, brooding on the unfairness of life, when he heard shrill voices pierce the volcano's bass rumble – "Mocha – paddle faster!" With a sick feeling of dread he remembered the conspiratorial whispering of the little gang at supper and realised they had been planning a dangerous escapade. Cursing the self-preoccupation that had blinded his Sight, he snatched up a torch and raced down to the plateau for help. But there was no-one there – every one of the clan members had moved to the new village – he would have to rescue the children alone.

Horribly aware that time was running out, Tom leapt from the plateau onto the top of the dam and practically flew across the slippery surface. He had almost reached the far side – in fact he was actually over the tunnel – when he heard a scraping sound. It could have been pebbles shifting on the beach, but he knew instinctively it was far more sinister than that.

The ironwood battering-ram had been pounding underwater for days, each blow vibrating through the remaining stretch of tunnel.

Scapa had said at supper that they were nearly through, and when the work stopped for the night the pressure must have continued to build. Every rock and stone, every pebble and grain of sand remaining in the tunnel had been shifting, and now the blockage was going to tear itself free. He saw Aran and Farr on the beach and followed their gaze to Mocha, a small frantic figure paddling furiously on his pathetic little raft, with the moon shining on his wet skin like a searchlight.

There was no time even to get to the beach – the ominous rumble beneath Tom's feet told him that – so he jumped off the bridge onto the volcano itself and slid right down to the water's edge yelling, "Come on, Mocha – you're nearly there!"

Mocha heard Tom shout and tried to steer towards him but he couldn't manoeuvre the waterlogged raft – it was clear it wouldn't even stay afloat for much longer.

Then there was a roar and the mouth of the tunnel exploded. A wave of murky river-water mixed with gravel spewed out halfway across the lagoon, and Mocha was directly in its path.

Tom's torch-lit dash across the lava bridge had alerted others, and there were arms to catch Aran and Farr before they could be knocked off their feet by the backwash, but when the brown wave subsided, Mocha had vanished. Tom stared in anguish at the cloudy water, convinced that Mocha was dead – and then he heard a child crying out for help. Aran and Farr were safe, so it could only be Mocha, lying at the bottom of the lagoon and still alive – but not for long.

This was what Tom's underwater dreams had prepared him for, and he knew he had to try – without further hesitation he took a deep breath and jumped off the volcano. His body plummeted straight down, and when his feet hit gravel he waded just as he had done when the crocodile caught him, searching for Mocha with his feet as well as with his mind. He could feel the child's life-force fading but it was impossible to see anything through the muddy water. His own body was cooling fast and he knew he couldn't hold his breath for much longer, but he sent out a final mental shout, "*Mocha!*" and a hot little hand clutched his ankle – against all the odds he had found him.

His lungs screaming for air, Tom heaved the little boy over his shoulder and headed up the slope to the beach. The moment they emerged from the water Sasso grabbed Mocha, but the small body lay limp and lifeless in his arms. Burying his face in his son's neck he howled with grief, but Chert snatched his grandson and held him upside down, thumping his back repeatedly until Mocha brought up a stomach-full of dirty water and coughed back to life.

Sasso took him back and raced to the village, where he dumped him right in the middle of the fire until he glowed with heat, then wrapped him up and tucked him into bed, too thankful he was alive to scold, and fed him sips of a hot drink like a baby.

Just before his eyelids drooped shut, Mocha whispered, "Did you see me, Father? I went to the moon and back."

Meanwhile Tom sat cocooned in blankets beside a roaring fire in the guest hut, taking sips of tea

Noyau had laced with wood spirit and brushing off the praise of a stream of visitors.

He didn't feel entitled to praise when he knew his silly quarrel with Verda had clouded his Sight and nearly cost Mocha his life. Verda was beside him now, and when he put out his hand she grabbed it quickly. Drawing her closer he whispered in her ear, "I'm sorry."

"It was me as much as you," she replied, kissing his cheek.

"It's good to see you two have made up your squabble," Noyau said complacently.

"Oh Mother!" Verda protested, but she was laughing, and Tom thought she had never looked so beautiful – he had to make sure of her before she returned home. Instinct told him now was the moment and he held her gaze, willing her to read his mind. Her brow furrowed briefly in puzzlement, but then he felt her relax and saw her answer flare joyfully in her green eyes. Turning to her father, Tom said formally, "Zircon, sir, will you give permission for us to be betrothed?"

"What – tonight?" Zircon said with mock severity. "I'll have to think about it."

Noyau kicked him. "Shut up, you old fool! Of course they can be betrothed – we've been waiting for weeks for Tom to ask her."

Verda kissed both her parents ecstatically. "That means we can be Bonded at next summer's Festival."

"My thoughts exactly," Tom grinned, "Then we'll be together for the rest of our lives."

Verda hand shot out to grab a lump of firewood. "Touch wood, Tom! It's tempting Fate saying things like that," and she wouldn't rest until he had followed her example.

Once the shock of the near-tragedy had worn off, Scapa was delighted with the success of his tunnel. The initial burst of gravel-laden water had scoured the roof to a perfect curve, and by morning the river was flowing smoothly, eight feet deep, through its new outlet. Scapa could return to his desert quarry satisfied with a job well done – a tunnel dug under circumstances no man had ever tackled before – and his name would be woven into legend.

Yakan too was thrilled with the result. Not only was the lava causeway dry, the stepping-stone islands at the ford were once again above water – a trader with a loaded camel would be able to cross in safety. When his men had tidied up the towpath, visitors from the north, south and east would flock to see the volcano, and the profits he'd anticipated when it first erupted would be his for the taking.

CHAPTER TWENTY – BASALT THE PEDLAR

Sasso and Chert took Mocha home the next day, back to his mother and to Roca's ministrations. "No offence meant, Tom," Sasso said apologetically, "But Roca's had more experience with near-drownings than you have."

"This is the second time I've almost drowned," Tom said, "Perhaps I should come with you." He was only half-joking – Verda was also leaving, and it was much too soon. He managed to wave them all off with a smile, but his heart was heavy, and when he trudged back through the village he saw Aran looking equally miserable.

"Mother says I've got to stay where she can see me," the child complained, "Will you play five-stones with me?"

Having nothing more urgent in mind, Tom agreed, and the simple game lifted their spirits. They had embarked on a second round when Ness came over and asked if he could join them. This was the first time any of the clan's young men had sought

Tom's company, but he hid his surprise and made room for him. As Ness lowered himself gingerly to the ground, Tom said, "You're still very stiff, I see – do you need another pot of salve?"

"Yes, please," Ness said, "Sima slaps it on as if she's greasing a joint of meat." He sat back on his heels and observed, "You're not just a medicine man though, are you? Jumping into the lagoon like that was the bravest thing I've ever seen."

Tom threw the five-stones to cover his confusion. "I couldn't let Mocha drown – and the water was warm."

"Maybe so," Ness said, "But none of us would have dared."

"I saw it all from the beach," Aran cut in eagerly, "Tom's a hero."

"He is indeed." Ness picked up the stones for his turn and said no more, but Tom soon discovered Ness and Aran weren't his only fans. All through the day people made a point of clapping him on the back with a hearty, "Well done, Seer!" and his sensitive ears picked up an undercurrent of talk everywhere – their new Seer might be smaller than average, but he had been man enough to leap into deep water and snatch a child from certain death.

The real bonus of this unexpected admiration was that Tom's peers started treating him as one of them. He was often invited to join the other young men when they gathered to while away the hours with talk and games, and as autumn winds and rain stripped the leaves from the trees, in their congenial company he felt the absence of Verda less keenly.

*

One day Tom and Ness were chatting in the village square when Aran and his friends came hurtling out of the forest, dropping armfuls of firewood as they ran. "We saw a monster!" Aran screamed, "Twenty feet tall with horns and great humps all over it!"

Tom was about to scold him for being over-imaginative when the monster actually appeared. It was nearer fifteen feet tall, not twenty, but a frightening figure nonetheless, with deep folds of grey skin and three horns sprouting from a furry head. Several of the young men snatched up their spears, and then the monster spoke. "Is this where I'll find the new volcano?"

Standing as tall as he could, Tom stammered, "Yes, it is, and I'm the Seer – what do you want with the volcano?"

"Just to see it," the apparition said, and began to shed its skin. As the layers dropped away, the monster was gradually revealed to be only a man, but what a man! He was the tallest man any of them had ever seen – well over twelve feet, made even taller by the fur hat her wore. His 'horns' were three poles that opened out into a tripod which, when he draped it with his huge waterproof poncho, became a tepee – a traveller's simple shelter. The man obviously knew the effect he was creating as he unslung his various packs in front of his growing audience and put them inside the tepee. "I am Basalt, travelling pedlar," he declared, "Carrying many fascinating goods for your delectation – but first, Seer, show me your volcano."

Having duly admired the volcano – "It's spat out a lot of babies for such a small thing" – and the tunnel – "This wonder will make a good fireside tale for the winter" – Basalt refused the offer of a bed in the guest hut, saying he'd rather sleep in his tepee. "It's small enough to warm up quickly with a Firepot," he said, "And I don't want to get winter-soft yet – I've got another month of travelling before the Sleep." But he did accept the use of the guest hut to display his wares.

Basalt presented Yakan with a soft sealskin blanket for his grandson, which secured the Leader's unstinting hospitality for the night, but a visit from a pedlar was such a rare treat that he sold a great deal of his other stock. For the women he had goat hair cloth woven in Whitewater, a village on the Ridge Path where he had seen one of the Shore volcano babies, and he had sheepskin moccasins made by clans in the far north. He also carried a selection of jewellery, and Tom traded two pots of salve for a gold ring set with an emerald from the northern mines. The Shore men bought iron spearheads and knives, while the children clamoured for the spinning tops and bamboo whistles Basalt carved as he travelled. The clan paid him in salt and ham and hard sausage, smoked fish and dried seaweed, and Tom spotted him filling a bag with gravel from the beach to sell as 'volcanic mementoes'.

But what made the pedlar a truly valued visitor were his stories. During supper he regaled the assembled clan with the news he had picked up on his travels – which clan had new babies and who had died, who was betrothed and who had been Bonded. Tom was particularly pleased to hear that Bala and his group had reached Twin Lake safely via the Ridge Path – Tabor's story of his lost Wolf Clan had touched him deeply. But when Basalt talked about the northern mines and of seeing snow on the mountains beyond them even further north, the vision that had haunted Tom for months came rushing back. "Could there be a lake in those mountains?" he asked eagerly, "One that freezes in winter?"

"Now you mention it, that might explain the gulls I saw so far inland," Basalt replied. "They could have been flying up there to fish in a lake." He paused thoughtfully. "And the two big cold rivers that flow into Twin Lake come from that range."

Tom was so thrilled to have found a possible answer to his puzzle that he turned instinctively to tell Verda, but of course she wasn't there. Basalt spotted the desolate expression that washed over his face. "Did I say something wrong, Seer?"

"Not at all – in fact you might have solved a mystery for me."

"So what's troubling you? Missing that Forest girl you bought a ring for?"

"Are you sure you're not a Seer, Basalt? I *am* missing Verda – I haven't seen her for weeks."

"Then go and visit her – what's stopping you? The volcano? Yakan?" When Tom shook his head Basalt said briskly, "You should come with me tomorrow. I'm going through to the prairie and can set you on the right path. The prairie route to the Forest village will be warmer than the towpath this late in the year – it gets the sun all day."

*

The track that led south through the forest to the prairie was clear enough to follow, but Tom was glad of Basalt's company – it was damp and gloomy under the trees after the clear salt air and sunshine of his coastal home. Basalt seemed unaffected by the atmosphere, but Tom's slighter body slowed down in the cooler air, and he hugged his Firepot just to keep warm. The ground was spongy with moisture too, and his weight caused him to sink with every step – an unpleasant reminder of his dreams in which people disappeared into a sea of mud. After trudging through the forest all day, it was a tremendous relief to reach the clear air of the prairie at sunset.

While Tom erected the tent Yakan had grudgingly provided – "Don't you dare miss the raft home, young man" – Basalt put up his tepee in half a minute then demonstrated how to build a fire inside dirt walls. "One careless spark could sweep across the prairie and kill all the animals," he warned, "And then what would people eat?"

"I'll be careful," Tom promised. "Which way do you go from here?"

"South to Estuary village then north-east through Oak. If I can get over the pass before the snow there's a woman, Isola, who runs a nomads' shelter where I can spend the winter Sleep." Basalt's voice softened when he mentioned Isola, and Tom felt certain the trader would cross the pass in plenty of time. They spent the night camped in the lee of the forest, facing south across the prairie, sharing a meal and swapping stories until bedtime.

The following morning they parted company. Tom watched until Basalt's tall figure faded into the distance, looking remarkably like the monster Aran had taken him for. Then he refilled his Firepot with glowing embers, tied the rolled tent on top of his backpack, and set off north-west towards the Forest village and Verda, relishing the freedom to stride out after the narrow forest tracks that surrounded the Shore village. For the first time in his life he was truly alone. On his left the forest stretched beyond the river and hundreds of miles northwards along the Ridge mountain range; spread to his right were the countless acres of windswept grass of the prairie.

Around mid-morning the roar of a lion drew his attention to some nearby hills, and he saw a group of apes running from a pride of lions, but to his astonishment they were running upright. He held his breath as two of them were caught, and was so intent on the drama that he sensed the fear of the victims and felt the crunch of lions' teeth on his own neck.

Experience had taught Tom that herd animals usually fled when one of their number was killed, but these apes were throwing stones, clearly trying to drive the lions from the kill – Tom found their behaviour puzzling. He screwed up his eyes to focus more clearly and saw that these apes had no fur on their limbs. One of them was carrying a completely hairless infant, and with a shock he realised he must be seeing Humans – Grandfather's stories were true after all! He only moved on after the Humans had abandoned their dead and fled the scene.

By dusk he had covered a hundred miles. He camped beside a stream and built a careful firewall before making a hunters' stew from water, dried meat and a handful of beans, just as Flint had taught him a few months – and a lifetime – ago.

Wrapped in his blanket beside the fire, he listened to the whoosh of the wind through the long dry grass, fancying he heard a faint echo of the waves that washed the cliff beneath his ledge. Uneasily aware of the vast emptiness beyond the circle of firelight, he closed his eyes and tried to visualize home – his cave with its comfortable pallet and dancing fire, the infant volcano linked to the land by its lava bridge, and the cradling lagoon enclosed by a curve of white water on reef rocks. He sent his spirit adrift to visit his Sanctum, but the Mother had other plans.

She pulled Tom northwards, over the forest and far beyond the desert into the now familiar land of his nightmares. Instead of the green and turquoise of the Ocean, he was hovering over the cold blue water of that freezing lake, and instead of the foam of breakers on the Shore reef he saw ice floes. Huge gulls dived for fish in the frigid water, and far down in the inky depths a line of fire burned. It was clear that the fire threatened some kind of disaster, for why else would the Mother have brought him here so often?

"What can I do?" he cried, "I don't know where the lake is, let alone the fire!" But when he woke up in his lonely camp on the prairie, his question remained unanswered. Shivering as much from his dream of ice as from the night air, he built his fire as high as he dared and crawled into the tent, where he rolled himself tightly into his blanket and lay awake for a long time, wondering how it was possible for there to be fire underwater.

*

Tom's time with Verda crawled by swiftly – although the individual hours seemed endless, the days sped past in a blur. They set out together each morning to collect plants and seeds, roots and slivers of bark for medicines, and as long as they were back for the noon meal Verda's parents were happy to let the betrothed couple roam unchaperoned. In the warm autumn evenings they sat beside the communal fire with the rest of the Forest Clan, but Tom spent his afternoons with Roca, learning how to prepare what he had gathered and creating a stockpile of medicines to take home.

One afternoon he was pounding some rocks to make clay for cuts – a boring but necessary chore. The rhythmic thud of pestle into mortar had a soporific quality, and he performed the task in a semi-trance. Once he had reduced the rocks to powder he began adding water, stirring in a few drops at a time with his fingers, until the mixture acquired the consistency of thick mud. The yellow-ochre powder matched his own skin so perfectly that it was hard to tell where his hand ended and the clay began.

Watching his hands move through the glutinous mess, he let his mind wander.

Thinking about it afterwards, Tom could never decide whether the bowl of clay grew or he shrank, but the effect was the same. One moment his fingers were stirring the mixture, and the next moment he was surrounded by steep walls, as if he was inside the bowl itself. The air was thick with panic, his ears rang with a thousand screams, and he was digging through the gritty clay in a frantic search for some lost treasure. His fingers closed on a small, hard object and, fighting against the drag of earth that seemed determined to swallow him, he pulled it out. After rubbing off the dirt he found he was holding a ring set with an emerald – the ring he had bought from Basalt and given to Verda. Now he had the ring but not Verda – he had lost her! He tried to dive into the mud to search for her, but it was mud no longer and his body hit solid ground.

The shock jarred him back to consciousness, gasping in panic, and he looked up as Roca took the bowl from his un-resisting hands. "If you knead that clay any longer you'll dry it out," she said, then she noticed his expression. "Are you all right?"

"I lost Verda," Tom said, his heart still pounding with residual terror. "She sank into mud that turned back into solid ground before I could rescue her."

"That's what comes of daydreaming while you mix clay," Roca said with a smile. "Handling rock in any form is a sure-fire route to dream-land."

Tom released his breath in a long sigh – Roca was right, of course. He had mini-visions all the time, and he must learn not to treat each one as a premonition of disaster.

CHAPTER TWENTY-ONE – CHO & THE SLEEP

Chert took the final raft of the season down-river two days later – Tom's visit with Verda was over. When they kissed goodbye, Verda made one last attempt to keep him. "Are you sure you won't stay here for the Sleep? Mother says you can."

"I must go back, sweetheart – I'm the Shore Seer."

"Sometimes I wish you weren't," she said, blinking back tears, "I won't see you again till after the Sleep, will I?"

Tom wiped her face tenderly and swallowed a lump in his own throat. "I won't be far away, and I'll think about you every time I wake up."

"So will I," Verda said, making a brave attempt at a smile. "Winter won't last forever and next summer there's the Festival." She didn't have to voice what was in her heart – the Festival was when they would be Bonded, never to be parted again.

*

Cho launched into a scolding the minute Tom arrived. "About time you came back, young man! I thought you'd decided to stay the winter with that pretty green girl and I'd be stuck here alone."

"Weren't you ever in love, Cho?" Tom asked

"I've had my moments, Tom – just never got caught," the old Seer smirked, but then his face dropped again. "You forget that it's boring with nobody around, and soon you'll be joining the clan for the Sleep. It's time I went home."

"So you trust me to manage without you now?" Tom grinned. "I'll miss you."

He felt a hint of pressure as Cho patted his shoulder and said, "I expect you'll make a few mistakes, but the Mother says I've got to go."

"I'm surprised She let you stay this long – how did you manage it?"

Cho shuffled his ghostly feet and admitted, "Truth is, I shouldn't have stayed at all. When I knew I was dying I broke my big toe off and left it here. I wanted to stay till another Seer arrived." He looked so shifty that Tom chuckled but Cho said huffily, "It was no laughing matter, I can tell you. Froze the toe in cold water first, of course, but it rutting well hurt all the same," and he vanished in a tetchy puff of vapour.

The next day Tom glanced at his collection of lava pebbles and frowned. He had saved one from each birth so there should be eight, not nine. He counted them off on his fingers – the Guaza Clan's babies Riva and Onyx, the Forest baby and the Lake one made four. Then there were the two Yakan had tried to steal followed by Zan and Crystal's daughter, and finally Yakan's grandson – eight in all. Tom was wondering where the extra pebble came from when he heard an exasperated sigh beside him and Cho said, "Oh, for heaven's sake, boy – look at them properly!"

Tom checked the shelf again and suddenly light dawned. Right at the end of the row was a worn cylinder of grey rock, unmistakeably toe-shaped. "That wasn't there before today," he said, "How did you manage that?"

"Mind over matter, my boy, and it wasn't easy, I can tell you! I left it there before I died but Banca chucked it out onto the ledge when she was sweeping up. It was hard work getting it back on the shelf, but I knew you'd never find it otherwise."

From the old Seer's expression Tom guessed this was the moment he must say goodbye. "I've got used to having you around," he admitted, "I'll be lonely up here without you."

"Get away with you! You'll be asleep soon and next year is the Festival – you'll be too busy planning for that to miss me," said Cho, but he looked gratified nonetheless. "I'd like one last wander round the old place before I go. Stick my toe in your pocket."

Tom obediently pocketed the old grey toe. "All right – where do you want to go?"

"We'll start at the old caves. It's good the clan's moving back into them for the Sleep – caves hold the heat much better than those new-fangled huts."

On the clan's old empty plateau Cho nipped in and out of every cave like a nosy neighbour, and then perched on the very edge of the rocks, leaning so far over that Tom had an irrational urge to grab him. "I don't suppose you fancy taking me on a raft, do you?" Cho said wistfully, "I used to love crossing the lagoon as a boy."

"Not a chance. I've had enough of water to last me a lifetime."

"I'm not so sure," Cho said, but when Tom asked what he meant he shrugged his pale shoulders. "I can't make it out, son – I don't see visions now, only shadows."

At suppertime in the new village, Cho's ghost wandered round alone, peering at every face and flitting back to tell Tom, "He's aged a lot," or, "That girl turned out prettier than I expected," but he quickly became bored, and as soon as Tom had finished eating Cho said, "I don't belong here any more – take me back to our ledge. You can do the deed after dark when they're all asleep."

Making sure he still had Cho's toe in his pocket, Tom stood up. Yakan was accustomed to people waiting for him to move first and he snapped, "It's a bit early for bed, isn't it?"

"Sorry, Yakan, but I'm really tired," Tom said, stretching his arms wide and yawning. Suddenly everyone else was yawning too and heading for bed.

"What's happening here?" Yakan frowned as Tarifa folded their blankets. "Oh well – I suppose there's no harm in an early night for once," he said and followed Tarifa indoors, leaving Tom alone in the village square with only Cho for company.

"That was a clever trick," the old man said admiringly. "Grab a torch and let's go up."

Down in the village Cho's ghost had faded until it was almost transparent, but once they were inside the Sanctum he regained strength and they sat for a while talking.

"I loved this place the moment I saw it," Cho said, gesturing round the small, glistening cave, "It can be a great comfort in times of trouble, as you'll discover."

"You said something earlier about water," Tom reminded him. "I know there's trouble coming and it's to do with that frozen lake – what do you know about it?"

"Not a thing, son," Cho said despondently, "I told you I can't see visions any more – probably because I'm one myself!" He forced a laugh. "And the Mother's summoning me home now. I've a feeling She's going to need more Seers' souls next year – it's time I went."

"Up to the cairns, I presume?"

"No, son – you're going to put me in that volcano. I knew last year it was coming and I reckon I've earned a proper look inside it. Chucking my toe into the crater will be the quickest way to send me back to the Mother. You'll need your sling."

When Tom slid down onto the causeway the volcano was so quiet that he was worried there'd be no lava, but Cho said, "We'll be fine – just head for the crater."

With the fragment of Cho in his pocket and his voice urging him to hurry, Tom scaled the side of the cone and peered over the edge. A dark crust covered the lava pool, but at regular intervals a bubble formed lazily and popped to release a few glowing drops of lava on a spurt of gas. Apart from that there was no movement – as he had anticipated, the volcano was going to sleep.

Cho hung in the wavering air beside him. "I hope you haven't lost the knack with that sling, son, because you've got to get me inside one of those bubbles."

"I haven't used it for months – are you sure this is the only way?"

"I have every faith in you, Tom, and the Mother will help. Now get on with it – never did hold with long farewells."

Swallowing a lump in his throat, Tom slipped the toe into his sling and took careful aim at a large bubble. As it swelled with lava he recited the final prayer of the Cairning ceremony, and when the crust split open he let fly. He was relieved to note he hadn't lost the knack, though he might have had some help – the old Seer's toe arced straight and true through the sulphurous fumes towards its goal. Tom felt Cho brush past him and heard him say, "Good luck, young Seer," before the stone landed perfectly in the exact centre of the bubble and sank into the golden lava. When every last spark of the miniature eruption had died away the night seemed very dark, and Tom trudged back to his cave knowing that he had lost a true friend.

*

A week or so later Yakan invited Tom to share his seat at the evening meal – a rare honour – and draped a heavy arm round his slim shoulders. "Well, my boy," he boomed, "Winter's nearly upon us, and you'll need a place to sleep." He clamped his huge hand on Tom's knee. "You'd better move in with us."

Tom was caught off guard. He knew he couldn't stay in his own cave – it was courting disaster to spend winter alone – but moving in with a Leader who still insisted on calling him 'my boy' would be almost as bad.

But Banca came to his rescue. "Tom's welcome to share with us," she said.

Aran piped up to add his voice, "We'll need someone to help with the fire duties now Father's dead, and I'm still too small."

Tom smiled at them both and eased out of Yakan's suffocating embrace. "Helping Banca is the least I can do after she's fed me all year," he said, and Yakan could do nothing but to agree that it was the best solution all round.

CHAPTER TWENTY-TWO – THE LAST VISION

After Tom had assured Yakan that the volcano would remain dormant for the winter, the Shore Clan moved their possessions back to the caves that had been their homes until the eruptions drove them out. For days there was constant traffic along the track between the village and the cave plateau, as the women carried pallets and blankets and bundles of clothing, while their children moved stacks of firewood, even the toddlers staggering along with a log under each arm.

The men hunted increasingly scarce and wary prey, and the air on the plateau was redolent with the rich smells of spices as the women smoked joints of meat over constantly-burning fires and filled huge covered jars with preserved food – even during the Sleep the clan members had to wake regularly to eat and to refuel the fires.

Gradually the new village acquired a desolate air as one by one the families swept out their log huts and made them secure for the coming winter. After glimpsing strange creatures in the forests, some clan members suspected Humans were more than mere myths and took even greater precautions against thieves. Remembering those strange apes on the prairie, Tom was inclined to agree with them.

The horizon over the Ocean became a mass of clouds that thickened with each passing day until, a few weeks after Tom had returned Cho to Mother Earth, the temperature plummeted overnight and the rains came in earnest. The heat-loving people shivered, only venturing out into the relentless downpour to collect fuel from their woodpiles. The fur-blanketed pallets in their caves began to look more and more inviting as their bodies slowed down.

One morning, after days of wet weather, Yakan's father put his breakfast bowl down with a clatter, rose stiffly to his feet declaring, "You youngsters can stay up if you like but I'm ready for the Sleep," and staked his claim to the cosiest corner at the rear of the cave. Soon the old man's snores were rumbling out onto the old plateau, and Tarifa drew a heavy leather curtain across the cave entrance against draughts, weighing down the hem with rocks. During the remainder of that day, Yakan shifted his log-pile to block the cave's main entrance, leaving just enough room to squeeze through, and other Shore men moved sluggishly to follow his example. Performing the same task for Banca, Tom remembered helping Flint to block the entrance to the cave on Guaza Mountain only a year ago. Hoping to pay one final dream-visit to his former clan, he made himself a palm-leaf umbrella, took a flaming brand to light a fire, and made his way up the muddy track to his ledge to spend one last night alone.

Wrapped in blankets with his feet on a heated rock, he leaned against the wall of his Sanctum and prayed for the Shore Clan to come safely through the Sleep. He expanded his prayer to include Verda and the Forest Clan, and then, as the flames of his fire flickered over the green-streaked walls, he was drawn into a vision.

It was not the hoped-for trip to Guaza Mountain – far from it. He was riding Mocha's little raft as it lifted off the surface of the lagoon to fly up the beam of silver light towards the moon. When the volcano had dwindled to a glow in the distance, the raft veered north through increasingly cold air and Tom, with a sinking heart, guessed where they were headed. Although he knew this vision wasn't real, Tom was a Rockman before he was a Seer, and when he was dumped up to his chest in freezing snow, the cold that seeped into his stones terrified him. Even in his vision he fought to free himself before the heat of his body melted a path to oblivion. Flailing his limbs in the cold wet horror and grunting with effort, he swam upwards until the snow released its grip and he was on the surface, standing beside the lake of his earlier visions.

But there was a difference this time – instead of hands and feet he had broad paws, and his entire body was covered in white fur so dense that he no longer felt the cold. He was a white bear – a hungry one – and he lifted his muzzle to sniff the air for food. Then he heard a squeal of terror and whipped his head round to see a cub – which he knew somehow was his cub – sliding helplessly towards a steep drop. Instantly he plunged after it, his strong, padded paws pounding the snow in a desperate race to save the cub. He had just caught its head in his mouth when the surface gave way, and they were both enveloped in the choking, roaring vortex of an avalanche.

Tom's jaws held desperately onto his cub's head, struggling to breathe in the stinging snow. They fell for what seemed like an eternity, until finally they crashed with shattering force through thick ice into the numbing waters of the lake. As they sank towards the bottom Tom tried to swim, but when his limbs wouldn't obey his commands he realised the impact had broken his back. There was no hope of walking out of this lake as he had with Mocha, Tom thought, and as the icy water rushed into the bear's lungs, his spirit left the bear's body to float alongside it.

The two white bears drifted down into the ooze, past strange fish with lights in their bodies and tiny transparent creatures trailing gossamer threads. Tom drifted with them, watching in wonder, until finally he saw what the Mother had brought him to see. He had only glimpsed it in previous visions, but now he was just an arm's-length away he could see it clearly. There was a crack in the lake wall, and deep inside the crack lava was flowing – a river of fire that even this huge amount of water could not extinguish.

In the freezing depths of the lake he was bathed in heat, and as he bobbed with the bears' bodies in the warm current, the underwater fire erupted and the lake-water exploded upwards in a huge wave, taking him with it.

When he awoke, the fire he had built in his Sanctum was dying and he was shivering. Rousing himself with an effort, he carried the embers through to his outer cave and built the fire up high before lying down on his pallet, but he couldn't shake off the awful vision. He pulled his blankets closely round his shoulders and sat with his feet in the fire, still aching from the memory of his plunge through the ice. He heated up a bowl of cereal, fumbling the spoon as if he still had paws, and after eating he fell asleep where he sat.

*

Aran had to shake him hard to wake him the next morning. "Come on, Tom – Mother's making special Sleep porridge this morning."

"You don't sound anywhere near ready for the Sleep," Tom grumbled, "I hope you're not going to keep us awake all winter." Aran simply giggled and helped Tom to douse the fire with dirt before escorting him down for breakfast.

"There you are, my boy!" Yakan called across the entire width of the plateau, "Everything all right with the Mother's world?" Tom looked at the crowd of sleepy faces and remembered his vision, but what danger could possibly be posed to these people by a lake hundreds of miles away?

"Everything's fine," he told them, and sat down to a bowl of Banca's special porridge.

The rain had stopped overnight and many women, including Banca, took the opportunity to give their blankets a final airing. Tom brought his pallet down from his ledge and made up his bed next to Aran's, but conversation was desultory and they retired early.

"I'm not getting up tomorrow," Banca told Tom, "So after this you'll have to help yourself from the stew-pot when you wake up."

A stove in each cave kept a cauldron of stew simmering, and when a drop in temperature woke adults to refuel the fires, they would scoop out a handful of food, and mothers would spoon the thick gravy into their slumbering children's mouths.

By the end of that week every cave on the plateau was filled with sleeping Rockmen. Like many other creatures, from huge mountain bears to tiny burrowing animals, their bodies were tuned to synchronize with the earth – to slow down and hibernate to conserve their heat and energy while the Mother slumbered.

Many of Tom's Sleep-dreams were those of any young man separated from his girl. Dreams of exploring the forest with Verda and picking herbs became mingled with memories of playing the Firegame. He also suffered nightmares about lizards that turned into crocodiles, of trying to remain afloat on a disintegrating raft, or dreamed of children drowning. The vision of the frozen lake haunted him all winter, and every time he awoke shivering he knew he'd been dreaming again of the place of fire under ice and huge white bears.

Upstream, the Forest villagers had doubled the thickness of their walls by stacking their firewood indoors, and every hut was snug with the smell of sap.

Smoked hams and sausages hung from the rafters, ready for slices to be cut by whoever woke to refuel the corner stoves. Verda lay wrapped in furs in the corner of her parents' hut, dreaming of Tom and the coming Festival at which they would be Bonded. Roca had put her Sanctum Tree outside her hut, where it stood as dormant as its larger relatives, waiting for spring. The Forest Seer's Sleep-dreams were, as always, awash with green, and when she dreamed of water she sensed no danger, but simply went out to her small tree and gave it a drink.

In Grand Oasis the Desert Clan was only just entering the Sleep, for winter came later to the desert. Their homes now resembled a neat row of sand-dunes, because the clan saved fuel by heaping sand over them. On his last day awake, the Seer Donax visited his own Sanctum – a grotto inside High Rock – and as he prayed that his clan would come safely through the Sleep, the light of his torch appeared to become trapped in the waterfall at the rear of the grotto. A more sensitive Seer might have seen these liquid reflections of fire as a warning, but Donax dismissed his frisson of fear as the fancy of a tired old man, and went to claim his customary winter place in the Leader's hut.

In their cave halfway up a mountain the Guaza Clan also slept, although not as deeply as some. The twins Onyx and Riva were only six months old and still needed to be fed every day. They always woke at the same time for their mothers to feed them from a pot of soup kept hot over the steam-vent, and any dreams Hekla had that winter were scattered by the babies' cries.

All over their vast continent the Rockmen slumbered. From the mountainous western shore to the white chalk cliffs of the far east – from the wave-battered south coast to the frozen north, other creatures – two-legged as well as four-legged – roamed forests and grassland undisturbed by the large hunters.

Lava simmered gently in the volcanoes that dotted this young land, waiting for Mother Earth to wake again and send more children for Her volcanic race. But no tremors disturbed the Rockmen in their beds and the danger that threatened their lives lurked unseen.

Deep beneath the earth, pressure was building, slowly and inexorably, between two continental plates. Unheard by any ear, million-ton rocks groaned and, hidden in the frozen lake of Tom's vision, a glowing rift widened.

*

End

Printed in Great Britain
by Amazon